Rebel Earth

Dale E. McClenning

Milton, Ontario
http://www.brain-lag.com/

Brain Lag Publishing
Milton, Ontario
http://www.brain-lag.com/

Cover artwork by and © Thomas Budach

Library and Archives Canada Cataloguing in Publication

Title: Rebel Earth / Dale E. McClenning.
Names: McClenning, Dale E., 1962- author.
Identifiers: Canadiana (print) 20210327588 | Canadiana (ebook) 20210327596 | ISBN 9781928011637
   (softcover) | ISBN 9781928011644 (ebook)
Classification: LCC PS3613.C55 R43 2022 | DDC 813/.6—dc23

To my mom. Dedicating a book to her hardly makes up for all she has done for me. Thanks, Mom.

Chapter One
About One Boy

The wooden door, pulled by the spring at the top, slapped the wooded frame as it closed. Without turning, Miriam called over her shoulder, hands still wet in a sink full of dishes. "Is that you, Wilmont? Make sure your shoes are clean before coming in this house or you'll have to wash the floors."

When no reply came, Miriam called again. "Wilmont? Wilmont. Answer your mother."

"Mom," came back in a weak voice, causing Miriam to immediately take her hands out of the sink and make her way to the door across the wooden flooring, dripping water and soap as she went. When she came to the door, a gasp flew out of her lips. Standing just inside of the door, Wilmont leaned on the wall, head resting against it, while blood ran in a slow, steady stream from his nose. His face looked pale and his eyes were unfocused.

"Wilmont! What happened?" Heedless of the soap, she ran to her son and placed her hands on either side of his head.

"Don't know," came the slurred voice. "Just started."

"Sit down." All but carrying the boy almost her size to a chair, she leaned his head back over the back of the chair. "Did you get hit or something?"

"No."

Miriam looked into the boy's eyes and shook her head. "Stay right there!"

Running to the door, Miriam grabbed a set of keys from a peg in the wall and hurried through the door. She looked frantically around the farm.

"Agnar! Agnar!" she yelled.

A middle-aged man poked his head out of the barn door. "What?" It came with as much irritation as it did question.

"Wilmont's bleeding again!"

"Again?" The man walked out of the barn, wiping his hands on his overalls. "What he do this time?"

Miriam ran to the man. "He didn't do nothing. And he doesn't look good. His eyes are wandering around and his speech is slurred."

"Just put him in bed," the man said with a dismissive wave of his hand.

"NO! No, Agnar, we are not ignoring this. This is my son and we are going to get him treatment!" Her finger poked point-blank in the man's face, threatening as any gun.

"You want to take him to those heretic doctors? Not my family. What would the neighbors say?"

"When it comes to my son, I don't care! Everyone goes to them, you know that." Miriam poked her husband in the chest. "Even the town council goes to them when the town doctors can't do anything. Everyone knows that. Agnar, this is serious! He needs to get looked at." Miriam stomped her feet and put her hands on her hips.

"I ain't taking no son of mine to no heretic doctor!" Agnar said with equal force.

"Then I will! So either help me get him into the truck or stay out of my way!"

Agnar turned back to the barn. With a huff, Miriam turned, quick stepping back to the house. Once inside, she grabbed a small towel and hurried to Wilmont.

"Hold this under your nose," she said, placing the towel there. With her arms under his armpits, she lifted the boy to his feet, putting her arm around him for support. "Come on, I'm taking you to the doctor."

"Pa be mad?" the boy asked as his head lolled forward.

"We're not going to worry about Pa right now."

Almost falling three times, Miriam managed to get Wilmont into the truck. Once behind the steering wheel, she plugged in and turned the key. The engine came to life with barely a whisper. Pushing "D", she slammed the accelerator to the floor, though the vehicle accelerated in a smooth manner that ignored her urgency.

"Damn it! I'm in a hurry, you stupid truck!" she yelled.

"Is this an emergency?" a voice asked from the console.

"YES! It is an emergency!"

"Would you like to proceed to the nearest medical center at the quickest safe speed?" the voice asked in a calm voice.

"Of course I would!" Miriam yelled back.

Automatic belts wrapped around Miriam and Wilmont as the vehicle accelerated. The steering wheel lost all resistance as the vehicle drove itself down the dirt drive, slowing enough to make the turn onto the road at the last moment. Miriam put her hand on her son's chest. As she looked at him, she swore to herself that he looked paler than before.

"Hold on, honey, we'll be there soon."

Braking hard, the truck stopped in front of the entrance to the Chicago Medical Assistance Center, located just outside the barrier-wall of Chicago. Miriam had been struggling with her seat belt for a quarter of a mile, trying to get it off. With the vehicle fully stopped, the seat belts disengaged themselves from the passengers.

"The facility has already been informed you are coming," the console said in the same calm voice.

"Thank you," Miriam replied as she exited her door and ran around the vehicle. By the time she reached Wilmont's door, a robotic personal conveyance and a man were almost there.

"I'll get him out, ma'am," the man said. "Just in case his condition requires it."

"Please hurry!" Miriam held the door, restraining herself from helping the man but not managing to stand still. Once the conveyance was occupied, he secured straps around Wilmont and it tilted horizontal. Patient secured, the device headed back into the medical center. Miriam watched, following.

"What are his symptoms?" the man asked.

"He's been getting nose bleeds for no reason. He also gets dizzy and he slurs his speech when it happens." Miriam could not help looking past the man at the retreating gurney.

"What about his eye sight?" the man led her to the medical building at a calm walk.

"I don't know, we normally make him lay down for a while. Guess I never thought about his sight."

"Don't worry. We'll get him to a diagnostic platform right away." As they walked through the double doors, the man indicated some seats with his hand. "Please, take a seat. An assistant will be right with you."

"Can't I go with my son?" The first quiver of worry came into Miriam's voice.

"We'll let you see him as soon as possible but right now you would only be in the way. He will get treated faster if you stay here."

Breathing in and pulling herself together, Miriam nodded. "Okay, but please hurry."

As the man left, Miriam looked at the seats but couldn't bring herself to sit down. There were no windows to the area where they had taken Wilmont so she paced the floor. It wasn't until she had crossed it several times before she noticed that two other small groups of people also sat in the waiting area. They were both dressed in the Puritan fashion but she did not recognize anyone. They each gave her a strained smile when she looked at them and she managed to give one back, but no one started a conversation. The same worried look that must have been on her face was clear on the other ladies in the room.

As she thought about the others in the room, a lady in a white blouse and pants came through the door and walked toward Miriam. The lady held a easy smile on her face. Miriam didn't wait for the woman to speak.

"Do they know what's wrong with Wilmont yet?"

"He's being diagnosed now. When it is done, a doctor will come out and talk to you. Please, will you sit with me?" The woman made a smooth motion to the chairs.

"I... I don't think I can," Miriam said, shaking her head.

"I know you're worried but I'm sure your son will be all right. I've seen worse come in that door." The woman's eyebrows raised with a quick motion at the statement. "I'm Chalene by the way."

"Chalene?" Miriam shook her head. "I'm sorry, this whole thing has me totally upset. I didn't mean to react like that."

"You're fine. I know you're worried. Would you like something to drink?"

"No, I can't..." Miriam stopped herself and took a calming breath. "Yes, thank you. I probably better. Just some water."

"Of course." Chalene walked over to a wall and opened a door, removing a bottle of water. She twisted the top off as she walked back, handing it to Miriam.

The drink Miriam took was slow. When she finished and looked at the bottle, over half of the water was gone.

"Guess I was thirstier than I thought," Miriam said. She started to hand the bottle back to the lady.

"Keep it. You'll feel better if you don't dehydrate."

"I suppose so." Miriam felt weak to the point of exhaustion but sleep sounded like an enemy.

"Please, let's sit down." The woman walked the few steps to a chair. Sighing, Miriam followed. For some reason she now felt like she could sit down, taking the seat next to the lady.

"Thank you for being so kind. I was so worried—still am I guess."

The woman grinned. "I could just say it's my job, which it is, but I like helping people who come here. I don't know how to heal people but I do seem good at making them feel more comfortable while they wait."

"I'd say that's just about as important."

Taking another drink, Miriam finished the water in the bottle. As she looked in amazement at it, a woman in a long white coat walked out of the door they had taken Wilmont through. Miriam looked up with expectation. The woman walked over to her.

"Are you Wilmont's mother?" the woman asked.

"Yes. How is he?"

"Would you come with me please? We'll talk in private."

Her hands shaking and bottle forgotten on the chair, Miriam stood and followed the woman to a door at the side of the room. As she walked there, she stole a glance at the people in the room, receiving sympathetic looks in return. The door led to a room with four fully-padded chairs and a small table. The woman gestured toward one of the chairs and sat in a facing one. Miriam sat down, her knees threatening to give out as she did so.

"I'm Ordanza. I'm a doctor here. It's a good thing you brought your son in when you did."

"He's alive?" Miriam felt a wave of relief wash over her. Tears threatened.

"Yes, but he's in serious condition. He has a tumor in his head pressing on the left optic nerve. You know what a tumor is, correct?"

Miriam nodded. "Yes. I've seen them in animals."

"Your son's tumor needs to be removed. We can do it here but we need your permission."

"Of course, of course. I... I didn't bring any money to pay for the operation..." A new worry showed on Miriam's face.

"We don't charge you for our services." A kind smile filled the woman's face.

"Can he go home afterwards?"

"The surgery, while relatively simple to perform, is quite traumatic to the body. We need to keep your son here at least overnight. It would be dangerous if he was moved too much."

"But I can stay until you are done, right? And then come back tomorrow?"

"Of course. If you'll excuse me, I'll get the procedure started." The woman stood. "You can stay in here if you want or sit in the waiting area. Excuse me."

It was only a half-hour later when Miriam was led to another small room, but this one held a bed and equipment. Wilmont was in a bed asleep, a round bandage on the side of his head. It was much smaller than Miriam would have expected.

"How is he?" Miriam asked the man manipulating a holographic display.

"He's fine. We need to keep his head still for a while so we will keep him asleep until tomorrow." The man looked up after a few seconds. "You can kiss him gently if you wish."

"Thank you." Miriam did just that and then squeezed his hand. "He'll be fine now?"

"Good as new."

"Can I stay for a while?"

"Of course. Someone will tell you when you need to leave but you have plenty of time. There is a hotel across the road that you can use for free if you wish."

Miriam pulled a chair over to the bed and sat, holding Wilmont's hand. When the man left, the tears flowed freely.

Chapter Two
Unspoken

Waking up in a strange room caused Wilmont to panic at first. He didn't remember much after his mother put him in the truck. The walls and ceiling were whiter than any walls or ceiling he had ever seen. They also looked strange, not like walls and ceilings he was used to.

A firmness on his body made Wilmont look down at his chest. A strap ran across it and across his legs, holding him to a bed like one he had never seen before. The bed-sheets were also a stark white and a shining metal frame surrounded the bed, only adding to the strangeness. The straps were strong enough that he could not move against them. The straps added to his panic, but when he couldn't move, he decided to wait on the panic until it could be useful, when the opportunity to run away came around.

Footsteps caused Wilmont to look to his left. A woman in white, almost as stark as the walls and ceiling, walked toward him. She had blonde hair pulled back behind her head, no jewelry, and wore a smile.

"How are we feeling this morning?" the woman asked.

"What... where...?" Too many questions ran through his head to express any in a complete form.

"Here, let me get those," the woman said, reaching for the straps. "We didn't want you hurting yourself while you were asleep."

"Am I in heaven?" It sounded silly but beat at least one alternative.

"No!" the woman said with a laugh. The straps retracted below the bed as she unclasped them. "You're in a hospital. You had brain surgery to remove a tumor in your head. Do you feel better?"

Wilmont's eyes went wide as he looked away from the lady. He tilted his head one way and then the other. "Yeah! My head used to hurt all the time but it doesn't anymore. Wow, I got so used to it I didn't even think about it being gone." Wilmont moved his head some more in ever extreme motions.

"That's an improvement then. The doctor will want to examine you so she should be in soon. Do you need to use the restroom?"

"Yes!" Wilmont's enthusiasm came from the realized urgency that his bladder was yelling as if it were one of his little sisters. The woman helped him up and held his arm while he walked to the small room in the corner but let him go inside by himself. Inside there were rails on the walls to use as support. He wasn't sure that he needed them, but made sure they were close.

Feeling much better after leaving the restroom, the woman insisted that Wilmont lie back in the bed while he waited for the doctor. Since exploring the building wasn't allowed, Wilmont resigned himself to waiting and examining the room.

"Would you like to watch something while you wait?" the woman asked.

"Watch what?" Wilmont looked around the room to find something to watch.

"I meant on the display," the woman said with a giggle. "Display on."

Wilmont jumped as a three-dimensional image of a person appeared at the foot of his bed. The person looked real but was too small to be a real person, plus she floated in mid-air.

"What do you like to watch?"

"I've… I've never watched anything like that before." Wilmont was wide-eyed but couldn't look away, tilting his head at times.

"Really? What do you do in the evenings?"

"We go to bed when it gets dark. Sometimes we stay up to catch fireflies or have a bonfire, but that's only for special occasions."

"I see. Maybe something about nature."

The display changed to a tropical jungle. Bird calls and croaks came from the display. A large insect flew across the view.

"Expanding our patient's world view?" a woman's voice came from behind the nurse. Both the nurse and Wilmont turned to watch as Doctor Ordanza entered the room.

"Luck of the draw," the nurse said easily. She stepped away from the bed but didn't leave the room.

"Lay back, please," Ordanza said to Wilmont. She reached over him and drew a pad from the wall behind him. The pad extended until it was over his head and stopped. "Just relax and stare straight ahead. Most likely you won't feel anything but maybe just a little tingle."

Wilmont complied, afraid to even breathe. It seemed only a few seconds before the pad retracted back to the wall. The doctor looked over his head toward the wall.

"It appears that everything is fine. We need to get some food and fluids into you so I'll have them bring you something. Anything particular you want?"

"Ice cream?" Wilmont said in a soft but eager voice. "I love ice cream and we almost never have it."

The doctor laughed. "I'm sure we can get you some ice cream for dessert."

While not his mother's, the food was really good and the ice cream was cold and creamy. Wilmont was sorry to see it gone but didn't ask for more. The doctor came in again after he was finished and used the pad to examine him again. She smiled, giving the idea of being happy with what she saw, making him think everything was fine. Afterwards his mother came into the room. Her red eyes made it clear that she had been crying, something he had not seen her do often.

"Is he okay?" his mother asked.

"Good as new," the doctor replied with a smile.

"Can I take him home then?"

"Of course. We'll just need you to sign for services so they can be counted in the exchange." The doctor gave a quick look to Wilmont. "And we'll let him get dressed."

"Of course." A small amount of red appeared in his mother's checks.

"If you'll follow the nurse," the doctor said with a wave of her hand. Miriam followed the man from the room. As the doctor turned to follow, Wilmont spoke.

"Can I ask a question?"

"Sure." The doctor turned back to the bed.

"What if I don't want to go back home?"

The question caused the doctor to pause for a moment and look at the boy. "Where do you want to go?"

"I want to stay here, in the city."

"The city, of course, will not turn you away, but this is something you need to bring up with your mother." It was the first time Wilmont saw concern on the woman's face.

"You couldn't just tell her for me?" A slightly pained looked came across Wilmont's face. The doctor responded with a serious look of her own.

"If you are old enough to stay, you are old enough to inform your mother yourself. That's the deal." With a final look, the doctor turned and left the room.

"Darn." Wilmont sighed.

Wilmont found his clothes on a table near the bed. They were freshly laundered and pressed but not stiff as they would have been at home after pressing. Even clean, he was keenly aware of how dull they looked compared to the ones he had just taken off. Maybe it was because he was leaving, but the whole room looked cleaner than any room had been in his house.

"Do all the houses in the city look this way?" he asked himself. With a shrug, he walked to the door. The nurse was waiting outside the door to lead him to the waiting area and his mother. The rest of the building was more of the same white walls. The carpet in the hallway was soft under his feet. The air even smelled like pine trees. Since he saw no trees he wasn't sure where the scent was coming from, but he didn't ask. At least the building didn't smell like animal dung. While he was still taking in the surroundings, they turned into the room where his mother waited.

A hug was the first thing his mother gave him, a long one that included some swaying. It made Wilmont tense a little. His mother must have felt the tension because she withdrew to arm's length and gave him a look of concern.

"Is something wrong? And don't tell me I'm embarrassing you. I'm your mother and I get to hug you after almost losing you."

Wilmont paused for a few seconds and looked at the ground, everything making things harder. Finally he took a deep breath and spoke without looking at his mother.

"I don't want to go back home."

"What?" His mother's face froze. "What do you mean you don't want to go back home?"

"There's nothing for me there! There's not enough land to divide between me and my brothers and I'm not much of a farmer anyway." Looking up, Wilmont paused a couple of seconds before the next statement. "Besides, I won't miss Pa hitting me over the side of the head. Plus Stephen started doing it too!"

Wilmont could see the doctor behind his mother open her mouth for a moment, but then shut it again.

"But, but where would you go if not with your family?" his mother said in a weak voice. Sadness filled her eyes.

"I'd stay here, in the city. You know they'd take me in. And you could come visit me anytime you want. Ma, I want to learn things! I want to learn about the world! I don't want to be stuck on a farm digging in the dirt for the rest of my whole life. There's things even on the farm no one will talk about, things in the ground and insects and plants that no one seems curious about, even things we see every day. It drives me crazy that no one will talk about them! I just get told to not worry about it and think about church stuff. Didn't God create the world and the earth and the bugs and the plants? If so, what's so wrong about learning about them?"

During the whole speech, Wilmont's mother gave him a look he had seen before, but only briefly. This time it stayed and continued even after he quit speaking. She looked a little lost, but also a little sad and maybe a little hopeful. Tears formed in her eyes but did not run down her checks. He just stared back and waited for an answer.

"I know," she finally said. "I know you have always been more curious than your brothers or sisters. And I know you've been punished for it over my objections to your father in private."

Miriam reached up and tousled her son's hair. "What am I going to do with you? I'm your mother, I've always worried about you and I always will. But you are growing up and you have to find your own way. I just wish it wasn't so far from home. But you're right. You can't stay on the farm and there's no land close for you to take over. Either way, you would be making a home of your own soon. I just wanted a few more years before I wasn't your mother anymore."

Another hug came, this one even tighter and longer than before. When it was done, Miriam turned to the doctor.

"You'll make sure they take care of my boy, won't you?"

"Of course. He'll be well taken care of. And you can visit him any time you want, you or anyone else in your family."

Miriam returned a smirk to the comment that left the doctor with a questioning look. Miriam turned back to her son. "You take care of yourself and don't do anything stupid, you hear?"

Wilmont nodded. "Of course, Mama. I'll make you proud of me, I promise."

"I always was proud of you," Miriam said with another hug, "even if pride is against the church's teaching."

Miriam gave her son a kiss on the cheek and then quickly turned and walked away. Wilmont watched, heartbroken but hopeful at the same time, lost to know how he could be both. He was thankful there wasn't anyone else he knew in the room. When the door closed, he turned to the doctor, loss on his face.

"Come on," she said. "I'll take you to the processing center. Since you've already had a full medical examination, it should go quickly."

Back home, Miriam got out of the truck as her husband walked out from the barn, wiping his hands on a rag. He looked into the cab of the vehicle.

"Where's the boy?"

"He didn't make it," she replied without looking at him.

"It was God's will," the man said without emotion as he turned back toward the barn.

Chapter Three
Big Change

"You like those?" the nurse asked Wilmont. He had changed his farm clothes for a pair of blue pants and a yellow-and-green shirt that was divided in a diagonal line across his chest. They were much softer than his old clothes but did not feel delicate.

"They're very comfortable," Wilmont replied.

"I'm sorry we can't let you keep your old ones. Pest control, you understand." The woman gave him a strained smile.

"Sure." Wilmont gave a shrug that indicated he did not understand. "You can keep them. I like these a lot better."

"The family that we are placing you with can help you pick out more and will help you get anything else you need, like a hairbrush." The woman made a flipping motion with her hand.

"How many more sets of clothes can I have?"

"That's between you and them, but I won't go too wild with asking." She shook her head like he should take her suggestion.

"Like, three?"

The question caused the woman to laugh. "Oh, more than three I'm sure. Now, on to more important things."

The woman walked over to a table and picked up two small items. They were crescent-shaped and about the size of a large pea pod. When she came back, Wilmont could see that they were shiny like they were made of metal. She held them up to eye level.

"These are your interfaces. They will be your communication with other people who aren't with you at the time. They're like a phone. They also do a lot more than that, but for now we'll just worry about communication. They're placed just over the ears." The woman pulled back her hair to show one over her left ear. "They don't hurt, though it may take a while for you to get used to them being there."

The woman reached up and placed one device above each of Wilmont's ears. It did feel a little strange to have them there, but they were soft and fit right into the crevice above his ears. She twisted a wire around the back of his ear and up into his ear canal.

"The wire will secure the device to your ear and has a speaker directed into the ear so you can listen to people who are talking to you over the interface."

"Will people hear what I say?"

"When you are talking to someone over them, yes. Just speak normal. The devices actually sense the vibrations in your head to communicate to others. Just give your head a small twist to the left when you want to use them to talk to someone and another when you want to stop talking to them." A serious expression came over the woman's face.

"How will it know who I want to talk to?"

"Just say their name and the computer will connect you to the person. Now, here is the important part. Never take them off. And if we are ever visited by aliens again, for sure don't take them off. Do you understand?"

"Sure," Wilmont said as his head jerked back slightly with the forcefulness of her voice. "Why not?"

"Because the devices include shields that will deploy if any telepathic communication is detected, if they are not activated manually. Did you know that the aliens communicated telepathically?"

Wilmont shook his head.

"Do you know what 'telepathic' means?"

Wilmont shook his head again as his cheeks turned slightly red.

"It means their minds can talk directly to our minds without speaking." Wilmont's face twisted as one eyebrow went up and one went down. "It's how they spoke to mankind before. We are not sure if they could control people with the same ability or not, but we do know they killed at least one person with it."

"Just by looking at them?" Wilmont asked, his face going from red to white.

"Without being in the same country."

Wilmont felt a small amount of sweat go down the side of his face. "Don't worry, I won't take them off. Wait! What if I take a bath or go swimming?"

"They're waterproof, so don't worry. In fact, they're about everything proof, so most likely you will even forget they're there. Just leave them there and don't worry about them, right?"

Wilmont nodded.

"Okay, let's get them turned on."

"Computer," the woman said into the air, "please turn on Wilmont's interfaces and register them to him."

"I'd be happy to," a voice said from somewhere Wilmont couldn't see. He couldn't tell if the voice was male or female, but then he didn't know if a computer was either.

A small amount of noise, like rustling grass, came to Wilmont's ears, then disappeared. But then he felt a movement from the device.

"That's strange," the woman said as she stared at him.

"What?" Wilmont's eyes moved nervously.

"The shields deployed." The woman looked back into the room. "Computer, run a diagnostic on Wilmont's interfaces and make sure they are working correctly."

"Shields?" Wilmont asked.

"Both devices are working within specifications," the disembodied voice said.

"Then why are the shields deployed?"

"What are shields?" Wilmont asked, tilting his head to try and get the woman's attention. He felt up by his ears to find that flat plates had extended themselves along the side of his head.

"They are deployed when telepathic signals are detected to protect your mind from them. But computer, there are no aliens on the world, correct? So there are no telepathic signals."

"You are correct that the aliens have not returned to Earth, but the devices are registering telepathic signals just within detectable range."

"How is that possible? Do you detect any signals?" The nurse looked more and more confused.

"No, I detect no signals. The strength of the signals indicated by the interfaces would require the source be very close to the devices."

"But I'm standing right next to him and mine are not detecting anything. That would mean..." The woman stopped talking and looked at Wilmont with wide eyes.

"Did I do something wrong?" Wilmont asked as the woman stared, a small amount of fear entering his voice. She stayed that way for longer than made him comfortable.

"No," she finally said weakly. "You did nothing wrong. We need to go speak to someone."

Grabbing his arm, the woman walked Wilmont from the room.

"Where are we going?" he asked.

"To speak to someone a lot smarter than me," the woman replied.

Chapter Four
Head of State

Clothed in full military dress, minus the medals, the general walked in to the President's office without knocking. The room was not an oval like the traditional President's office. The engineers who had designed the building had proclaimed an oval too space inefficient. Because the building was round, the room had curved inner and outer walls, looking more like a pie section out of which someone had already taken the best bite. The door was located in the middle of the inner curve and provided those who entered with a grand view of the whole room with a backdrop view of Denver through the glass on the outer wall. The whole effect could be stunning on a clear day and more than made up for the non-traditional room layout.

The furnishings in the room, though, were more traditional. A large, wooden desk was positioned to one side to provide anyone who sat behind it a view of the room and the city. It was not the historic desk, which had succumbed to time, but an exact replica. Most of the furniture were replicas, like the carpet with the President's seal, though a few were antiques. The paintings on the walls were masterpieces, with a large painting of colonial America hung across from the President's desk.

The traditional accouterments were accompanied by modern, less noticeable, security features, computer interface relays, and a three meter diameter holographic display unit that projected into the middle of the room. Realistic enough when used, a visitor could find themselves talking to someone without knowing they were not actually there. Several had been caught trying to shake the hand of a hologram, which had turned into a favorite gag played on newbies.

Carefully treading on the carpeted floor, Tigen walked up behind the President in complete silence, an accomplishment given his two meters in height and over one hundred kilos in weight. His long service in the military had taught him many things, one of which was how to be unnoticed. It also helped that the President was preoccupied with the latest legislation that had been sent from Congress. Wrapping his arms around her, he used one hand to turn her head to meet his and planted a full kiss on her lips. When the kiss ended, she opened her eyes and looked into his.

"And why do you think you can just walk in here and kiss the President?" she asked with a playful tone.

"Because I have been kissing her for thirty years," the man answered smugly.

"I like that answer." Worthia Amster turned and gave the man a kiss of her own, long and meaningful. "You have any plans later tonight?"

"Not yet. Does my President require my services?" General Tonsten asked.

"Oh, she does." Worthia's eyebrows rose and fell. She traced her finger along the line of the striping. "You know how I love a man in uniform."

"Yes," Tonsten said with a grin, "but I'll let you remind me."

The door to the office slamming open ended the conversation and caused the two to separate. A breathless aide came through the door.

"M. President!"

"Yes, Tom?" The exhaled sigh only emphasized her disdain at being interrupted.

"You're needed in the communications room right away!"

"Is it really that urgent?" Worthia started to slowly walk toward the door.

"You'll definitely want to hear the news from Chicago." The young man nodded for emphasis.

"What is it?" she asked.

"I don't want to say, in case they're wrong."

"Fine, let's go find out what's so urgent." With a resigned sag of her body, Worthia followed Tom from the room and into the hallway. Tigen took his place in tow a step behind her as was his habit. As they walked, Worthia noted that some people whispered to each other as they watched the two pass. The ones whispering looked as if they were expecting something from her.

"Word travels fast around here, doesn't it?" she said.

"It's a small place," Tigen responded.

"Not as small as it was two hundred years ago," Worthia retorted. "In fact, it is several times larger."

"True, but it's not too large to prevent news traveling fast. I think the fact that the floor plan is round only helps. Besides, people carry interfaces that interact at the speed of light. Not a good situation to keep secrets." A slight tremble showed up in his voice.

"I must say that is true." Worthia heard a sigh of relief from her shadow.

The doors to the communications room opened automatically to reveal a small host of people. The room was situated on the opposite side of the building and was larger than the office they had just left. The table and chairs had been withdrawn into the floor, leaving only a few chairs along the outside wall. The holographic display was at the clock-ward end of the room and was surrounded by those in attendance. They parted as Worthia entered and walked toward the display.

"Good afternoon. To whom are we speaking?" she asked.

"The Chicago Chief Scientist, Hars Lensin, is waiting to brief you," Secretary of Information Lorda Rans said before stepping out of Worthia's path. Worthia continued to the display and looked into the eyes of the image of the man standing at the front of the display. Behind him were several others who couldn't seem to stand still or maintain eye contact with anyone for long. Mr. Lensin was the only one who faced the President in a calm, professional manner, though his mouth twitched with eagerness.

"Chief Lensin, what have you decided to pre-empt my evening with?" Worthia crossed her arms.

"M. President. We had a young man come into the medical center yesterday for treatment, then ask to stay…"

"Yes, yes," Worthia said, rolling her fingers in front of her. "Get to the point."

The man cleared his throat. "When he was fitted with his interface, the telepathic shields activated. Upon examining him, it appears that he is sending out the faint telepathic waves. They are not strong enough to communicate with anyone and are not detectable more than a few centimeters from his head."

Worthia straightened and her eyes opened wide. After a few seconds, she said, "He's creating them?"

"Yes. All indications are that they are coming from him, though they don't appear to correspond to his thoughts or speech. They just appear to exist without purpose." The man kept a tight control of his emotions.

"Can he control them?"

"It doesn't appear that he is even aware of them. He has demonstrated no conscious control of the signals."

"M. President," Secretary of State Url Pernent interrupted, "we need to have that boy sent here right away."

"Agreed!" Worthia responded without looking. "Chief, get that boy on the fastest plane here, immediately."

The man appeared to relax slightly. "Yes, M. President. We assumed you would want him sent to Denver. We have a plane prepared already. It will leave right away."

"Thank you, Chief."

The image of the man disappeared.

Worthia turned back to the gathering. "Do I need to call a meeting or are all the salient people here?"

A chuckle went through the room and smiles appeared on faces.

"I will assume by that response that you are all here. Can I also assume that we are already preparing for the boy's arrival?"

"Of course, M. President," Pernent said.

"Good." Worthia scanned the room. "I want him treated like a person, not a test subject. How old is this boy?"

"Fifteen," Pernent answered.

"Then I want him treated like a fifteen year old boy. Remember, he just came in from the Puritans so he's going to be more lost than a visiting citizen. He'll need companions, not just researchers staring at him all the time. I'm sure that can be arranged?"

"It won't be a problem."

"What will be a problem will be making him feel normal. I want all tests to be as unobtrusive as possible." She held up her hand. "I know, that will make them take longer, but this is a boy and not a lab rat. Got it?"

Heads nodded all around.

"And I want to greet the young man when he gets here. Now go do your jobs."

As people started to slowly process from the room, Worthia turned to the Secretary of Information. "Lorda, I'm sure you thought of this already, but could this be what the aliens were looking for when they were here last?"

Lorda smiled. "Of course it's impossible to tell, but I would say that, given their own abilities, this is exactly what they are looking for in the human race."

"And with our luck, that means they'll be back soon," Worthia said with a sigh.

"It has been a hundred and sixty years since they left. Every year only makes it more likely that they will return, this boy showing up or not."

"I know." Worthia shook her head. "It's just nothing ever seems to happen by itself. This feels like that music that starts up in story-holos when something important is about to happen."

"I know how you feel." Lorda's head made slow, brief nods. "Hopefully we will have a little time before they arrive to figure out what's going on with this kid and the human race as a whole for that matter."

"What did the boy come into the medical center for in the first place?"

"Brain tumor."

"Could the two be related?" Worthia's voice strained as she asked.

"God, let's hope not. I'd hate to think I'd have to get a brain tumor to become telepathic." Lorda let out a small chuckle.

"At least we would know who was getting the ability instead of them hiding it." Worthia rolled her eyes, but then became serious again. "Are we worried that there may be more Puritans that have this ability? The boy's family for instance?"

"We already tasked Chicago with checking the family under the pretext of checking them for brain tumors. If they cooperate, we might learn something. If they don't..." Lorda shrugged.

"And we can't check everyone, I know." Worthia exhaled, her head falling back to her right. "I guess we won't know until the aliens show up and start taking people, maybe. And here I was hoping for a quiet second term and a pleasant retirement."

"The signals from the boy are barely detectable within a few centimeters from his head. I don't know how the aliens would be able to detect them from any distance."

"That's the problem," Worthia said with a firm voice as she returned her eyes to look at Lorda. "We don't know."

Chapter Five
Welcome to Denver

The plane entered vertically through the opening in the top of the transparent dome. As Worthia waited, it descended to the landing pad directly underneath in a smooth motion that ended with a gentle touch on the concrete. As the whine of the engines lowered in pitch, the wings retracted into ground position. By the time the engines were a low rumble, the door opened on the side and transformed into stairs. First out was a man in military uniform. He was followed by a boy approximately five feet nine inches tall with a face full of freckles and wind-swept brown hair. Even from a distance, Worthia could see the boy's wonder looking around and his caution at stepping onto the concrete. It took a large amount of self-control to wait for the boy to come to her.

"Welcome to Denver," Worthia said with a gentle voice and an outstretched hand as the boy drew near. "I'm Worthia Amster."

The boy's hand stopped short of hers as he looked up in wonder into Worthia's face. "You're the President, aren't you, ma'am?"

"Yes, I am, but I try not to let it go to my head," she replied with a smile. The boy took her hand and shook it once.

"Why did they insist I come here?" the boy asked as his hand disengaged. "My mom can't come see me all the way here. She won't be able to find me!"

"Don't worry, if your mother wants to see you, we'll fly her here. It's much safer for you to be here than at home or even in Chicago.

Shall we go inside?" Ignoring the tension in the people behind her, Worthia kept her voice even and pleasant.

"Can I go around and see the city? I've never seen anything like it. They didn't let me see much of Chicago." The boy continued to turn in place as he looked up at the buildings.

"I'll have someone set that up right away. I thought you might want to see where you will be staying. Besides, we need to get off the landing pad." Worthia gave a small nod of her head toward the plane.

"Oh, sorry, sure. I'm not used to such things, though I was surprised at how smooth the ride was. A lot smoother than even our truck."

With a wave of her arm, Worthia turned to the landing pad exit. The boy fell in beside her, but was still distracted by the sights, even those she would have considered mundane. He kept acting like he wanted to stop to examine things, making Worthia give a small laugh. "I've seen all of this so much I guess I never thought how it would look to someone who's never seen it before."

"They don't let us have technology on the farm. We're supposed to keep things simple. They say it's good for the body to work hard, though I always figured there could be a lot of other things we could be doing if we didn't spend so much time on the simple things machines could do." Wilmont talked without looking at her.

"We can do many things, though there are some people here that still like to plant their own food or flowers and make their own things. We even have some people who weave fabrics on old-fashioned looms." The group that had come with Worthia fell in behind the two.

"Why would they do that?"

"I think it's basic human nature to make things. Besides, it gives things a personal touch that can be lacking with things made by machine."

The boy huffed and shook his head. "City folks are strange."

"Everyone is a little strange." Worthia pointed to a transport waiting along the road.

"You mean like these signals coming from my head?" The boy stepped into the vehicle after the door opened. Inside were two benches with enough room for two people with room to spare. More vehicles waited behind the first one to which the people in the group behind them headed.

"Everyone's a little different in some way. It's what makes us… us." Worthia stepped into the vehicle and took the facing bench. The door closed when she sat down.

"All those people going to follow me around all the time?" Wilmont asked, leaning slightly forward, face plastered on the window, looking at each building as it went by. The forward motion of the vehicle could barely be felt.

"Most of them were following me," Worthia said, leaning forward slightly herself. "I'm used to it and don't really notice, most of the time."

"For the preacher back home not liking you, you seem like a nice person."

"I sure hope I am!" Worthia's head came back upright. "Why doesn't he like me?"

"He says that a woman shouldn't be in charge of men." The words came out with reluctance.

"Well, the men helped put me in charge so you'd have to blame them too." She gave the boy a smile.

"What does your husband think?"

"My 'husband' is the one who insisted I run for the office."

"Why would he do that?" The tone of the boy's voice made it clear that he was trying to understand instead of condemning.

"He always said he liked me because I was so smart and that the country deserved the smartest person they could find as president. Besides, I don't think he wanted the job. Too many people asking him to do something for him."

The boy responded with a small scoff. "My ma would sure make a better president than my pa." The comment caused Worthia to laugh. "What does your husband do?"

"He's a general."

"So you're in charge of him? Because of your job I mean."

"Technically, yes. But he's a pretty smart guy too and I trust him a lot."

"Still, my pa would never go for Ma being in charge of him. Have a fit, he sure would."

"I have the feeling your pa doesn't like anyone in charge of him." Worthia nodded up and down slightly.

"You got that right, though he can't say much about the preacher without getting in trouble." The thought brought a small smile to Wilmont's face.

The vehicle came to a halt and the door opened. When he exited, he boy stood in front of a glass building that appeared to reach halfway to the dome. Plants, some in bloom, were arranged in front of the building and people walked by, giving him only a momentary glance. They were dressed in all kinds of clothes, from those much like his to some that looked to be made of shiny, flexible metal. There were even a few that looked to be made of material that he would find at home. Everyone wore the devices above their ears, but theirs did not have the shields deployed. It made him more conscious of the devices when people noticed his and stared for a few seconds. His hand went unconsciously to one of the devices.

"I'll see what we can do about those shields. Maybe we can turn the sensitivity down a little so they don't deploy all the time." Wilmont looked up to see Worthia smiling at him.

"I'd appreciate it. They feel kind of weird and I don't like people staring at me." He looked at the building in front of him. "Where are we?"

"Where you will be staying. We found a family with kids about your age. We didn't think you would want to stay by yourself." Worthia raised one eyebrow as she looked at Wilmont.

"Do I get my own room?"

"Of course, we wouldn't do that to you." Worthia smiled.

"That's better than at home." Pausing, Wilmont got a sheepish look on his face. "I do appreciate it though, ma'am."

"This way."

With an outstretched hand, Worthia led Wilmont into the building. He was relieved to see that people stared at her instead of him, though they did look briefly at him. Many shrugged when they did. As they came to a wall, a doorway opened into a small room. After they had stepped inside, the door closed and Wilmont could feel the room moving upwards.

"Have you been in an elevator before?" Worthia asked.

"No, ma'am, though I've heard of them, mostly in 'heretics are so lazy' sort of stories. Well, jokes really."

"Do you think people back home would want to walk up fifty sets of stairs to get to their room?" A small chuckle came with the question.

"No, I don't," Wilmont said with a chuckle of his own.

The door opened and Wilmont was led around a central open area to a door to the right. As they stepped up to the door, Wilmont heard a chime much like a wind-chime sound on the other side of the door. "It's strange, things happening without having to do anything."

"You get used to it. In fact, until you said something, I hadn't thought about it since I was young."

"Is someone watching us?" Wilmont's eyes darted around the interior room.

"Something. Computers keep track of people and activate the doors, etc. as needed."

"Could someone be watching also?" A small amount of fear came through his voice.

"Since I ran for my first public office, a lot of people have been keeping track of me since I am the President. They'll only watch you if they think you might be in trouble or need the attention for some reason."

"Don't they trust you?"

"More like they worry about me. It's like having dozens of moms." Worthia watched the shiver go through Wilmont's body.

"I don't even want to think about that. One's enough for me."

The door opened and a woman who looked about as old as Wilmont's youngest aunt opened the door. She wasn't wearing a skirt like his mother would have been, but pants, and had a pleasant smile on her face. Her eyes sparkled a little.

"Welcome! We're very excited to have you in our home, though we'll try to contain ourselves. Oh, sorry, I'm Renna. Oops, Ms. Daunet, I mean Mrs. Daunet." The woman shook her head as she looked up. "I have to get used to using the right terms."

"I'm sure you'll do fine," Worthia said. "Now, if you both will excuse me, I'm sure there are many people waiting for me to give them some of my time."

"You're leaving already?" Wilmont looked up at the president.

"Don't worry, they're good people." Worthia leaned down and whispered at him. "And I'm pretty sure you can take them if you need to, farm boy. They're city and soft, you know."

On her way to the elevator, Worthia activated her interface. "I want a twenty-four hour security detail for the boy."

"Already done," came the reply.

"And get someone over here to adjust his ear-pieces. He doesn't need them causing people to stare at him."

"Won't that make him more vulnerable?" came a different voice.

"Right now, he sticks out like we set him on fire. He needs to blend in if the whole world isn't going to follow his every movement." Worthia had trouble keeping the bite out of her speech when she felt she was stating the obvious.

"Yes, ma'am." The voice sounded reproved.

"Any report on the rest of the family?"

"Nothing to report, at least yet. It's a big family and most don't want to cooperate."

"Well, find some incentive. We have to at least monitor anyone with the same abilities of our friend here, even if they don't volunteer to join us."

"We'll get it done."

Chapter Six
Different Neighbors

Wilmont walked into the park, brushing his hand over his right ear to make sure his hair was in place. The ear-piece's shields no longer deployed, but the devices still felt funny on top of his ears. He had on new clothes that were even softer than the last ones that had been given him, making him pat his body to reassure himself they were actually there.

"You're either new here or it's the first time you've been let outside your whole life."

The comment made Wilmont turn to find a girl about his age standing behind him. She was very thin and wore clothes that Wilmont could not decide if they were pants or a dress. Her thin, long, auburn hair moved with every breeze while her auburn eyes remained on him. Smiling, she giggled at him when he looked at her. Her friendly eyes caused Wilmont to relax.

"I didn't expect all these plants in town. They're so... healthy."

"Of course they are, we won't want unhealthy ones around." The girl giggled again, swaying as she talked as if not able to stand still. "I'm April. You just come into town from the countryside?"

"Yes." Wilmont couldn't help but stare at the girl's thinness. "Are you all right?"

"Well, yeah, why?" The girl scrunched her eyebrows.

"My mother would say that you're so thin you look sick." Wilmont said the statement with ease but immediately became uncomfortable. "Not that I'm saying there's anything wrong with you. I mean, I just don't know and, well, you know…"

The girl burst out laughing, covering her mouth with her hand. "You're hilarious. Your face gets so red when you get embarrassed."

Wilmont looked at the ground as if trying to decide if he would not draw more attention to himself if he ran away. He made small kicking motions in the grass with one foot.

"I'm sorry," the girl said as she suppressed her laughter. "I really shouldn't have laughed. Thank you for being concerned about me, it's really sweet, but no, I'm fine. I've always been thin. Mom always said I was too busy doing things to eat too much. Guess that's true. Where're you from?"

Wilmont looked back up and gave her a weak smile. "Just outside of Chicago a ways."

"Chicago?" The girl's eyes flared. "What are you doing here? Do you have family here?"

"No." Wilmont shook his head and looked around. "It's kind of a long story. What do you guys do here? In the park I mean."

"Do you like games?" The girl started to bounce a little. "Come on, I think they have a game of Slider going right now."

The girl grabbed Wilmont's arm and started pulling him toward the center of the park. Wilmont went with her, if not enthusiastically.

"What's Slider?"

"You've never played Slider? Don't worry, it's great, you'll love it." After a few seconds she added, "You aren't afraid of getting wet, are you?"

"No." Wilmont thought for a few seconds. "How wet?"

"REALLY wet!" April's eyes glowed with the statement.

Sitting on the grass, Wilmont dripped water and panted. His clothes didn't absorb much water so it was mostly only his skin and hair that were wet. His shoes sat close by, taken off before the game started. April flopped down next to him.

"Fun, right?" she insisted through gasps of breath.

"Yeah," Wilmont said with a twist of his head, "but I think I lost."

"Lost?" April asked the question as if she had no idea what the word meant.

"Lost, as in didn't win. I was getting smeared out there."

"But that's the fun part of the game!" April laughed again, something she seemed to do a lot. "You can't get someone else all wet without getting wet too."

"But then how do you decide who wins?"

"Wins what?"

"The game!" Exasperation came through Wilmont's voice.

"I don't understand." April's smile had faded some.

"Back home, boys in particular are always competing against each other: who's the faster, who's the strongest, who can wrestle the other guy to the ground. There's always a winner and a loser, someone who gets to brag and someone who gets shamed."

"Why would I want to shame someone?" April sat up and twisted her hair, quickly draining water from it. "We're just here to have fun. We all have fun so I guess we all win. Unless someone gets hurt that is, that's no fun, but that almost never happens. Usually only when someone is stupid."

Wilmont stared, his brow furrowed and his head tilted to the right. April finished wringing out her hair and stared back.

"You were allowed to have fun, weren't you?"

"I... I don't know if I even knew what it was. We worked all the time, until sundown most days. Not Sunday, though. We went to church on Sunday, all day long."

April's head came up and she straightened her back. "You're a Puritan?"

"I was. I mean, my family was, at least. I only paid attention as much as I had to. I had too much else to worry about."

It was April's turn to cock her head. "Like what?"

"Like my brothers or their friends beating me up, or Pa getting mad at me for something. Things like that." Wilmont's eyes scanned the surroundings as if looking for danger.

April leaned in. Her eyes shifted back and forth several times before talking. "Would he beat you? I heard Puritan dads do that."

"Of course he did." Wilmont watched her eyes grow wide as he said it. "If you weren't beat some time in your life, you were called spoiled."

"That's awful!" April shook her head with purpose. "Well, no one's going to beat you here, we're civilized. We don't do awful things like that."

"That's good." It was Wilmont's turn to chuckle. "I don't think you could take a beating."

"Who'd want to?" April leaned back in shock at the suggestion, but then she bit her lip and leaned back toward Wilmont. "Do you have any scars? Can I see them?"

"Am I allowed to show you?" Wilmont whispered back.

Chapter Seven
The Real Question

"Tell me you have something, anything." Worthia controlled her voice to an even keel while her face told a different story. Those in front of her shuffled from one foot to the other, most looking at the ground, even though the President had met them in their own lab to try and make them less nervous. The man in front took a small step forward and cleared his throat.

"I'm afraid not much." The man looked down and back up. "Scans of his brain don't show us anything of value. The variations in his brain are within normal human variation. Without more examples like him, we can't tell which variations are important and which aren't."

"Assuming that you can even know what to look for and that any of the variations mean something." Closing her eyes, Worthia shook her head. "Don't you have any good news?"

"It's still early. We've been studying the boy for less than a week. These things take time." The man's voice had a note of pleading.

"Ha! Scientists always ask for more time when faced with something they don't understand." Worthia waved off the man as she turned away, stopping his objection. "The fact is, people, we don't know how much time we have. Every day is one closer to the aliens coming back to Earth. For my money, this is exactly what they came to Earth for. Somehow they knew or they implanted it in us and have been waiting for it to appear, but you can be sure they will be back.

And they will want what they have been waiting for."

The man appeared to shrink, his shoulders slumping. "We will work on it as fast as possible."

Taking a breath, Worthia tilted her head back and tried to exhale the tension. Still facing away for the group, she said, "All your efforts are appreciated. Please let me know if you find anything we can use."

"Of course, M. President."

Worthia listened to the group as she left. Once gone, she cupped her forehead in her right hand. She couldn't help but shake it some more once she removed her hand.

"You shouldn't scare people like that," a voice behind her said. "They are trying to help."

"I know," Worthia said with a sigh. "It's all just so frustrating. What happens when the aliens come back and we know no more than we did before they left?"

"We know a whole lot more than when they left, partially thanks to them. The domes, the new weapons, the mind shields, they all are a result of the aliens' arrival even if they didn't help our scientists create these things. They came from the aliens' technology. The human race had stagnated. They were the disruption we needed. We're stronger now. We can take on the aliens when they come back and we can win!"

"If they don't bring more than one ship, that is." Worthia turned to face Secretary of Defense Chadan Mantarida standing just behind her. The small man looked half-starved with his sunken cheeks and thin limbs, even though he ate twice what anyone else did, at least in public. His hair was equally thin, as were his eyebrows and nose. His diminutive size was in contrast to his intellect and his passion. "Your faith in our military is well known, Chadan. Not everyone is as confident as you."

"Which is why I am Secretary of Defense, right?" The man gave a mischievous grin.

"Or it might just be a 'chicken or the egg' thing." Worthia shrugged, but her face relaxed a little. She turned back the direction she had been heading and started walking again. "I can't help thinking that looking for telepathic abilities are why the aliens were here."

"They would be very useful in several areas. At least to my way of thinking, but then I am not EO-AY." Chadan tilted his head and rotated his hands.

"But the EO-AY were already telepathic…"

"With the aid of machines, of that we are pretty sure. They may have needed the machines to communicate in the first place. No one ever recorded them physically speaking. They may be incapable."

"But if they wanted someone to speak for them, couldn't they just telepathically tell them what to say?"

"We have no idea what using the machines took out of them. Maybe that is the reason for the long pauses between actions and communication. If they found a race that had natural telepathic abilities, maybe the EO-AY could talk to them directly on their own without the use of machines. My guess is that it would make things a lot easier."

"Not to mention the advantage telepaths would have in negotiations, particularly long ones if they could only use their machines for a limited time." The words came out with a blend of disgust and envy.

"And other areas." Chadan turned and moved to walk next to the woman. Doors opened for them as they made their way outside to a group of security that waited for them.

Worthia moved back to her vehicle. "Did you ever wonder why the President still has so much security wherever I go?"

"You're the President, reduce the number in your detail." Chadan said the words as if the answer was easy.

"I tried." Sighing, Worthia continued the conversation once seated. "What other areas would telepathy be an advantage?"

"Think of the advantage in hand-to-hand fighting if you know what your opponent is going to do." Chadan took a facing seat.

Worthia let out a laugh. "Definitely. Not that I think Tigen needs it. He already acts like he knows what the other person is going to do. Have you seen his training bouts? I'm surprised anyone still fights him."

"Or stealing information?"

"If you could read their minds without them knowing it." Worthia's head nodded.

"Or even just knowing what people really want, the things they don't tell anyone. You surprise someone with their secret heart's desire and imagine the impact that would have." Chadan relaxed into the chair.

"If you don't use it as blackmail." Worthia's tone had a hint of darkness.

"Yes, that is another possibility."

"But couldn't you just set up detectors to know when they were using their telepathy?"

"You're assuming a technologically advanced race. If they were less advanced…"

"They wouldn't even know what was going on. Would fit a profile of being manipulators of lesser races. By the way, why did you come around in the first place?" Worthia's head came up to look at the man.

"I thought you might need someone to talk to." Chadan smiled. "You've looked stressed since we found out about the boy and I know involving you in a discussion always seems to help."

"And impart a little wisdom along the way?" One of Worthia's eyebrows raised.

Chadan made a small bow. "I am your humble servant."

"Ha!" Worthia shouted. Her mood lightened for the first time. "I am sure neither of those words apply to you, my friend."

"You wound me." Chadan put a hand to his heart as he gave a friendly smile.

"From that slight graze of truth, I am sure you will recover. Now, unless you have something else you need from me, I am sure there are people waiting for my attention. There always are."

"I will take my wounded soul and retire to my office." Chadan made another small bow, hand still on his heart.

"Wounded soul my ass," Worthia said in a small voice as they stepped out to the Warrence Donnest Government Building which held all the federal offices. It was fifty stories high to represent the original states, or so they said. "I would say ego, but I'm sure that's impenetrable. Kate!"

Worthia waited a few seconds for a reply from her interface. *"Yes, M. President?"*

"Did you ever wonder why they didn't move the government back to Washington, D.C.?" Worthia started into the building.

"History says that the Puritans burned down the buildings after they took control of the city."

"Yes, but I mean after things had settled down and the citizens were back in control, mostly."

"By that time, the District of Columbia had been absorbed back into the states it had been made from. The city didn't exist anymore."

"It could have been done."

"They probably figured it wasn't worth the effort. Besides, the weather there in the summer is awful."

"True. It was built on a swamp. I could never figure out why people do that with cities. Who's waiting for me now?" Her private elevator was waiting, open, for her.

"You have some choices..." The voice trailed off.

"Great. That's *always* a good sign."

Chapter Eight
Intrusion

"We just lost Kuiper Belt monitor number three."

"What?" Captain Moraine Harjo turned toward the Space Command monitoring station number twenty-three. The facility was in the third basement of the government building, a fact that continued to strike Harjo as ironic. Fifty stations monitored satellites in the Kuiper Belt, each major planet, the asteroid field, and eight satellites around Earth for any activity in space. Most of their time was spent tracking comets or meteorites and destroying old space junk as practice with the space-based lasers. "What do you mean we lost it?"

"The transmissions stopped." The man tried to sound calm, but his voice was edged with concern.

"What do the records show just before the signal was lost?" Captain Harjo made purposeful steps toward the station.

"Nothing definitive." The man's voice cracked slightly at the end as if in anticipation to the next statement.

"We're supposed to be monitoring space, God dammit! What good are we if we don't see anything? Play back the last images, three-sixty view."

Harjo walked up to the holographic display as the last two minutes of the signal went by and stood in the middle. If the room had been dark, it would have felt as if she was standing in space itself on top of the satellite. "Again, and rotate!" The view rotated ninety degrees to the vertical, putting the two edges of the images in front of her instead of to her side. Again, images passed by but in a different direction.

"What's that smudge?" Harjo asked. "Give me the last two minutes." As two minutes of recordings played, the smudge came and went, never more than a smudge. "What is that?"

"Could just be a rock or comet."

"How fast is it moving?" Harjo asked as if the answer should have been given already.

"We can't tell. We only have one frame of reference so we don't know how far away it is." The man gulped at the end of his statement.

"Damn budgets," Harjo muttered. "Space is too damn big. Keep rotating.

"There! What's that?" Harjo pointed at the display.

"What?"

"That small bit of red on the side of the monitor." Harjo walked over to the man's station and pointed.

"It looks like a reflection," the man said slowly.

"A reflection of what? Change the phase angle and filters of the display to the reflection's source."

The man's fingers manipulated the view, rotating it in various planes and changing colors. "It's mostly below the monitor, directly below. There's only a partial image."

"Show it."

After more manipulation, the view stopped. It showed a thin red line, blurred, sweeping a small arc.

"Damn it!"

"What?"

"Send me that file!" Ignoring the man, Harjo brought her interface up to her mouth. "This is Captain Harjo, Space Command. I need to talk to the President as soon as I get there."

Harjo strode into the President's office almost at a march. Back straight, she executed a precise salute two steps into the room.

"At ease, Captain," Worthia replied, a slight quiver in her voice.

The office was not used to that amount of formality shown by the captain. "What do you have?"

Harjo, still rigid, walked to the display control on the desk and transferred a file from her interface. The image from the Kuiper Belt monitor appeared above the desk, large enough to block the women's sight of each other. Worthia studied the image for twenty seconds before speaking.

"And what do you think this red streak is?"

"I've seen images of the alien warriors when they were here last. My opinion is that it is one of their flaming swords." The words were delivered without emotion as Harjo maintained her military posture.

"And the other thing?"

"I would place my bets on their ship. The warrior would have to have come from somewhere." Even Harjo's words were still at attention.

Sighing, Worthia walked around the desk. "Your at-ease posture is not well developed, is it?"

The comment brought Moraine's head around in a quick jerk, followed by a relaxing of her shoulders. "Sorry, ma'am, force of habit."

"Our families are old friends, you know," Worthia said with a kind smile. "We should be too."

"But... you and the general. It might not be... appropriate." The precise military voice was replaced with a halting one, softer, without the crisp diction.

"I said we should be friends. You and General Tonsten are another matter."

The comment caused Moraine to let out a small laugh, her head dipping for an instant with the laugh. The rest of her body relaxed more. "I can see why people like you so well."

"Part of the job," Worthia replied with a flip of her head and hands. After one last smirk of a smile, her face got serious again. "So, if this is a flaming sword, that would mean the guardians don't require air to breathe?"

"We always suspected that they were not organic, or at least living beings as we understand them, though they could have organic matrix parts. If you reviewed the records of the attack on the ship, the one that took damage did not bleed blood as we would know it."

"A lot of people don't bleed when getting hit by particle fire." Worthia turned her attention back to the display.

"And many do. It is not conclusive evidence, just a noted fact."

"At which I am sure you are good at. So," Worthia turned to the woman, "if this is a guardian, where is the ship?"

Moraine shifted on her feet. "If this is a guardian, their implied range from the ship would be significant. Either that or the ship is able to hide itself from our sensors, at least at long range."

"Which, if it could, there would be no need to destroy our satellite. What we know about the aliens, though, they could have sent the guardian on a one-way suicide mission. Wouldn't be the first time they sacrificed one. Any verification from other satellites?"

"No, ma'am."

"Worthia," Worthia corrected her.

"Worthia." The name came out slow and unsure.

"If we are going to be friends, you have to call me by my first name, Moraine." A small amount of shock caused Moraine to let out a small gasp. Worthia smiled. "Don't be surprised I know who you are. I make it a point to know everyone."

"I just never imagined…"

"Besides, our families have history, remember?" Turning off the display, Worthia walked back around the desk. "So, Captain, what is our next move?"

Returning to her rigid stance, Moraine spoke in a military voice. "I have put all our sensing stations on high alert. Those near the lost satellite have been commanded to spend more time in that respective direction, but not exclusively."

"In case this was a distraction?"

"Exactly."

Worthia gave the woman another smile. "I'm sure other people are making less disturbing suggestions."

"Yes, ma'am. Random particle strike with the red streak being caused by the red-shift due to its speed."

"So hope for the best and prepare for the worst."

"Exactly. It's what the military does."

As she spoke, the door opened again and Secretary of Defense

Chadan Mantarida entered, shutting it manually afterwards even though it was not necessary. Once the door was shut, he turned to Worthia. "Started the briefing without me?" His voice was good-natured.

"Not my fault if you are late," Worthia said with a flip of her hand. "So, if this is an alien ship, how long before it's here?"

"That takes a lot of assumptions," Chadan said with a raised finger, walking toward the desk. Before he spoke again, he looked toward Captain Harjo. "That will be all, Captain."

"Yes, sir," Harjo said with a crisp salute before executing a military turn and leaving at a brisk pace. Chadan did not talk again until the door was closed.

"You dismissed my guest. I was just getting to know her," Worthia said with a half-pout.

"And I hope you get time to do that thoroughly." Chadan straightened as he turned to the president. "To answer your question, if they proceeded here at their previously demonstrated speed, they could be here in a day. But seeing as we now have sensors covering the solar system and are thus looking for their return, they may be more cautious. As you remember, the aliens never seem to be in a hurry to do anything. It might be a week, it might be more."

Worthia rolled her eyes and she walked out from behind the desk. "Or they might let us stew for a while and relax our guard." She waved her hand over her shoulder. "But that is how humans think. The aliens showed so much of what we would call arrogance before, they might not care if we know they are coming or not."

"Then why destroy the satellite?" Chadan's eyebrow went up as his head tracked the president's pacing.

"You're the military adviser, you tell me." Worthia turned, her arms crossed on her chest, her pacing stopped.

"It was something new," Chadan said easily. "It might have just been sent to investigate and only destroyed the satellite when it realized what it was, seeing it as a threat to the ship."

"How did it get so close without us seeing it?" Worthia resumed her pacing.

"It has been one hundred and sixty years since they were here last, and we have no guarantee that they demonstrated all their technology while they were here. The how is not something I consider worth worrying about. I am much happier about what their return tells us." A huge smile grew across the man's face and his eyes twinkled. The comment caused Worthia to turn back to the man.

"And what is that?"

"That wherever they took the people who went with them, it is not more than eighty light-years away. Narrows down their possible home location significantly."

"Unless they were using the people to seed another planet." It was Worthia's turn to raise a finger. "If it was that close, wouldn't we be able to identify it?"

"We can identify possibilities, but we don't have the technology to actually look on the planet surface to see what it's like, at least not yet." Chadan tilted his head and maintained his smile with the comment. Worthia waved it off.

"I assume all of the defenses are getting a shake-down."

"Of course."

Taking a deep breath, Worthia looked out the window. "Then I guess we are doing all we can for their return. Wait, what about those outside of the domes?"

"Those over which we have authority are being recalled, though they are not being told why."

"Good. Last thing we need is a panic, though I know the scientists won't be happy." The comment came with a snicker.

"Are they ever?" Chadan gave a snicker of his own.

"When they are left alone and well funded, usually. Trust me, I know the type."

Chapter Nine
The Other Side of the World

"What have we got?" The man asking the question looked more European than east Asian. At six feet, four inches tall and a shoulder size of nineteen centimeters, Mr. Smith stood stiff-backed straight in his three-piece, looking more like a statue than the head of security for Ishisun Industries. His lower, booming voice caused more than the normal amount of cringing from those under him.

"One of the American satellites was taken out." The man, one of a dozen monitors in the room, did not look away from his display as he spoke.

"And our satellites? Do we have a record of the event?" Mr. Smith's voice gained irritation.

"Yes, sir." The display changed to a view that, at first, only showed dark outer space, but then zoomed in to show an alien creature with four faces approach a satellite from below. As it came close, it drew a sword handle, activated the flame, and slashed through the satellite.

"Do the Americans have this data?"

"We have not sent it to them. Do you want us to?"

"No." Smith took a slow breath. "I meant would the American satellites have this view?"

"We do not believe so." The man's voice croaked as he spoke.

"Do they know about our satellites?"

"We do not believe so, sir."

"What about the alien ship?" At Smith's question, the display was changed to one that followed a elongated blur. "How fast is it moving?"

"We estimate at least 0.75c."

"Send me the data." Smith walked from the room and into a hallway with white stone on all sides. He turned the direction where the floor sloped up, walking with his hands behind his back. At the top of the slope, he turned to his right down a hall equally as white but with stone only on the floor. The hallway appeared to have a dead end, but pressure on the wall revealed a hidden door that led to a large room. The room had a more modern appearance and was decorated in manufactured jade and red. Drawing attention only from security guards, Smith crossed the room to a door trimmed in gold. The secretary in the adjacent room glanced but said nothing as he walked across the floor to the even more elaborate doors on the far side. After a couple of seconds of standing, the doors slid forward ten centimeters toward Smith and then sideways to allow entrance.

Smith walked into a room that contrasted with the rich decor of those he had walked through. The floor was bamboo. The walls were mostly glass with a view of a garden. The desk was glass-top with silver metal legs. The chairs were comfortable but not of any designer or historical note. At the table sat Eiji Hata, Chairman of the Western Conglomerate. Dismissing a display, Eiji looked up at Smith as he walked to the other side of the desk.

"The aliens have returned," Smith said in a plain voice. "They sent a creature to take out one of the American satellites near the Kuiper Belt, an attempt to hide their approach I assume."

"But it was picked up on one of ours," Eiji finished.

"Ours are much better hidden." Smith stood through a silence for a moment. "Do we share our data with the Americans?"

"I am sure they know by now and have guessed the cause." Eiji sat back into his chair. "Are we tracking the ship?"

The first movement by Smith since taking his stance was a slight shifting of weight on his feet. "It is proving harder to find or is already traveling at near-light speed. As they get closer, they will not have as many opportunities to hide from view."

"Assuming they dropped off this warrior while at speed, how long before they will be here?”

“Sixteen hours minimum, depending on how close they are to light speed and how long it took the creature to go from the ship to the satellite. Most likely more, but also depends on how cautious they are being.”

“Not much time.” Eiji placed his hands fingertip-to-fingertip and his elbows on the table. His thumbs beat together. “Quietly go to level three security alert. Nothing visual from the outside but I want all defenses activated. Call it a drill if you want. And I want all high-priority assets sheltered.”

“Of course, chairman.” Smith executed a small bow.

“And I want to know as soon as possible where that ship is going.”

“Of course, chairman.” Another bow.

The small table in the middle of the garden was surrounded by the smell of flowers and the songs of birds. As Smith approached, Eiji swallowed, placed his silverware next to the plate, and wiped his mouth with the cotton napkin. Looking up, he relied on his eyes to ask the question.

“We have spotted the alien ship making an approach to Earth.” The lack of nervousness in Smith’s voice was telling.

“Do we know where it will land?” Eiji placed the napkin on top of his plate.

“Not at this time. It is too far away.”

“Jerusalem again?”

“Doubtful. Their current course takes them over America and us, so either is possible.” Smith looked less confident.

“How long?” Eiji sat back into his chair, his shoulders relaxing.

“Within the hour.” Smith endured a pause. “Should we inform the Americans?” The question was asked with no emotion or hint of suggestion.

“They will find out soon enough. Besides, then we would have to explain how we know, wouldn’t we?” The question went unanswered. “And we are sure there is only one ship?”

“Yes, one hundred percent confidence.”

“First Jerusalem, now maybe America. Jerusalem made sense since it was the seat of the World Council. But why America, and if so, why not Denver, or Washington, D.C. location at least?" Eiji looked up at Smith. "Conjecture?"

"The clear reason would be that they are after something, or someone, specific. There is always the possibility that they will make a course and land somewhere else, but at their high rate of speed, their ship would be forced to slow considerably before doing so." Smith's posture or his focus just above Eiji's head had not changed during the whole conversation.

"Keep our forces on alert but reduce it to level two. No need to burn resources unnecessarily."

"Yes, chairman." Smith bowed, made a military-style turn on his heels, and walked from the garden.

"In some respects, it is too bad the aliens are landing in America," Eiji said to himself as he stood up, a smile crossing his face. "It would be interesting to watch Mr. Smith meet them in hand-to-hand conflict."

The hour passed slower and faster than any hour in Earth's history. Eiji stood, watching a wall display tracking the progress of the ship. A double-digit numeric counter next to Tokyo showing the probability of Tokyo being the destination continued to rise until it hit ninety-nine and held there. As it did, Eiji turned from the display and walked from the room, a horde of people following him. As he entered a transport in the city tube system, the one that waited for him at all times, the horde hurried into other transports. Not all made it.

"Dome edge," Eiji said when the doors had closed. Smoothly accelerating, the small vehicle made a direct line to the dome surrounding the city. "Viewing platform," Eiji added. The platform was restricted. The government didn't need a crowd of tourists or someone doing something stupid at the platform. It was one of only three that existed. The others were larger to accommodate crowds of dignitaries. The one he traveled to held three people comfortably and was the private venue of the chairman. It was not used often.

When the transport stopped and Eiji stepped onto the small

balcony on the inside of the dome, he was not surprised to find Mr. Smith waiting for him in a firm but relaxed stance. Smith did not look happy.

"Are you going to advise me not to go outside?" Eiji asked.

"I don't think I need to," Smith answered.

"I will not hide behind a dome. One must face their enemy and I will be no exception." As he walked, his hands went to the sides of his head and removed the devices from the tops of his ears.

"Now you have me concerned," Smith voiced.

"Let your enemy know as little as possible," Eiji replied, handing the devices to Smith.

"That would seem to be the opposite of what you are doing." He held the devices in his open palm as if ready for Eiji to change his mind.

"Let them try to read my mind." Raising his chin, Eiji continued to the door embedded in the dome. A military guard opened the door as he approached and closed it after he had exited. Alone, Eiji turned in the direction the alien ship approached.

Thousands of people watched from much less advantageous points as the alien ship slowed over the mountains, causing a wave of clouds to disperse ahead and to the side. The wave rolled over the countryside as if it were a statement, thin by the time it reached Tokyo. Eiji let the water condense and stay on his face, dripping as it may. It was several minutes before the ship moved again, this time toward Tokyo, at an apparent slow pace. Stiff as a statue, Eiji waited. When the ship was close enough to be imposing, it stopped.

From the top, one figure exited and made its way to Eiji. It had only one face and no obvious weapon. There was no sound or motion of wings as the messenger flew, and it stopped and stood effortlessly as if on the air itself three meters before Eiji.

"We have come for those who are ours." The words appeared to come from the messenger, his lips moving while they sounded.

"Anyone outside of the dome cities you can have. Those inside are ours." Eiji glared at the messenger, still as stone.

Time passed. "You would attack us if we attempted to enter," the messenger said without emotion.

"Yes." An equally emotionless reply.

"Why?"

"We are not your slaves, we are not your property. We are intelligent beings in charge of our own lives. If there are those who wish to go with you, so be it. But we wish only to be left alone by you to live as we desire."

"And yet you do not apply that equally to all who live here."

The insight of the statement caused Eiji to consider. Feeling nothing, he shook off the feeling. "Not everyone's desires can be accommodated, there are too many and conflicting desires. We do as well as we can."

"Some people's desires are more important than others." The blatant statement was made without accusation.

"True," Eiji said, staying stoic.

"Are yours the most important?"

"Not necessarily."

The messenger stood before Eiji, motionlessly, for several minutes. The wind did not even ruffle its robe. Eiji replied in kind as if it were a contest. Those inside held their breath. Outside, the lack of sounds made it seem that nature did too, waiting for the messenger to speak again. Finally, it did.

"We could force you to do what we want."

"Control my mind?" Eiji scoffed. "In my veins runs royal blood. I fought twice as hard to attain my position because of those who opposed me because of that blood. No one or nothing stands in my way. If you wish to try to control me, go ahead. I am no weak-minded fool to be your servant."

Again the messenger stared. Minutes went by with Eiji feeling nothing. Those inside waited without motion also, including the snipers on the messenger and Eiji. The wind whistled as if to start a conversation, but all ignored it. The messenger broke the silence.

"For now, we will look for ours outside of your cities. For now."

Turning, the messenger left much faster than it had arrived, though Eiji felt no effect in the wind of its leaving. When it was out of sight, he turned and re-entered the dome. Smith handed him the ear-pieces, a questioning look on his face.

"For now, they will leave us alone." Eiji put the ear-pieces on. "Give our allies a full recording of the event."

"There is no audio of the messenger."

Eiji's head nodded. "I am not surprised. Send me the recording and I will add what they said."

"Yes, chairman."

"We should be doing something!" Face red, Agnar was all but shouting as he stood in front of all the men in and around the town called to an assembly to discuss the news about the return of the alien ship and its meaning. No one under eighteen years old had been allowed.

"When God wants us to do something, He will tell us." The reply came from the older, longer-bearded, man in the front row. His calm eyes remained unruffled during the whole town meeting no matter who spoke or how loud.

"This is our time!" Agnar's arms waved into the air. "It is time we took revenge for all the insults and indignities the city folk have heaped upon us."

"And do what, exactly?" The questioner, Martook, gave Agnar an unsure look.

"Attack the city, of course."

The comment brought laughs from the assembly as well as shaken heads. Bartholomew, the elder in front, spoke. "We cannot win against the city. Our tools are no match for their weapons. We can't even break through the shield they have around the city."

"But we must do something. What will we say when God arrives and asks why we did nothing?" Agnar looked at different faces in the crowd. Most looked away.

"Again," Martook asked. "What?"

"We... we..." Snapping his fingers, Agnar rolled his lips over each other, then spoke in a hurried voice. "We'll stop all shipments of food and goods into the city."

"Simple, since they have closed the city anyway." Bartholomew's eyes rolled in his head.

Agnar pointed at the man. "Maybe we can sneak someone in."

"Not possible," came a voice. "It was tried years ago."

"Which is why they won't be expecting it," Agnar countered.

"And it's exactly what they will be expecting," Bartholomew said in a dismissive voice. "The only people getting in are those in those flying machines of theirs."

Opening his mouth but then closing it again, Agnar turned and took a few paces before turning back to talk. "We can show up in force at the gate and make demands. Even if they don't listen, at least we can tell God we did something."

"And I suppose you will volunteer to lead this group to the gate and make the demands?" Suspicion overflowed from the words as Bartholomew spoke them.

"Someone has to!"

"And what demands are we going to make?" Bartholomew raised an eyebrow. "Any that have a chance of even being met?"

Agnar's face contorted and his hands began to shake as the muscles in his arm clenched. After a handful of seconds, he said, "Do I have to think of everything?"

Chapter Ten
My Kind of Town

Gliding to a smooth stop, the vehicle halted just behind the Chicago turret tower and opened its door for Cedynia to exit. The crushed stone crinkled under her boots as she walked to the door and stood with her face in front of the dark glass panel. The panel reflected her round face, thin nose, and modest brown hair that took any breeze as an excuse to show off.

"Welcome, Servicer Cedynia Altone," a warm male voice said as the door opened. As she walked in, the voice continued, *"Welcome, Servicer Wray Wellington."*

"I don't see why we are doing this," Wray grumbled, ignoring the door. He was only a couple of centimeters taller than Cedynia and his hair was longer, though tied behind his head into a pony-tail. His hair was also more yellow, lightened by the sun the more he was outside. His classic square jaw was holding up a frown, making it more square in appearance. "We just gave these things their semi-annual check two months ago."

"Because we were told to, that's why." Cedynia stepped onto the lifting platform and waited for Wray to shuffle on. Once settled, the lift accelerated upwards, slow at first, but faster with time until it reached the programmed speed. "It's our job."

"It's like they didn't trust us to do it right the first time," was the mumbled response. "Command has been acting strange for three or four days now. Something has to be up or else someone is going for a promotion.”

“Or they are trying to make sure you don’t become a creature of habit,” Cedynia responded with a smile. It was a pleasant smile, but Wray stayed determined to not let it change his mood.

“What’s wrong with habits?” Wray’s mouth held the opposite profile as Cedynia’s.

“They make you sloppy. Who knows, they might have disconnected something just to see if you find it. Been known to happen.” With a small shrug, Cedynia turned away from her companion. There was nothing to look at but wall, but the lift started to decelerate.

“Yeah, Mickeals would do that, wouldn’t he?” Wray rolled his eyes.

“If you’re so bored, why not ask for a transfer to something else?” The lift was substantially slower now and the lights of the turret were within easy throwing distance.

“Maybe I want to be bored.”

“HA!” Not being able to suppress the outburst, she turned away as she put her hand over her mouth. “No one *wants* to be bored.”

“Maybe I have other things to think about.” Wray raised his chin and turned his head to one side.

“Oh, of course,” Cedynia said with faked shock as she rolled her eyes. “I am so sorry, I should have thought about that.”

Huffing in response, Wray walked off the platform and approached the left wall. Once there, he used his interface to open an otherwise hidden access panel. As he did, Cedynia walked to the auxiliary controls. A quick glance at the displays showed no irregularities.

“Computer,” she said, talking to her interface, “access turret eleven controls and run diagnostics.”

“Of course, Servitor Cedynia,” a voice replied, female this time.

“Last time we were here the computer was male.” Cedynia watched her display as data filled the screen. “I swear they assign random voices to cycle through these things.”

“Don’t want you forming any habits,” Wray called out from behind her.

“Funny, very funny.” Cedynia watched until the screen was filled. “All normal here.”

"Here too. Like I said, no reason to be here." Wray shut the panel manually so that it slapped in place.

"Hey! Want to go outside?" Cedynia turned, her eyes lit up.

"Out there? A hundred and fifty meters in the air? Why?"

Cedynia would have sworn she saw a shiver go through Wray. "For the view, of course! Don't worry, you can't fall off these things, they made sure of that. Unless you are really trying, that is. Come on!" She waved as she headed to the outside access door.

"Well, trying is not something I'm going to do, that's for sure." Wray's pace was more tentative and he let Cedynia get all the way outside before even standing in the doorway. Sticking out only his head, he looked both directions and at the outer walkway.

"Oh, come on! There's more than enough room for two people to walk side by side. I promise I won't push you off." Cedynia put her hands on the rail and leaned over, letting the wind catch her brown hair. It flew in chaotic swirls and flutters.

"The fact that you even thought to mention that makes me nervous." Wray walked out the door and stood with his back pressed against the wall of the turret. Just watching Cedynia rotate her head in the wind while her feet were barely touching the floor gave him the willies and he turned to look out over the countryside.

"Come enjoy the updrafts," Cedynia encouraged. "They're great!"

"I'm fine just where I am, thank you very much." Wray appeared to be trying to use his hands as suction cups on the wall.

"You're not scared of heights, are you?"

"No, I'm scared of hitting the ground at terminal velocity. Kind of fatal, you know."

"Stick in the mud," Cedynia taunted.

"Why would someone put a stick in the mud anyway?" Wray scrunched his face.

"It's just an old saying." A head roll accompanied the eye roll.

"I know, just asking where it came from." Wray stood up straight, back off the wall.

"Who cares. We'll probably never know. Besides, it's only used to express an opinion just like calling someone 'bug in the code.'" After some silence, she continued. "Wray, are you listening, I was talking to you. Wray?"

Turning, Cedynia found Wray walking toward the railing, head slightly up, mouth open, and eyes focused far into the distance. "Wray? Wray, what is it?"

"I think we need to get inside, and I mean now."

"Why?" Cedynia cocked her head. Wray's only response was to point. Following his finger with her eyes, Cedynia saw a long silver cylinder in the sky about one finger joint wide. Watching for a few moments, it was clear the cylinder was drawing closer.

"What is that?" Cedynia asked. "It doesn't look like any air vehicle I have seen."

"I think you'd have to be pretty old to have seen this one. Come on! We need to get down to ground level before the turret goes into action."

"Action? Why would it do… Crap!"

A foot race ensued to the lift.

"How did the thing get so close before we saw it?!" Captain Zaheia Gint, command of Defensive Forces, Chicago, knew she was shouting, but did not look as if she felt it was justified.

"Captain, I have no idea. I would have to know how their technology worked to answer that question." Ensign Taggert Estron made frantic motions in the display, trying to call up information faster than it arrived.

"Errrr." Zaheia clenched her fists, her arms shaking. "Sergeant, at least tell me the defensive systems have responded."

"Yes, Captain," Sergeant Nerkin responded, looking over his displays one more time. "All turrets are actively tracking and powered up."

"Are the panels closed?"

"Yes, Captain, all panels are closed." Nerkin checked their status again after the comment.

"Then we are as prepared as we can be. Please tell me someone called Denver."

"Aye," came another voice.

"Thank God. And I didn't mean the aliens. Ensign, what is the ship's heading?"

"It appears to be headed for Wheaton," Estron replied.

"Wheaton? Why the hell would it head there?" Zaheia emphasized the first word with vigor.

"It is a rather large Puritan settlement," Nerkin replied.

"Fine," Zaheia said with a single laugh. "They can have them."

"Captain," a private said as he fast-walked up to her. "The mayor is calling for you."

"Of course he is. Surprised it took him this long." Zaheia raised her interface. "Put him through."

Chapter Eleven
When God Returns

The ship was like a giant moon moving across the sky, the dark side displayed for those on the ground. Miriam and Agnar Bridge stood just off their covered porch and watched the ship come ever closer. Sent inside the house, the children watched from the best available windows. Opposite reactions ran through their parents' bodies. Restless, Agnar's feet moved almost without pause and his hands swung across his body. In contrast, Miriam's head was tilted and bowed, looking at the ship through the sides of her eyes, and her hands wrung in front of her.

"I can't believe they're here! I can't believe they're here!" Agnar all but bounced as he talked. "Our faithfulness has been rewarded. We might even be selected to be taken to their home."

"What about our family?" Miriam asked, her voice filled with concern.

"Of course they would take the whole family, why won't they? You don't think they would leave the kids behind, do you?"

"They didn't take whole families last time." Not looking at her husband, Miriam kept the sharpness out of her voice.

"That was different. We hadn't been living in accordance with their teachings. Now we have whole generations raised under the truth." Agnar's arms went wide as if to encompass the community. "The heretics have been locked up in their cities for years. God will see our devotion."

"I'm worried about the children. What if they want to take the children from us?" An edge of desperation entered Miriam's voice.

"Then they will be most blessed." When Agnar's head turned to his wife, a wide grin decorated it, but it was greeted by a frown. The smile became uncomfortable. "Don't worry, it won't happen."

Overhead, the ship grew ever closer, stopping over Wheaton, eight miles to the east of the farm. The horses and cattle stared after the ship for a few minutes and then went back to eating grass or chewing cud. The dog looked up at the couple, intermittent wags of his tail and pout asking what he should do. Agnar waved him off and the dog wandered off into the fields. Even with chores waiting, Miriam could not tear herself away from watching the ship and dared not speak.

With no clearings except corn fields, the Bridges were not surprised when the ship did not land. What did surprise them was when streaks could be seen radiating out from the top of the ship. Straining their eyes, they watched as one streak came closer, landing near the church down from the farm. After a few moments, the church bell started ringing.

"Gather the children, we're going to church," Agnar said as he turned toward the truck.

After a quick glance at her husband, Miriam hurried to the house and opened the door. "Kids, get your shoes on, we're going to church."

The sound of four pairs of feet running down the stairs was followed by the chaos of searching and putting on shoes. Of course, some of them had to be thrown at siblings before they were put on. Abigail was standing in front of her mother first, as always.

"Why are we going to church? It's not church day."

"Didn't you hear the bell, little one?" Miriam checked over her daughter's head. "Hurry up in there."

"Does it have to do with the spaceship?" Big brown eyes looked up at her mother.

"I'm sure it does. Now go get into the back of the truck like a good girl." The other three followed soon, shooed out by their mother, who came on their heels. After making sure all the children were seated in the back, Miriam got into the cab. Without looking,

Agnar started the truck and put it into gear. As they turned onto the road, Miriam saw other vehicles headed the same direction.

"Looks like everyone is coming," she said as she watched.

"Of course they are. The bell means everyone is supposed to come." Agnar scoffed.

"Doesn't mean they always do." The comment was said in a flat voice, not quite a condemnation.

"Then they wouldn't be selected to be blessed." Agnar turned down a road. "God knows."

Keeping herself from reacting, Miriam looked out the window and watched the church get closer. Others had already arrived and were entering the building.

When the truck was parked in the grass outside the church, Miriam gathered the children, keeping the two youngest close to her. The boys, being older and seeing their friends, walked with a slight swagger toward the church. Abigail clung to her mother's arm, head against her body. It didn't prevent the eyes of some of the boys her age looking at her. Miriam put her arm around her daughter, between her and the boys.

Sitting room disappeared fast and Agnar led them to a spot standing against the left wall before it was all gone. He planted his feet and crossed his arms in front of his chest as if making a statement. Putting the kids between them, Miriam kept Abigail next to her. The pastor stood at the podium, waiting without looking hurried. There were a few nods and waves between those who entered and those already in the church, but no conversations started. Nervous tension made babies fussy and little children squirm.

The last people to arrive were forced to stand in the doorway. As the foot-traffic subsided, the pastor cleared his throat and placed his hands on the podium.

"Believers. We are blessed today because we have a visitor from God. He has some instructions for us from God. I know you will listen carefully and do all he asks."

To the intake of breath from many, the pastor retreated from the podium, stepping to the side. At the same time, as if cued, the door to the back room opened and a man-like figure walked to the podium. Dressed in a floor-length white robe with two wings tucked behind its back, the being's nondescript face held no emotion as it scanned the crowd once before stopping a meter behind the podium.

"We have come for those desired. Each of you will be examined. Those that are found desirable will be welcome to be with the EO-AY. Those that are found lacking will be left behind."

With a nod to the pastor, the angel stood in place while people were led one at a time to the angel. The examinations were not dramatic. Placing his hands around their faces, the angel would stare into the person's eyes for a few moments before releasing them. One by one, people were examined and dismissed. Most appeared disappointed, but enough were relieved that Miriam did not feel alone in her anxiety. Eager people tried to move ahead of others but they were controlled by the deacons. Order would be maintained no matter how religious someone might be.

Much of the room was cleared out before Agnar moved to take his place in line, wordlessly expecting the family to follow. His delay surprised Miriam, who had looked at him several times when small opportunities to enter the line could have been taken. Smiling and taking bold steps, he did not appear nervous or hesitant.

"Daddy wants to be dramatic," Abigail whispered to her mother.

"Who made you so wise?" Miriam responded with half a giggle.

"Not Daddy," Abigail responded with a giggle of her own. Miriam shushed her but then gave her a squeeze around the shoulders.

When his turn came, Agnar stood, back straight, shoulders square, as if a medal was to be pinned to his chest. His shoulders slumped as low as they could go when the angel dismissed him with a wave of his hand and he didn't even watch as their oldest son stepped up to the angel. He did a whirlwind spin when he heard the angel speak.

"You are acceptable."

"What?" Agnar appeared more shocked than the boy. "How can that be?"

Without addressing the man, the pastor directed one son away and the next to the angel. Though ushered by the deacon, the boy watched with anxiety as his brother was examined.

"You are also acceptable."

The relief on her oldest son's face was in opposite magnitude to the shock and horror of Miriam's husband. The sight brought a small smile to her face for a brief moment, then worry showed up in her face. Her oldest daughter was next.

Shaking, Beth stepped up to the angel. A slight flinch was her response to the angel's hands but she held her ground quick enough. She put on a brave face but Miriam could see her quiver. After a short pause, the angel waved her away. No one was more relieved than Beth, with Miriam close behind.

Not letting go of Miriam's arm, Abigail walked up to the angel. The angel didn't object to the contact with her mother. He only insisted that she straighten her head so he could place both hands around it. Miriam held her breath for the next fifteen seconds.

"You are acceptable."

Miriam never felt so panicked. After a quick look to her daughter, she turned back to the angel, almost unable to breathe. "Please… please. Let me go with her, even if I am not acceptable. She's only a child. At least until you leave. You can always leave me later. Just let me help her adjust."

The angel waved her forward. Praying harder than she had ever prayed, Miriam closed her eyes. The pause felt long, then she decided it was longer than the previous ones. With an intake of breath, she opened her eyes.

The angel still held his hands on either side of her head, just touching it. His eyes, though, were not focused on her, but appeared to be looking over her head as if he was listening to something she could not hear. Hope went through her body like lightning. Maybe her prayers had been heard for the first time she could remember. After more waiting, the angel lowered her hands.

"I must bring you to the EO-AY for their decision."

If the angel had lips, Miriam may have kissed him. Hugging Abigail to her, she shrieked with joy. The boys looked surprised, but also grew bright smiles.

"Wait. Wait." Agnar was waving his hands and shaking his head. "You're telling me this… gift… comes from her side of the family? The Keralas? It can't be."

"No one cares about your ego, Agnar!" Her voice was an ax splitting Agnar's anger like a vengeful spirit. He took a step back, his mouth slack. "For once, think about your daughter. You will be the only one she has to depend on. Can you do that?"

Overcoming years of inertia, Agnar's head bobbed up and down, slow at first but gaining speed. Beth's eyes had gone wide with surprise, and then pride at her mother, but transitioned to sad as she thought about what lay ahead.

"Beth, you're going to be the woman of the house at least for a while. You know how to do things. I have no idea if I will be back or not, but you are old enough to take over. Understand?" It was Beth's turn for her head to bob up and down. Miriam watched the mixed emotions go across her daughter's face. "I am sorry this is your transition into womanhood. I wish it could have been more... normal."

"It's okay, Momma. I'm ready." Standing straight as she breathed in, Beth drew up the corners of her mouth into dimples. Miriam responded with a smile of her own.

"I know I can count on you. Take care of your father. He'll need it."

Turning, Miriam walked Abigail to her brothers. A family hug comforted all. When it was over, she turned to the angel.

"We're ready to go."

"Where is your other son?" the angel asked.

"He died," came Agnar's voice from behind the being.

"No, he did not. Did he, Miriam?" the angel asked.

All of Miriam's joy evaporated. She looked at Agnar, guilt replacing everything. Just as quickly, it evaporated into anger. "What do you care? You thought he was weak, a drain on the farm."

"You lied to me!"

"He deserved better than you!"

"Where is the boy? He must be examined." The angel's voice held none of the emotion being thrown around the room.

The words came slow. "I left him in the city."

Unphased, the angel turned toward the back of the church. "Follow me."

Chapter Twelve
They Know

With the full cabinet, military personnel, and scientists standing in the room, the war room was as crowded as Worthia would allow before she started kicking people out. Nervous looks were shared by most except the military, some of whom looked stern enough that it made them look as if they were itching for a fight.

"Thank you all for coming," Worthia said as she walked into the room toward her chair, "though I doubt any of you would have stayed away."

The comment brought a few single guffaws from some and nods from others. General Tonsten held out her chair and assisted as she sat down, causing Worthia to smile at the prerogatives he took with the cabinet. No one ever argued. She gave time for him to settle.

"Lorda," Worthia began with a nod toward the woman, "our visitors didn't waste any time getting here. Give us a complete update."

"Thank you, M. President." Lorda cleared her throat. "A ship identical to the one here one hundred and sixty years ago, as far as we can tell, has settled over Wheaton, Illinois. This is the same area that the boy who… is our guest came from. We have not observed any beings leaving the ship nor has it settled, but as we all know, that does not limit the aliens' communication with those below. Last report is that it is still hovering."

"What do we know about Wilmont's family?" Worthia's voice was calm and even.

"Almost nothing except what Wilmont has told us." Lorda looked around the table once in a nervous manner. "The family has not cooperated at all, rejecting to even see the doctor that was sent regardless of the excuse provided. The town wasn't any better either. You would have thought we were the aliens."

Worthia gave the woman a small smile. "Does he have an extended family in Wheaton?"

"Our records indicate that they do, but it's not like they are updated or the most reliable."

"I would have thought they would screen the immediate siblings, would have been the most likely candidates for similar... ability," Secretary Pernent stated.

"If they can detect the ability, then they may have traveled directly to that person's location," Lorda replied.

"Do you really think they can detect something so faint? We can barely detect it ourselves more than a few feet away." Url gave her a strained look.

"We have to assume they can," Tigen inserted.

"Correct," Worthia said firmly. "There may be someone there with the same abilities or the descendant of someone from that area who went with them may have developed it and they are returning to their home town."

"I find that unlikely," Secretary Mantarida said. All eyes turned to him. "You must remember that the aliens are capable of near light-speed travel. Assume they cannot travel as fast or faster than the speed of light, which we believe to be impossible, the one hundred and sixty years they have been away would have been much shorter than that for them. Plus it gives us an area for their possible home base, but that is not germane to this discussion." Chadan gave a self-pleased smile.

"And if our scientists are wrong and they do have faster-than-light travel?" Lorda asked.

"Well, things become less interesting," Chadan replied.

"All of which is unimportant detail at the moment." Worthia's voice was as firm as her stare. "Let's deal with the relevant. Are all cities secured?"

"Yes, they are." It was Url's turn to be firm.

"And our personnel that were outside the city?"

"Luckily, most were not too far away. Those that were either have been collected or are in the process of being collected with help from the military." Tigen's voice wasn't as firm as Url's had been. "Luckily, it doesn't appear we need to worry about anyone in the Chicago area, but the western states in particular are still retrieving people. And then there are those on ships. A couple of the navy ships will have to seek port with our allies. Merchant shipping will be slower. They are the biggest worry."

"Can't be helped, I suppose." Worthia couldn't prevent a sigh with the statement. "I assume we are in constant contact with them until they are safe?"

"It was deemed safer for them to remain silent, but we know when they should reach port and will report in as soon as they reach their destinations, and if something untoward happens of course."

"The loss of regular shipping is going to concern a lot of people," Secretary of the Interior Anne Coons stated with concern in her voice.

"I would think an alien ship would concern them more," Chadan countered.

"It depends on how long it's here," Coons replied, turning her head to Chadan and giving him a stare. "I'm thinking long term."

"The city military bases have maintained emergency stores," Tigen added into the discussion, "as well as the cities' own reserve. We shouldn't have a problem for a month at least."

"People get used to their comforts." Coons lowered her eyes and sat back in her chair.

"The loss of some comforts is something they will have to endure if the aliens stay that long. We are not endangering anyone for the sake of comfort or providing negotiating chips to the aliens." Worthia looked at all the faces at the table to find dissent but found none. Satisfied, she relaxed and sat back in her chair. "Anything we have forgotten?"

The question was answered by silence. Allowing twenty seconds to pass, Worthia spoke again. "Good. What's our next step?"

"We wait," Chadan said. "If we are lucky, the aliens will take what they want from the Puritan communities and leave. If not, life gets busier."

When no one stated another option, Worthia stood. "I see we have few other options. Thank you all for coming."

The participants nodded as they stood and left the conference, except for two. Tigen stood behind Worthia as if standing guard. At least he had a pleasant smile on his face all the while. The other was Chadan, who took his time standing and let everyone else leave before him. Not turning to look, Worthia assumed that had earned him a frown from Tigen.

"I see you've been putting a lot of thought into our visitors." Worthia smirked as she gave in to the intended conversation.

"You know me." A shrug accompanied the words.

"So what interesting insight did you wish to share?" Retaking her seat, Worthia settled in.

"I don't know if you ever thought about it," Chadan started, his legs beginning a pace and his right fore-finger pointed up, ticking with the words, "but I found the timing of the aliens' visit interesting."

"Timing?"

"Yes, timing. At the height of our technological development, when technology was so integral to everyone's life that they used it constantly throughout the day without even thinking about it, the aliens show up and demonstrated that our technology was incredibly inferior, hopeless in the face of theirs. At the same time, they demonstrated how powerless our political institutions are, the same ones that had united the world in peace."

Watching as Chadan paced, Worthia spoke as the man's arms went wide with emphasis. "So you think they wanted us to revert to an agrarian society?"

Chadan returned a smile, one that could have been worn by a teacher in a classroom. "An agrarian society has many advantages for them."

"It makes us more peaceful, or at least easier to handle," Tigen added with a neutral voice.

"Not only that," Chadan said with a nod of his finger to the man, "but agrarian societies marry sooner and have more children…"

"Increasing the pace of genetic changes in the society," Worthia finished.

"Exactly!" Triumph sounded in Chadan's voice.

"But wasn't it a gamble that we would react in that manner after they left?" Worthia led the man with what she figured was the expected question.

"Who is not to say that they implanted or encouraged the idea in people's heads, at least a few key personnel like Valesco?"

Tigen huffed. "Not like he would have needed much encouragement."

"So?" Worthia asked with emphasis. "What does all this do for us?"

Chadan spun on his heels to stare straight at Worthia. "Imagine their surprise when they find our walled cities that their telepathic abilities cannot penetrate."

Worthia sat back in the chair and drummed her fingers on the arm. She could feel Tigen stiffen behind her. "They might not be too happy. Depending on how well they think they know humans, they might be rather incensed about the whole situation. They did appear to be quite possessive the last time they were here."

"The same conclusion I came to." Chadan nodded his head as he gathered his arms to his body.

"Fine, Mr. Thinker, give me your recommendations then. How do we handle the situation?" Worthia's voice took on a tone of seriousness.

"Carefully, of course." Chadan hugged himself. "Assume nothing about them, take nothing for granted, and don't trust them in the least."

"That's assumed," Worthia countered.

"I was getting the easy things out of the way," Chadan said with a wave of his hand. "Further, it might take them some time to decide what to do, if history is any indication. Of course, we can expect them to test our defenses. After that, after their warriors prove ineffective against us, well, that is the question."

"And the answer?"

"That's the question that keeps my mind churning, M. President.

Do they have other weapons? Do they call others of their kind? Do they have other, more lethal, ships? I don't know the answer."

"Let's hope we don't have to find out," Worthia said as she shook her head. "We like to think we are prepared. Finding out that we are still outclassed would be a rude awakening."

Chapter Thirteen
Their Problem

The hands of the man at the monitor shook more than normal. He had almost gotten used to Mr. Smith's presence, but now Chairman Eiji added to the pressure. Sweat trickled down his neck and threatened to make his fingers unnoticeable to the monitor's holographic interface.

"Wheaton," Mr. Smith said.

"Which is…?" Eiji asked.

"A few kilometers outside of Chicago. The greater city, not just the dome."

A step toward this monitor was heard by the attendant, a soft one indicating Chairman Eiji. He could feel the sweat increase in volume as it ran down his neck.

"I don't suppose we have an intelligence asset in Wheaton?" Eiji asked.

"No. It is a small town of, before now, no consequence. We do have assets in Chicago, of course, but the city has been sealed." Calm and even as ever, Mr. Smith's voice was low enough not to carry farther than it was needed while not requiring Eiji to strain to listen.

"So the question is why the aliens are there." Eiji rubbed his chin with one hand while its elbow was cradled by the other. "Conjecture?"

"On their previous trip here, the aliens took a variety of people from all over the globe, including a representative sample for

America." Smith spoke of the events as if they were common conversation. "It is assumed that this allowed them to sample the population to narrow down the area where... whatever they are looking for would be most likely."

"So is their target really Wheaton or do we believe it is Chicago?" Eiji walked away from the monitor. The attendant breathed again.

"Impossible to know. We do not even know if they are targeting a town or a general area. Exact locations such as specific towns may be meaningless." Smith still had no emotion in his voice.

"Did anyone that was taken before come from this area?" Eiji asked.

"Several came from the general area..."

"I mean this town, Wheaton." Eiji's voice became more firm.

"Precise World Council records of those who were taken were destroyed in the riots after the alien ship disappeared."

Eiji gave Smith a look that expressed disbelief.

"It seems that many who did not make it on the ship blamed the World Council for delaying them to the point of missing inclusion. Totally unreasonable, of course, but apparently the desire to join the aliens was very high in a significant portion of the population. In the first wave of riots, the security forces held the upper hand, but then the rioters got more creative. Somehow they managed to destroy government systems from the inside, most believe with inside help. Computer databases were physically destroyed."

"No backups?"

"In an ironic twist of logic, backups in other locations were not made in an attempt to keep the information more secure." The statement brought a sustained laugh from Eiji though Smith did not join the response.

"Thus proving the incompetence of the World Council," Eiji said when he had recovered. "Our representatives did not secure a copy?"

"They did not have time to secure the detailed information, only general information. From the reports, we lost an asset in the riot that destroyed the database."

Eiji's head bobbed up and down. "Regrettable. It would be very useful. Continue to monitor and inform me of any significant developments."

"Of course, Chairman." Smith started to bow.

"By the way," Eiji stopped walking and looked over his shoulder, "how many people from our areas of interest joined the aliens?"

"In total, just under a thousand," Smith replied.

"So a number less than would be represented by our population."

"Much less, yes, Chairman."

"Does this work to our advantage in avoiding contact with the aliens?"

"It would be a reasonable assumption, though lowering the odds would be meaningless if they found what they were looking for in any of those taken."

Eiji's mouth drooped. "Your adherence to precise logic can be discouraging at times, Mr. Smith."

"I only try to serve effectively, Mr. Chairman." A deep bow followed.

Chapter Fourteen
Selections

There was so much to take in. The inside of the ship was nothing like home and yet it felt warm and inviting. Miriam was sure that the boys hadn't stopped eating since they had discovered the food table, taking some with them as they explored the ship. They were so excited that she didn't want to spoil the moment by reproving them for selecting too many sweets. Abigail had been more restrained, but she had found a fruit gelatin that lit up her eyes and Miriam didn't have the heart to tell her she had had enough.

"If they make themselves sick, we will treat them."

Turning, Miriam found a man, or being, that looked human standing behind her. He was dressed in white robes like the others but his was lighter, less full and he had a full head of hair, unlike the others. His smile radiated kindness.

"Thank you," she responded, turning her head down for a moment. "They are so excited."

"Of course they are. It is natural."

"I'm sorry, but you are…?"

"The Subordinate."

With all the shocks that had occurred that day, this one hit Miriam the hardest. She could only stare for a moment, wordless. Moving for a while before any words exited, her mouth came around to finding a voice. "My lord, I… I…"

"Please." One hand came up and was laid lightly on her shoulder.

"We want to be friends. Can we talk as friends?"

"Of course, of course." Cheeks reddening, Miriam did not trust herself to look at the Subordinate. "Thank you for letting me come."

"Thank you for agreeing." Sweeping his hand toward some seats, the Subordinate led her to a bench, sitting at one end while she took the other. "You are interesting. Your children have inherited a great gift, though yours is so faint it almost cannot be detected by us. Taken together, though, it is more than we could have hoped for."

"What is this... gift?"

"The ability to speak to each other without words." The Subordinate's hands flared out with the statement. "Of course, your children's gifts are still very faint so they cannot talk to each other yet, but in time their future generations should develop the ability."

"Is that what you came looking for? People with this gift?"

"It is a sign that humans are developing into who they are supposed to be, into who we have guided them into being. We have been waiting many years. But we are good at waiting." Smiling broader, the Subordinate nodded in small motions.

"Why?" Miriam's head tilted to the left.

"Why what?"

"Why would you do this?"

"Because we care about you. We want you to share in our world, to work beside us as we travel among the stars." The words were delivered too easily for Miriam.

"Why couldn't we do that before?"

"The universe is nothing like this world." The Subordinate leaned back a little. "Here you are protected from harm and those that would take advantage of you. When you leave, that will change. You must be ready. You must develop into who you are meant to be."

"Won't you protect us?"

"There are... agreements... that are kept. These agreements change depending on where you are and what you know. Once you go into the stars with the other races, many more things are allowed."

The comment drove away Miriam's smile and caused her to shake a little. "But we will be safe with you?"

"Of course."

Miriam took time to recover and the Subordinate did not appear to be in a rush to continue the conversation. "So, will I be going with you?"

"We are still considering all the advantages and disadvantages."

"What if one of my children doesn't want to go?"

"Then they will be returned, of course." The words were said easily enough, but something made Miriam scrunch up the right side of her face.

"I am sure the boys will want to go, but Abigail is very young. She might be afraid to leave home." Miriam's head tilted down a little and she looked through the top half of her eyes.

"We will do all to reassure her."

A quick thought went through Miriam's head, but when the Subordinate's face started to change, she banished it to the far reaches of her mind. The Subordinate appeared to relax. Many thoughts demanded attention in her head, but Miriam kept them all at bay.

"Thank you again for everything. Are we going to go get Wilmont now?"

"We will send a messenger for him." The Subordinate re-positioned himself on the bench. "Your husband is making the case that since he is the boy's father, the boy will do as he says and that we should take him along to invite the boy."

"That may be true," Miriam said carefully. It was her turn to shift on the bench.

"But you doubt it."

"Agnar was never very kind to the boy. He always saw him as weak. I guess we now know why. Wilmont seemed very happy to stay in the city and he was never very religious. I don't know if he will want to leave."

"We will do all we can to show it is best for him."

The nervousness again went through Miriam, but she did not explore why. Standing, the Subordinate executed a bow and left down one of the hallways. Miriam was joined by Abigail, who was finishing a bowl of the fruit gelatin. Hugging her daughter, Miriam tried not to think.

Chapter Fifteen
Prep

"Look, I'm just saying it's a cute several hundred year old song I found in the music library…"

"That's about little furry creatures in love?" Wray asked the question without bringing the binoculars down from his face.

"No, it's about two people in love." Cedynia hit Wray in the shoulder with her fist.

"Who dress up as little furry animals?" Wray still sounded confused.

"Pfft, you're taking this song way too seriously." Cedynia swung her feet as they dangled off the edge of the building.

"I think whoever wrote that song didn't think enough. I have no idea what a muskrat is anyway."

"What's going on out there?"

"Some guy is driving up to the gate in a truck. Now he's getting out." Wray leaned forward a little over the railing he was sitting behind next to Cedynia. "I think he's… talking to someone."

"Who?"

"I don't know, he's the only one there." Wray handed her the binoculars. "Here, you take a look."

Cedynia took the binoculars and placed them in front of her eyes. The device automatically adjusted to her eyes. "Hmm, you're right. You know, I'm really proud of you sitting on the edge like this."

"We're only six stories up," Wray said easily.

"You'd probably be just as dead if you fell off."

"Yeah, but the other day we were sixty stories up. That's a lot more time to think about what's going to happen."

"He looks like he is talking to someone, Captain." Ensign Estron's voice was unsure as he twisted his head to the side.

"Who else is out there?" Captain Zaheia bent over the ensign's shoulder to view the display.

"No one," Estron said in a slow voice.

"Are you sure?"

"All our sensors only indicate one person and the audio is only picking up one voice. But I'll tell you," Estron said with a slight laugh, "he sure thinks someone is there, so either he is crazy…"

"Or we have just confirmed one of the suspicions from when the aliens were here before." Zaheia straightened back up.

"Captain?"

"That the messengers sent out by the aliens were only telepathic projections. Haven't you read up on the last visit?"

"I've been a little busy, Captain. What do you want me to do?"

"Record and log the audio for analysis. What is he talking about? Tap me in."

"He mostly seems confused about why the messenger won't talk to the city. Look, he's stepping toward the communication port. Now he stopped. Now he started again. Stopped again."

"Poor sod doesn't realize that thing isn't really there." They watched for a few moments more. "Guess he's leaving now."

Zaheia turned to the room. "Computer, tie in everyone in the room. Listen up! It is very likely that we will soon have a visit from one of the aliens' minions. I know everyone will want to view in, but we cannot allow ourselves to be distracted in only one direction. Eyes up and sharp, people."

Walking from the room, Zaheia talked in a quieter voice. "Computer, get me Denver command."

The room shown in Zaheia's viewer, as large as it was, was full of people above her pay grade. Remaining at attention throughout the report, her voice brought it to a crisp conclusion.

"Thank you, Captain," President Worthia, front and center in the display, responded with a calm, almost gentle voice. "We appreciate the work your command is doing there. Do you feel you can handle any incident or would you like to request assistance at this time?"

"We are as prepared as any city can be, M. President. Thank you for the offer."

"I am sure you will keep us apprised. Thank you for your time."

With that statement, Worthia turned back to the crowded room. The view of Zaheia went blank. Taking a deep breath, she scanned the room once for reactions, then spoke. "So the aliens undoubtedly know that they cannot read our minds by now. What is their next move?"

"If history is any indication, caution," Chadan offered. "Particularly if they did not anticipate this situation."

"Some of us might disagree with you." Tigen took a small step into the center of the crowd. "The last time someone from Earth denied the aliens what they wanted, they got very violent."

"When they were technologically superior, yes." The comment came with a small nod of Chadan's chin.

"You don't know that they still aren't." Pernent's voice held a small nervous shake.

"I know we are worlds ahead of where we were before." Chadan's chin came up a small measure.

"And maybe they are too," Pernent countered.

"With their speed, assuming during their whole flight, they might have only been gone a couple of years from their perspective." Chadan chuckled. "And we know they are slow to do things."

"All of which gets us nowhere." Worthia's voice rose above the others, shutting down the conversation and turning all eyes to her. "I don't want to just react, I want to take action ahead of time. We need a plan."

"We have a plan." The words came out of Tigen so smoothly that it was met with shocked looks.

"We do?" Several voices expressed the same question.

"Of course. The military always has a plan. It's what we do." Tigen almost laughed with the response.

"Care to let the rest of us know about it?" Anne Coons' voice was almost a laugh.

"All the steps we have already taken are part of the plan. In addition, forces are being moved to strategic locations near the aliens' ship. Close enough but not too close. The Chicago defenses have all been verified and placed in ready mode. At the President's word, we can start moving civilians into more secure locations inside the town. If the ship moves, we will adjust as needed."

The following silence was short but filled with those not in uniform staring at the statuesque general whose posture appeared to be chosen to radiate confidence. Army General Matilda Ruaridh, Navy Admiral Kedar Amster, and Air Commander Vessa Geshan all assumed the same posture in inseparable increments during the silence.

"Space Command?" Worthia asked.

"Remaining as unobtrusive as possible."

"Good idea." Worthia's head bobbed up and down. "Not that I am sure the aliens can't tell what those satellites are for, but the fact that they haven't taken them out is a good sign for us."

"I assume they don't want to start a war right off the bat," Chadan added. "Plus the fact they are designed to be hard to find."

"Let's hope they stay that way." Worthia took another deep breath and a couple of steps, all the room allowed. "Anne, Lorda, how are our citizens holding up?"

"I think about as well as can be expected when a large alien ship appears out of nowhere," Lorda replied. "Of course people are nervous, but they also seem to be very curious. No one alive today has seen aliens or their ships, of course, which adds to the curiosity."

"As long as it doesn't go too far. Anyone express the desire to leave the cities?"

"Not that we have heard, and I am pretty sure we won't. It's my feeling that people have chosen their side by living in the cities or at least not leaving as soon as the aliens showed up."

"More than likely true, but they might change their minds."

"We will be watching the gates closely, of course," Tigen offered to the conversation. "If someone leaves, it will be with the clothes on their back and definitely no technology. The last thing we want the aliens to get is one of our telepathic inhibitors."

"Right." Worthia lowered her head and took a breath before raising it again. "Anything else?" When nothing was said, she added, "Thank you all for coming."

As people left the room, Worthia turned toward the display, hung her head, and rubbed her eyes with her hands. Tigen gave the military commanders a head nod, asking for privacy. The last of the people gone, Tigen went to Worthia and placed his hands on her shoulders.

"It's just a headache," she said softly.

"The same one?"

"It never seems to leave since the aliens showed up." Worthia leaned back into Tigen's back, taking his hands and wrapping his arms around her.

"Did you see the Surgeon General?" The question caused Worthia to slump in his arms.

"No."

"Then we are going now." His voice was firm but gentle.

"I take it by the way you said that that it's definitely happening."

"Definitely, even if you were only my President."

The giggle had been suppressed as long as it could be, but when Surgeon General Stanley Wahls turned around, it escaped.

"Something you find funny?" the thin, gray-haired man asked as he placed the sensor in his hand down.

"It's just that doctors still wear white overcoats. I mean, how many millennia have they done that?"

"It tradition," Stanley said, turning back around and giving her a smile. "Plus they are very handy will all these pockets."

"Not like this room." Worthia looked around at the fine mesh surrounding the room and listening to the slight hum it emitted. She gave Tigen a smile when he came into view, standing stoically to the side.

"I have to take the inhibitors off for the examination. To which I have a question. Who adjusted your inhibitors and why?"

"I did," Worthia said easily. "They were bothering me."

"In what way?"

"I didn't feel like myself. I... couldn't read people as well as I normally do, so I turned the sensitivity down. Why? What does that have to do with my headaches?"

"Do you have a headache now?" The doctor raised one eyebrow.

"I... No, I don't. Wait, what are you getting at? I didn't adjust them that much."

"No you didn't, just enough I'm afraid." Stanley turned to the table that held the devices.

"You're saying some of the aliens' telepathic signals are getting through? But I can't hear them in my head." Worthia gave Tigen an anxious glance before catching herself and looking back at the doctor.

"No, you didn't turn it down that much. Here, let me show you something." Stanley went to the display and pushed icons around. "Here is a normal human brain, totally quiet of course. This," he threw another graph on the display, "is our friend Wilmont. And this is you."

As his finger moved, another line was added to the graph. It was nothing like Wilmont, almost the opposite in fact, but more active than the typical human graph. Worthia cocked her head and furrowed her brow.

"What's that mean?"

Stanley turned back to his patient. "We probably would have never thought about it with Wilmont. Our research has advanced leaps and bounds with him around. Wilmont is a transmitter, which is why we must have him shielded at all time so the aliens do not find him. You, my dear, on the other hand, are a receptor."

"A receptor?"

"We should have suspected it all along." A small laugh accompanied the statement. "With your intuitive instinct about people, it should have been obvious."

"You mean I am reading people's minds?" Worthia quickly turned toward Tigen, who gave a quick knowing smile. Huffing at him, she turned back to Stanley. "But I don't hear people's thoughts."

"No, you are not that sensitive. But I think you feel what they think."

"Feel what they think? What does that mean?"

Stanley took a breath and put his hands fingertip-to-fingertip. "Let's try an example. How did you feel that first time you saw Tigen looking at you, I mean really looking at you, not as a politician or anything else?"

Worthia's head went back a little. Her mouth moved a little before speaking. "I felt like the most beautiful woman in the world. You're telling me I felt that because of what he was thinking?"

"And what were you thinking, Tigen?" Stanley turned to the man.

"That she was the most beautiful woman I had ever seen. I will never forget that moment as long as I live."

Stanley turned back to Worthia, shrugged, then turned back to the inhibitors. "We're going to have to put these back to total blockage."

"Wait, that means when we're... I feel... Wow, that explains a lot. Hold on, if you set those things back, I wouldn't be able to read people."

"You will have to cope like the rest of us." Stanley placed the devices next to the display. "Computer, put these back to factory settings, please."

"Certainly," a voice said.

"I just thought of something," Worthia said, raising a finger. "If I'm a receptor, couldn't we use that to listen in..."

"*No.*" The firm word came from Tigen. When she turned to argue, he repeated, "No. Too much of a risk. And you won't get anyone else to agree with you."

Huffing as her shoulders slumped, Worthia gave him a frown. "Sometimes I think you're too protective."

"If you really want to see protective, wait until I think you are in real danger." Tigen raised his eyebrows and lowered his chin.

Worthia rolled her eyes. "God, I hope that never happens."

"Here we go," Stanley said, placing the inhibitors back on her ears. "And no adjusting them this time."

"Like he would let me," Worthia said with a shake of her head toward Tigen.

Chapter Sixteen
A Visit

"We have radar contact."

Captain Zaheia rushed over to Ensign Estron's station. "What is it?"

"Small. Person size." The quiver in Estron's voice was noticeable.

"One of the four-faced creatures?"

"Getting visual as quickly as possible, but it's moving fast." Estron moved multiple cameras to focus on the object, then kicked in a computer program to interpret the view. A new picture slowly formed, which he expanded.

"Isn't that one of the escorts, the ones that were seen with the Subordinate?" Zaheia turned her head while looking at the scene.

"I didn't know they could fly." The indicator on Estron's screen came close to the city.

"No one did, but what we don't know about these aliens could fill a computer." Zaheia watched for a few more seconds, then straightened. "I'm going to the gate. Keep me informed."

"Of course, Captain." As the captain turned and left, he added, "Be careful out there."

"It's me they have to worry about." Picking a pistol off the wall, Zaheia pushed it into the holster at her side as she walked out.

"You want me to handle this?" the captain asked as she looked at the mayor. If one looked closely, he was visibly shaking and his face looked pale.

"I... think that would be best, you being military and all." His shoulders sagged and the breath appeared to finally leave his chest.

"Stay here and if something happens, don't get in my people's way." Zaheia started walked toward the gate.

"You can count on that!" came the enthusiastic reply.

While one could see through the gate, it did not mean Zaheia was exposed. A thin layer of 'wing' material, as it was called by most, extended down into a slot in the ground just outside the gate. The micro-cellular stranded alumina-carbon matrix was stronger than the material the aliens had left behind, or so she had been told. She had seen video of a truck crashing into a layer of the material. While there had been some flexing, afterwards the truck had looked like it had hit the proverbial brick wall.

"Trust your tools," Zaheia said to herself as she walked within arm's reach of the gate. On the other side walked what had been designated as an escort, one of the creatures that had walked out with the Subordinate from the ship. With its wings already stored, it looked identical to the images in the videos. As far as Zaheia could tell, it carried no weapon. The creature walked up to the matrix material, tested with its hand, and then settled back.

Taking a couple of steps back, it stood with its hands to its sides and its legs spread shoulder-width. As they watched, the creature split along the front edge of its body, legs and arms, opening up like doors. From inside stepped a man. He was about a meter and a half tall, thickly built with only a little fat around the middle, and well tanned by the sun. He looked to be in his mid-forties and had a semi-groomed beard. The man walked up to the material and tested it for himself.

"Why have you barred me from entering?" the man asked.

"Hello, my name is Captain Zaheia Gint. What is yours?" Zaheia gave the man a smile, though strained.

"I am Agnar Bridge. Why have you barred me from entering?" No emotional inflection came with the question.

"You and those with you are not welcome here," Zaheia said flatly.

"Where is my son? Why can't I see him?" The question was asked without any movement of the head or change in voice tenor, almost not delivered like a question.

"We do not wish you to."

"You have no right to keep me from my son." Zaheia noted a slight pause between questions, almost as if the man was only a relay. "God has revealed to us that my wife was lying when she said my son died. I am here to demand that you return him."

"If someone in the city wishes to leave, they are free to leave. You son chose to be here, so I wouldn't count on us handing him back to you."

"How can we find the pure if God cannot invite them?"

Zaheia's back straightened. "You mean how can the aliens manipulate people's minds so that they 'voluntarily' join you? If anyone wants to join you, this time it's going to be truly voluntary. We're done with their tricks." As a reflex, her hand moved a few millimeters toward her pistol.

"They own this planet and they own the people who live here."

"So they say. Now hear what we say. Anyone outside of the protected cities are yours to recruit. Take as many as you want, I'm sure you'll have no lack of those who want to go. But everyone inside these cities is under our protection and we will defend them to the fullest extent."

Zaheia stood and stared at the man, unblinking. After a while she thought he would leave, having not moved, but he blinked and talked again.

"Where is the boy?"

Not able to suppress a laugh, Zaheia answered, "You have to be more specific. We have a lot of boys in the city."

For the first time, the man looked annoyed and angry. He took a deep breath and raised his shoulders. The volume of his voice increased. "Where is my son?"

Zaheia paused, then decided not to play coy since the creature would not understand. "He is not here."

"His mother brought him here."

"And an aircraft took him away shortly afterwards." Fighting to keep her statements measured and calm, Zaheia braced herself at the same time.

"Where did it take him?"

"I was not involved in his transfer or told of his plans." A small smile creased her face.

"WHERE IS HE!"

"I would not know. I tell you the truth that he is not here. That is all I can say." Hand drifting away from her gun, Zaheia appeared to relax.

Staring for a few seconds, the man turned and walked back to the creature. Stepping inside, the creature's body closed around him. Extending its wings, the creature shot from the ground as if fired from a weapon. Zaheia watched it leave before turning back into the city. As she came to the mayor, she could see sweat beaded on his forehead.

"Do you think they believed us?" the mayor asked.

"I don't see why not, but I guess we'll find out soon enough." The mayor fell into step as she continued to walk. "Of course the defenses will stay on alert while they are still here."

A few steps along, the mayor asked in a halting voice, "How do you think they knew about the boy?"

"From his family? Maybe they did tests and found similar traits among his siblings. The Puritans don't have inhibitors so it wouldn't be hard to get the full story from the mother, at least as much as she knew. Maybe his condition when he arrived was some kind of indicator. However they knew, they know now and will be looking for him, I'm sure."

"But wouldn't they expect you to be lying?"

"Or they are smart enough to know that the best thing for us to do would be to move him right away without telling anyone where he was going. I'm sure he went to Denver first, but who knows where he went from there. Some secret underground facility? Doesn't matter to us." Zaheia's head came back a little and her step lightened. "For once I am more than happy that information compartmentalization exists. Makes it someone else's concern."

"I sure hope so."

Chapter Seventeen
I Can Help

Agnar stood resolute in front of the creature, though inside he quivered with fear. Up close, the creature was more frightening than across the room, even if its human face was turned toward him. The other faces were still active, the lion snarling and the eagle constant in its search of its surroundings.

"Let me go and ask those inside Chicago." Agnar's hands were clasped together in front of him. "I am the boy's father, I have rights in the human legal system."

Agnar's words were cut off. "The boy is not here, your efforts would be worthless." The creature walked past the man without looking at him.

"But I can help." Agnar followed a couple paces behind.

"That remains to be seen. Go, leave us alone."

"But…"

The creature turned, his lion face coming to the fore. The malice in its eyes was unmistakable. The lion face growled, causing Agnar to take two steps backwards. "Do not presume, human. You are here at the pleasure of the EO-AY. That can change at any time."

The heavy footfalls of the creature as it walked off caused Agnar to miss the approach of his wife. "It would give me great pleasure to see you thrown off the ship."

His face filling with anger, Agnar turned toward his wife. "What did I ever do to you?"

"Do you really need me to answer that question?"

"I am only trying to do what everyone else wants, earn a ride to heaven."

"On the backs of your children?"

"Are you doing any different?" Agnar's stare became hard.

"I am here *for* the children!" Miriam leaned forward. Her right fore-finger came up and poked Agnar in the chest. "You know, those people who you never thought were more than just farm hands? And what about Beth? You left her, home and alone?"

"You were the one who said she could run the home." A shrug and frown accompanied the statement.

"I said run the house, not stay by herself. You know what will happen, don't you?" Agnar's blank stare was the only answer she got. "The boys in the town will not leave her alone, particularly if she is alone."

"They won't dare." Agnar's head went back and his brow furrowed. "The church won't let them."

"The church?" Miriam gasped and then laughed. "The pastor's son is the worst. They will just say that she invited them in or tempted them and his father will believe him because he has to or admit his son is the worst of them all. He might even call her a witch. Do you want that for your daughter?" When Agnar didn't answer, she slapped his face and left him there. It wasn't a dozen steps before she realized that Abigail was looking at her. Opening her arms, Miriam took the girl into her arms and hugged her.

"Why did you slap Daddy?"

"Because he deserved it. Let's not talk about him." She pushed the girl a small ways away and looked her in the eye. "Did you find any animals on the ship?"

"They have lots of birds and they sing really nice. Do you want to hear them?"

"Of course, honey. Let's go."

Letting her daughter distract her with the birds, Miriam tried not to think of her daughter or the fact that she had left too. Her smile was not real and the look on her daughter's face told Miriam that the little girl knew.

"Are you worried about Beth?" Abigail asked, a small songbird perched on her finger.

"Of course I'm worried about Beth. I worry about all of you."

"How is you being here different than Daddy?" The innocence in the little girl's eyes told Miriam the question was asked without malice.

"Well, first, I was invited to go before he was, which means he should have stayed home. Secondly, he would be a lot better at protecting Beth than I would. He's bigger and stronger than I am, and maybe the other boys would listen to him. I know they wouldn't listen to me." Miriam tried not to show the strain on her face while not lying to the child.

"So why didn't you stay after Daddy was invited?"

"Because I was here to protect you and I hate to say it, but your daddy isn't. I couldn't let my baby go somewhere without me, could I?"

The comment brought a frown from Abigail. "I don't like being called the baby."

"You'll always be my baby." Miriam gathered the child into her arms, causing the bird to take flight. "You're my last child and my precious little one."

"I thought Wilmont was your precious one," Abigail said with sadness.

"He was precious too, but I couldn't help him anymore. I don't want to lose both of you now, do I?" Miriam squeezed again.

"You should have stayed, Mommy," Abigail said through Miriam's clothes. "You are fierce."

Laughing, Miriam rocked back and forth with her daughter. "Thank you, little one. You are Mother's jewel."

After a moment, Abigail asked, "Will Beth be okay?"

"We have to trust that she will be, and we will get back to her as quickly as we can."

"Do you think they'll let us go?" A small amount of surprise came with the question.

"Mommy's working on that."

Chapter Eighteen
Here You Are Again

"**D**amn!" Looking away from Chadan, Worthia worked out her frustration in her mouth.

"It was only to be expected that they would find out," Chadan said, turning his hands over in front of him.

"I had hoped that they wouldn't. Call me an optimist." A small laugh accompanied the statement.

"He has siblings. We were unsuccessful in determining if they shared the same ability. The fact that they are looking for him, unhappy with those they found, would seem to confirm our earlier suspicions."

Taking a deep breath and letting it out, Worthia let her shoulders sag. "I assume that the captain in Chicago did not tell them where the boy was taken?'

"Of course not." Chadan shrugged. "We did not tell her where we were taking him, though I suppose she could have guessed. Should we move him to a remote base like Guam?"

"No." Worthia shook her head. "He's safer here. Guam is too far away for us to do anything if the aliens attack there."

"There are a lot more people here." Chadan's voice was stern.

"Yes, there are. But there are more defenses and the defensive satellites in orbit above us. There's not one above Guam." Worthia's voice was equally stern.

"We could reposition one, but it would take time." Chadan gave a small nod to the side.

"And who are you going to convince to give theirs up?" Turning, Worthia raised an eyebrow. It was Chadan's turn to shrug.

"There is that."

"My wife is right, as always," Tigen's voice boomed as he entered the executive office. "The boy is safer here. Our best troops and weapons are here. And I doubt someone would thank you for inviting the aliens down on their heads."

"I would think the military on Guam would love a crack at the aliens?" Chadan asked.

"There are a lot of civilians there too. In fact, we don't have a base that doesn't have more civilians than soldiers, besides Antarctica, that is. And that barely qualifies as a base for the purpose of stashing the boy." Tigen drew in a breath and expanded his chest.

"Which would make a good place to hide him," Chadan countered.

"Until they find him, then we might as well hand him over to them," Worthia put into the conversation.

Chadan sagged. "True. Just exploring options."

"Which remain extremely limited. Tigen, make sure that boy is watched and make sure he keeps his shields on at all time. Station a person in the apartment if you have to." Worthia's stare emphasized that it was not a request.

"It will be done. We could use more personnel here in Denver, particularly turret service personnel, for when the fighting starts. I would prefer to have one team per turret, which we don't maintain on a continuous basis."

"Budgetary?" Worthia asked with a note of disappointment.

"Of course." An eye-roll accompanied the statement. "The question is where do we take them from?

"Chicago," came the immediate response from Worthia. "The aliens have already left there so they should be safe. Extra infantry would also be good, whatever they can spare. Get them here as quietly as possible, but do it fast."

"Yes, M. President." Tigen gave a small, official bow, turned, and left the office.

"I find it surprising he lets you talk to him like that, you being married and all," Chadan said with a laugh after Tigen had left.

"I am the President, you know." Looking at the man from the top of her eyes and her authoritarian voice didn't phase him.

"Of course, of course. The military types I have encountered before have always seemed to want to be in charge."

"They asked him to run for President, you know. He won't do it. Recommended me actually."

"As I said, surprising." Chadan's head bobbed.

"You are dismissed, Mr. Secretary," Worthia said in a equally authoritative voice.

"Well, when you say it like that." Chadan left with a chuckle.

"We're tracking them, right?" More than hovering over her lieutenant, Captain Moraine Harjo spoke with a voice that was louder than required.

"Yes, Captain," the man below her answered. "The ship doesn't appear to be avoiding our sensors."

"Why should it?" Harjo said with disdain as she backed off. "They think we are inferior. Where are they going?"

"It… it doesn't appear they are going anywhere in particular." The man's hands flew over the interface. "The computer can't seem to find a specific destination."

"Search pattern, most likely." Harjo nodded her head.

"Not any I have seen." The comment was softer, almost under the man's breath.

"They are aliens, you know. Wait! Project that pattern in a three-dimensional space." Harjo stared as the computer display changed from overhead to isometric view. "Ha! See that!"

"Is that a three-dimensional search pattern?"

"Yes. They've spent too much time in space, the bastards. Wasting time changing elevation."

"Unless we don't understand how their sensors work." The man cringed for a second. "Just saying…"

"No, you're right." Harjo patted the man on the shoulder. "We can't assume anything and we can't underestimate them. Keep following them and let me know if they make up their minds as to their destination."

"Will do, Captain." The man inhaled and exhaled as Harjo walked away, visibly relaxing.

"Hey," the woman to his right said in a low voice, "don't worry so much. She's not that bad."

"Did you hear about the last guy who disappointed her and she decided to teach a lesson?"

"No," the woman said, not looking. "Why?"

"She had him meet her at the sparring ring. Poor bastard ended up in the hospital."

"Wasn't that Jones? He always was an idiot, didn't know when to quit. Probably his own fault."

"Yeah, but he's like three times bigger than she is. Someone like that scares me plenty and it has nothing to do with the fact she's a woman."

"You ever meet her grandfather?" The woman's voice had a lilt in it.

"No, why?"

"You'd know where she got it from."

Chapter Nineteen
While on the Other Side of the World

"Where are they going?" This time Eiji had a larger group, including the Minster of Defense, Foreign Minister, and several military commanders. The meeting was held in his office, using the large wall display run by Mr. Smith. While they hid it well, both nervousness and excitement could be felt from the crowd, the excitement from the military types.

"They seem to be executing a search pattern," Smith replied.

"Is this a general search or a specific search?" the Minister of Defense asked.

"We received information from one of our operatives in Chicago that several days ago a boy was brought into the city and then moved to Denver. Information was restricted, but I think the conclusion is clear." Smith made adjustments to the view to make sure the alien ship occupied the center.

"Have we learned any more about the boy?" Eiji searched the faces in front of him.

"No, Chairman," Smith replied.

"Then we are still not sure what the aliens are looking for in the people in that area."

"One of our operatives managed to exit Chicago and made his way to the Wheaton area." The Minister of Intelligence stood straight and proud as he made the remarks. "He reports that the aliens selected particular individuals to join them on their ship, but had no indication for what reason they were selected. Those selected tended to be from the same family, which would indicate it was a bred trait. But with the anti-technology stance of most Puritans, there is no way to know what the trait would be."

"But we have learned more." Eiji paced at a slow rate. "It is also curious that the American President has not shared any information with us."

"They may be holding it for a military advantage," the Minister of Defense stated in a firm voice.

"Or they may not know what the aliens are looking for either," Eiji replied with a wave of his hand.

"Maybe we ask the Americans about the situation in their country." The calm voice was Smith's.

"You may be correct. It would not cause undue suspicion for us to ask at this venture. In fact, it would be expected. Kenjiro, set up a call to the American President."

"Yes, Chairman," replied the Foreign Minister. "We must be careful how we ask the questions, sir."

"I am well aware of that." There was a sharp tone in Eiji's voice, but then he took a breath and his features eased. "If you wish to submit your suggestions, you may do so."

"Thank you, Chairman."

As Kenjiro exited, Eiji turned back to the others in the room. "It would be useful informing questions if we had some idea what we were looking for. Suggestions?"

The room was quiet for a moment with few daring to look at the chairman. It was Smith who spoke.

"Since we can safety dismiss technology as the object of the aliens' search, it thus insinuates that it is something about the people that they are after. Because they are taking Puritans, we can assume it is not their education level or mastery of science. Such traits would appear to have been discouraged by the aliens previously."

"How can you be so sure?" Eiji asked.

"I assume the aliens had some idea what their presence would do to the history of Earth and they did not discourage their worship when here. In fact, they took the historic appearance of Yahweh, indicating they encouraged such activity. Because such worship led to an anti-technology biased state, it would appear to be a fair conclusion they were not interested in human technology."

"Granted," Eiji said with a nod of his head.

"That leads to traits in the human body itself, supported by the claim that they started human life on this planet, if you believe such claims. Their selection of a sampling of the world also supports such thinking. Thus they were breeding, or expecting humans to breed, a trait in their interest." The others in the room watched Smith talk without comment or attempts to interject.

"And that trait is?" Eiji asked.

"Since the boy is of interest and he is not fully mature, I assume it is not enhanced strength or endurance. Any physical trait would not be fully developed at his apparent age. This leads me to assume it is a mental trait."

"Increased brain capacity of some sort?"

"Yes. Since the aliens took people before of increased intelligence and memory but did not target their family, I have discarded those as possibilities. If we ask ourselves what trait the aliens had that humans did not have during their last visit, the one feature that stands out is telepathy."

"You actually expect humans to develop telepathic abilities?" the Minister of Defense asked.

"It's not important if I do. What's important is if the aliens expect it," Smith countered. "At this point, it is all conjecture."

"An interesting conjecture," Eiji stated. "One that would make interesting conversation if I could bring it up with the American president, which I cannot. But it gives some lines of thought to follow. Thank you all, you are dismissed."

The crowd made a slow exit, Smith being last due to shutting down the display and watching until it was stored. As he exited the room and walked into the hall, he felt looks being directed his way, but no questions or comments came with them. Stiff-backed as always, Smith walked down the hall, ignoring the stares. When he reached the lift, the Ministry of Defense stood in front of the door, transmitting the hardest stare. The man did not move when Smith approached.

"Do you take exception with my conclusions?" Smith asked in a voice without emotion.

"I take exception to mix-breeds serving the chairman," the man responded.

"The chairman obviously disagrees with you."

"We have to protect the chairman from himself at times." The man's words were the verbal equivalent of a sneer.

"You assume too much." Smith returned his own stare. "If you were better at your job, you would have fewer concerns and garner more favor from the chairman."

The man took a deep breath, expanding his chest and drawing back his head. His stare turned more hateful. "Watch yourself, mixed-breed."

"I have no worry about my safety." Smith shouldered his way past the shorter man. After entering the lift, he turned back to the man and spoke as the door closed. "Do you?"

Chapter Twenty
To Tell the Truth

The faces stared through their holographic displays as effectively as if the people were sitting in the room. Those stares had melted opponents all over the world, but Worthia sat immune to them. She had dealt with the world leaders many times before and while she was president, but the resolve was external only. Inside, her slight muscle movements revealed internal agony at having to discuss the topic. Their anger was expected, though hypocritical. She was certain they would not have shared the information with her if it had been them.

"You were about to tell us why the aliens are searching your country, M. President." The comment came from Mabuso Kane, leader of the African contingent.

Taking a deep breath, Worthia brought her shoulders back. "We found a young man who has some... who emits very low telepathic waves. Let me emphasize that these signals are so low we could barely measure them and the boy was not even aware of them. He cannot read minds or send thoughts to anyone."

"And how were the aliens aware of this boy? I assume you took precautions." Mabuso looked dubious.

"Of course we did." Worthia tried not to huff with the statement. "We assume his siblings, which in Puritan families there are normally many, showed the same characteristic." It was her time to look at the man with a dubious expression.

"Did you not verify that his siblings had such ability?"

"No, the family did not allow us to check." This time Worthia stared at the man, daring him to ask the next question.

"You should have forced them!" Mabuso's already broad nose flared with the statement. He brought up his beefy hand and pointed a short, thick finger at Worthia.

"We don't do things like that here. *We* respect people." Worthia kept a calm but sharp tone, a small smile gracing her face. It caused Mabuso's eyes to widen and his nose flare more.

"There is no time for these squabbles." Maili Zaeim, the representative for the Arabian Qitea, interrupted the exchange. "With the aliens returned, we must keep our focus on them. It is too late to worry about who knew what and when."

"If the Americas knew that people had started to develop such abilities, they should have told us." Mabuso's voice was haughty.

"And how am I to know that any of you had not also discovered such individuals?" Worthia shot back.

Mabuso's mouth shut and his head turned to one side while his eyes never left Worthia. Instead of speaking, he leaned back into his chair.

"We are all independent contingencies and owe nothing to each other but courtesy. Complete information sharing has never been proposed or implied. Of course, at this stage, the boy could hardly have remained a secret anyway. Choose to believe me or not, the boy has no real abilities and cannot do anything different than a normal boy. But we will not allow him to become the subject of an alien experiment or anyone's experiment. He will be allowed to live his life by his choices. Our scientists have stated that with proper breeding, which we have no intention to initiate, and the best chances are assumed, a simple telepathic ability may show up in ten generations. That's if their assumptions are correct."

"You expect to wait ten generations and ask you again if you have anything to share?" Mabuso's voice left no doubt of his distaste.

"No." Taking time to look directly at Mabuso, Worthia paused a few seconds before saying more. "I don't expect anything from you."

A loud huff was Mabuso's response. Returning Worthia's stare for a few seconds, he turned his eyes to the others in attendance. "Is there anything else we have gathered to hear?" When no one spoke, he added, "Then I say goodbye."

Mabuso disappeared from view. One by one, the other delegates said goodbye in their own, more polite fashion and disappeared until Worthia and Maili were left.

"I believe that man does not like you." A sly smile accompanied Maili's words.

"Never has and quite frankly, I don't care. I think he feels he has something to prove. Exactly what, I don't know." Worthia gave a small shrug and returned the smile.

"That his contingent isn't the backwater that history considered them to be for so many centuries? I think he is still sensitive to the issue though one would have thought they would be over it by now." The question was full of implied opinion. "If he spent less time bullying people he might be better liked."

"They did have farther to go than the rest of us."

"That is true, but it is no reason for the man wasting his energy on image."

"My grandmother always said if you have to constantly prove something, it must not exist in the first place."

Maili's smile broadened. "Your grandmother was a smart woman."

"It runs in the family." Worthia waited a moment. "Is there anything else you feel that you needed to share?"

"Since you were being so open, I felt it only polite to tell you." Maili's gaze drifted downward. "We have also found individuals with similar... characteristics... in our area. As you saw, the ability is barely measurable. You can imagine that the appearance of the aliens and their search has us... concerned."

"I have a feeling that most of those who were present were concerned for the very same reason."

"It would be best to assume as much. Unless you think your and other people have superior breeding?" Maili's face came up, wearing a more pleasant smile.

"Well, there was a little interbreeding several generations ago that resulted in some significant individuals, as I remember." Worthia chuckled.

"A fortunate circumstance for us all. Maybe we should introduce your boy to one of our girls and see where nature takes things?"

"We can talk about cultural exchanges after the aliens are gone."

"Definitely." Maili straightened in her chair. "As always, it was good to speak with you again, M. President. Keep yourself safe from our visitors."

"You too, M. Zaeim. I look forward to tea at your home."

"It will be a celebration of our victory. Good day."

Maili's image vanished, leaving Worthia sitting in a round room by herself. "If we get to have tea, it will definitely be to celebrate a victory."

"I say we shoot the thing down now." Tigen's voice was the equivalent of a fist slamming onto the table, causing the non-military people to flinch. All except Worthia.

"How are we to know that our weapons will destroy the ship?" Worthia continued to lean back in the high-backed chair without any sideways movement.

"One sure way to find out." Tigen let a chuckle accompany the statement.

"Reckless." Chadan shook his head. The comment seemed to comfort many in the conference room, though Captain Moraine Harjo and Army Chief of Staff Matilda Ruaridh appeared happier with the earlier statement. "I am sure our allies would not be happy with such recklessness."

"I am sure they would not. At least if we didn't inform them of the decision beforehand." Worthia took in a breath and her gaze drifted upward.

"That would risk the aliens listening in." The statement was almost a mumble from Tigen.

"So," Worthia said as she swiveled the chair to the right, "where does that leave us? We have an alien ship executing a search pattern above our country. How do we respond? Do we respond?"

"I find it hard to believe that only one family in all of the Americas has children that have developed this ability." Lorda Rans leaned forward over the table. "Can it be that unique or are they just that greedy?"

"Maybe they are worried that some other aliens will find them," Anne Coons added. "Or what we will do with them if they are left here."

"Actually," Chadan cut in, "probability would indicate that the boy's family may be the only ones in the Americas, or maybe on the world today. Of course, it depends if this is a random occurrence or a planned attribute. Given the aliens' implied history with this world…"

"That's of no consequence," Worthia cut in. "We need a plan of action. I don't just want to sit by and hope they get tired and leave, but I also think half measures will only bring retaliation and loss of assets. We need something positive and effective. Any suggestions?"

Looking around the room at her cabinet, Worthia only found silence and uncertainty. Several even lowered their heads to hide their eyes as if in shame of not having an idea. When she had scanned the room twice without result, she exhaled and lowered her eyes.

"Anne, talk to the scientists and see if any of them have a workable idea, emphasis on workable."

"Yes, M. President." Anne's voice was steady but relieved.

"Everyone, get a good night's sleep. Hopefully someone will have a good idea tomorrow."

The room was given over to the soft sound of chairs being moved and people walking out. No one talked, at least until they were outside of the room. Tigen swung his chair around to face his wife and waited until everyone had left.

"No one has dealt with this situation before. You can't be mad if no one comes up with a brilliant idea." His voice was a low and soothing tone, though it did not appear to have much affect on her mood.

"I can't be the brilliant one all the time," Worthia retorted.

"But that's who you are." Tigen let a smile grow on his face. "I'm just a gun jockey who likes to give orders and shoot things."

"No you're not and don't ever say that again." Worthia's eyes came up and met his. "Every day we just sit here, I get more and more worried. You know this will come down to a fight, if not this visit, then maybe the next or the next. There has to be some other way or else we are rolling the dice and hoping our technology is up to the task."

"As in every war ever fought." Reaching over, Tigen took her hand in his. "Given fairly equal equipment, battles are won by determination and grit. And we know our weapons can best what they have, at least their warriors."

"Had. A lot of time has passed."

"A lot more for us than them. They have been traveling near the speed of light, remember, so their relative time has been much shorter."

"If our theories are correct and they don't have something a lot more powerful they didn't show last time." Worthia frowned, but did not let go of Tigen's hand.

"Granted, the unknown is a bitch. But lack of knowing doesn't prove one way or the other. We are as prepared as we can be and if the last one hundred and sixty years haven't worked to our advantage, then more won't either."

Taking a deep breath and closing her eyes, Worthia let it out slowly. "You're probably right. No matter when the confrontation comes, we will either be ready or not and we won't know until it does. And the longer it goes, the more they take from our world. The world needs to move on, which it won't until we kick some alien butt and make sure they don't come back and prove that damn church wrong. Imagine what we could have achieved if we didn't have those damned alien lovers."

"Maybe more, maybe not." Tigen nodded his head side to side with the comment. "We preserved the best minds in the cities and the situation gave a sense of urgency to everyone, which always makes things develop faster."

"The best minds then, but what about the last one hundred and sixty years? Which minds have we lost?"

"No one can answer that. Besides, I am a firm believer that great ideas don't come to only one person but multiple people. The one who gets famous is just the first to claim credit." Tigen leaned toward Worthia. "Like marrying you."

Worthia laughed. "So that is your great claim to fame? I don't think history will think it is much of an achievement."

Directing his chair so that they sat side-by-side and in opposite directions, Tigen gathered his wife up in his arms. "What do they know?"

Chapter Twenty-One
Mistake

The slow, irregular footsteps were the only warning, but they were enough to wake up Renna Daunet. Blinking to clear her eyes revealed Wilmont standing just outside of the bedroom doorway.

"What's the matter, Wilmont?" Renna rose from the bed with slow motions and stiff joints.

"I can't sleep," came the weary reply.

"Why not?" Renna walked to the boy, hoping he didn't wake anyone else.

"These… things on my ears. They bug me. I can't sleep with them on." Wilmont leaned his head against the door post as if it prevented him from falling over.

"You have to leave them on, dear. It's the only way the aliens can't read our minds." Putting her arm around Wilmont's shoulders, Renna led the boy back to his room. "I know it might be hard, but you need to sleep. Try lying on your back."

"All right, I'll try." Wilmont continued into his room while Renna stopped at the door.

"Goodnight, dear." Renna closed the door and headed back to her bedroom as Wilmont walked to his bed. Lying on his back, he stared at the ceiling.

"It's too quiet here," he said to himself. After staring for a while, he rolled over to his side. "Ouch!"

A tear formed as Wilmont sat up. "I can't sleep with these stupid things on!" Tearing the inhibitors from his ears, Wilmont threw them across the room, avoiding hitting the wall and making noise. His head freed, Wilmont lay back on the bed.

"That's better," Wilmont said quietly to himself, falling asleep soon after making the declaration.

"How did this happen?" Worthia paced the living room without looking at Tigen, who was still in his flannel pajamas. Whether he was the only one brave enough to tell her the news at two in the morning or if he had insisted on being the one, she hadn't asked.

"Apparently the boy has had trouble sleeping with the shields deployed for almost a week. Tonight he became desperate enough that he took them off." Tigen talked in a slow, even voice while watching his wife pace. Occasional glances at the more breakable objects in the room gathered ideas on how to remove them from harm's way.

"Wasn't it detected when he removed them?"

"Yes, it was, but it took a while to resolve the situation." Tigen swallowed, preparing for what he knew would follow.

"Then why did we station someone nearby if they can't do their job!" Worthia spun around, her arms beating downward in the air and then returning to grab the hair near her forehead.

"They did respond, but the boy was cantankerous and uncooperative, probably due to lack of sleep. He said the shields hurt him. They had to transport him to a facility with a shielded room."

"How long? How long was he unshielded?" The words were driven through the air like individual thrusts.

"Almost two hours," Tigen responded in a quiet voice.

"*Damn!*" Walking over to the wall, Worthia pounded it with the bottom of her fist once, the sound echoing in the room and down the hall. The spot had been repaired before. Leaning her head against the wall, she braced herself with both fists. "It was more than enough time. They'll have detected him, I'm sure of it. What is the alien ship doing?"

Shifting uncomfortably on the table he was half-sitting on, Tigen replied, "The ship has stopped. It's not moving."

"Then they know." With her arms lowering and her head coming off the wall, Worthia took a deep breath. "I had hoped we would have more time. Don't know why I thought we would get it. We should have put the boy in the secure facility as soon as they arrived. Damn it!"

"You were being compassionate," Tigen said in a gentle voice.

"I was being stupid. Now everyone here is at risk." Worthia's head came back to stare at the ceiling.

"We were always at risk. Even if no one had developed this ability, we can't say that the aliens wouldn't have come after us anyway. Last time they didn't let anyone come between them and what they wanted. Why would we think this time would be different?"

"I know." Worthia turned and slowly walked toward Tigen. "It just feels like I am responsible for all this. I could have sent the boy to a military base, I could have put him in a bunker, but I didn't."

"Because you are a good person." Standing up, Tigen put his arms around Worthia just below her shoulders, both arms completely circling her body. She nestled her head in his chest and let him support her weight. After a few minutes, she spoke.

"Why does the world always feel right when you hold me, no matter what's happening?"

"Because this is where you're supposed to be." Tigen kissed her head.

"We won't get much done in this position."

"You might be surprised."

Worthia punched him in the side.

Chapter Twenty-Two
We Can Only Wait

As many people filled the war room as was comfortable to allow a person to walk through. Everyone was there, including a few who must have been local politicians because Worthia did not recognize them. Military people stood toward the front, gathered around the displays, anxious and bored. Most of the displays showed a view of a round, metallic ship hovering above grassland. There were no lights or openings to show movement, but sensors verified the stillness of the vessel.

"How long has it been without movement?" she asked.

"Going on ten hours, M. President." The lieutenant that answered did not look away from her screen.

"Why haven't they moved?"

"Records show that the aliens do seem to take a long time to take action." Lorda Rans fidgeted her hands, moving them every five seconds or so to a different position. She hadn't noticed Chadan counting the number of unique positions from the corner of his eye.

"So how long before they do something?"

"No way to know." Lorda's hands changed position again. "Before, they typically did things at sunrise."

"Sunrise has come and gone and they've still done nothing. They waiting for tomorrow?"

"Maybe they didn't get a good fix on the boy's location," Tigen offered.

"Or maybe they are trying to figure out why they were able to make contact and then lost track of the boy again. You know, what it all means." The words came out easily from Chadan without stress of any kind.

"You know, the fact that you can be in a situation like this and be so nonchalant is why people hate you," Worthia replied.

"Jealousy is such an ugly thing," Chadan answered.

Attention went back to the displays, which refused to show anything different. Worthia switched her attention to a different display, which tracked military satellites. It showed two with fields of fire over the continental United States and a third being maneuvered into position, the numbers under the icon becoming almost zero. The target circles representing their final destinations overlapped at Denver.

Looking back to the main display, Worthia shook her head. "This is less exciting than watching paint dry and is getting us nowhere. I'm going back to work. I trust I don't have to tell you to call me if something changes."

"No, M. President," the lieutenant shot back, a look of concern crossing her face after saying it.

"Good." Worthia turned to the crowd. "All right, people, we can be a lot more useful today than standing around watching an alien ship hover over… where is it?"

"Kansas," the lieutenant said.

"When the aliens aren't in Kansas anymore, we'll let you know. So get before I have my Chief of Staff throw you out, literally. And trust me, he would enjoy doing it."

With muttering words, people turned and slowly left the room, many taking one last glance over their shoulders. When Tigen started to tap his foot, Worthia put her hand on his arm.

"Patience, dear."

"I'll turn them into patients, just give the word." There was too much glee in the words for them to be a joke.

"I said 'patience,' not 'patients.'"

"I must have heard wrong." Tigen smirked.

"We'll go with that. What's on for you today, given our visitors don't come calling, that is?"

"Surprise inspections." Another phrase with too much glee.

"Be nice. People are scared enough as it is."

"Do I have to?" A fake whine accompanied the question.

"Yes." There was nothing fake about the answer. "It's an order, if that helps."

"Helps make sure I'm nice, yes."

Worthia shook her head. "And they wanted you to run for President."

"Things would have been a lot different." Taking in a breath, Tigen resettled his shoulders. "I'd have to be nice and you'd have to be the hardball. Is why I didn't take the job."

"Because you wanted to be the one to be the hardball?"

"Because I didn't want you being the one to do it. I know what that's like. People don't deserve that!"

Worthia chuckled. "If we weren't surrounded by people right now, I'd kiss you."

"I do as my President commands," Tigen said in a casual manner.

"I'll remember that for later," Worthia said in a low voice. It caused Tigen to raise one eyebrow and blush.

A heavy sigh came from Wray, tempting Cedynia to look away from her monitor without success. It was followed by another one after a short amount of time, causing Cedynia to give a small one of her own.

"What." The annoyance was not hidden. "You only have a four hour shift. It's not going to kill you."

"I just wish that damn ship would do something besides sit there."

She could imagine in her head Wray rolling his eyes the way she had seen him do a thousand times.

"It's like they're intentionally torturing us by not moving, knowing that is what we are waiting for."

"Didn't you read the briefing, or at least listen to it?"

"The important parts." Silence ran between them for a few moments. "Okay, I fell asleep while listening to it. But it was soooooo boring."

Cedynia tsked. "Honestly, Wray, we have hostile aliens practically on our doorsteps and you can't stay awake to listen to something that might save your life?"

"Hey, give me one of those rifles and I'll be just fine."

The comment brought a laugh from Cedynia, which drew stares from those around them. "I've seen you shoot. Leave the rifles with those who know how to aim."

"That's those stupid target holos and I still say they don't always know when you hit them." Wray frowned at the screen because he was not allowed to turn his head.

"I was there, you missed!" Another laugh followed.

"Is there something you find funny?" The voice came from behind. Without looking, Cedynia answered.

"Him thinking he knows how to shoot."

"And what does that have to do with monitoring the ship?" The voice was sharp, military sharp, causing Cedynia to turn towards it.

"I'm... sorry, ma'am... sir... Captain." Cedynia made a quick swivel back to the screen.

"You're here to catch what the computers don't... both of you. Now do your job!" Footsteps going away followed the announcement.

A few seconds after the footsteps disappeared, Cedynia exhaled. "Thanks a lot," she said in a quiet voice.

"I didn't..."

"Stow it!" Her voice was almost as sharp as the captain's. "And no more sighing!"

"It sure is a big'un." John Stephens stared with his right hand over his eyes and his head thrown back. "What you think they are doing up there?"

"How the hell should I know?"

"Sybil, language!" John shot at his wife. "What if the children hear?"

"I didn't ask for someone to park a big-ass flying ship above our pasture." Sybil waved her arm for emphasis.

"Well, neither did I, but that's no reason to go cussing. What if these are the aliens the church told us about?"

"Then they should come down here and tell us what they want and stop scaring our cows! They've stopped giving milk."

John waved the ship off with his hand. "They'll be gone soon enough."

"How do you know that?" Sybil put her hands on her hips and set her jaw.

"Why the heck would they stay around here?" John gave an easy shrug and started walking toward the house.

Sybil looked back up at the ship. "And none too soon if you ask me."

Chapter Twenty-Three
On Our Doorstep

"It's moving!" The words were all but shouted as Tigen burst into Worthia's office.

Closing her eyes, Worthia tilted her head back a little. "Do I dare hope that it's not coming here?"

"It's headed straight here." Tigen's face was set hard. Lifting his shoulders, he took in a breath and settled on the balls of his feet. "Do I unleash the hounds?"

"Not yet." She watched his face drop. "I'm not starting a shooting war if I don't have to." Walking to the window, Worthia looked out over the city.

"Do you really think they will give you a choice?" The voice came from one of Worthia's guests in her office, who had been quickly forgotten.

"I hope so." A heavy sigh accompanied the words. "We have advanced so much since their last visit. Maybe it will be enough to convince them to let it go. Bullies tend to only fight easy battles."

"Are you sure we are not still an easy battle? If we don't attack right away, we may lose the element of surprise." Tigen walked over to the window, his heavy steps announcing his movements.

"If we are an easy battle, surprise won't matter." Scanning the city, Worthia shook her head. "I expect they'll talk first, try and convince us to give up the boy. If they have any sensors at all, I would think it would be clear they are no longer dealing with Earth from one hundred and sixty years ago."

"I still say open up on them with the satellites as soon as we can." The words were soft, but Tigen's voice made sure they carried.

"And if there are other ships in space?" Worthia turned to face him. The words caused Tigen's head to go back.

"We have seen no evidence of other ships."

"And they were on top of us before we saw them this time. Lack of proof is not proof as Chadan would say. If we take out that ship and then another ship takes out our satellites, where are we then?" She raised an eyebrow.

Recovering quickly, Tigen made a head bow. "As you instruct, M. President." Making a quick military turn, Tigen exited the room with long, purposeful steps.

"What do we do?"

Worthia was reminded of her guests for the second time. Turning to them showed faces filled with worry and bodies tense. She tried to give them a reassuring smile. "Go home. Tell everyone to stay home. If you show no threat, I don't think the aliens will bother with you. I am sure the military will be able to handle the situation."

"I hope so." The two men and woman stood, made abbreviated head bows, and left the room. To their credit, they didn't run. Worthia let them go in silence, which ended as soon as the door was closed.

"Computer, I need everyone here now." It almost came out as a shout. Taking some breaths, Worthia forced herself to calm down. She did not have long to wait. With the speed most people entered her office, it was clear they had already been on their way. Taking the seat behind her desk, she raised the elevation so people wouldn't have to look down as far as normal. With the room nearly full, she spoke.

"Tell me that everything is ready." She scanned the room.

"Everything is ready," Chadan replied.

"Are we sure?"

"Everything has been checked and triple checked."

"The boy is secured?"

"Yes." Tigen.

"Why do I feel like I am forgetting something?"

No one spoke for a few moments. Several looked at each other as if asking if someone dare say anything. Several shuffled their feet. Tigen dared to speak, to the relief of most in the room.

"Because you are worried."

"I should be worried. We are about to all but declare war on an alien race we know almost nothing about." Worthia paused, head turned down, then spoke again. "One thing I want to make clear to these aliens is that we are acting alone. No one else is to be dragged into this. If we are destroyed, at least they might learn from it."

Tigen grew a huge smile. When Worthia looked into his eyes, she thought she could almost see a tear forming in them. Her face relaxed and a smaller smile gathered on her face.

"Then, everyone at your stations." Command came back into Worthia's voice. "I'll be in the war room. Yes, I've just renamed it from the situation room. Seems appropriate." Her chair lowered and she stood. "Well? Get moving."

The rush out of the room was orderly. Worthia let everyone else leave before moving, but once outside the door, Tigen fell in line with her. "Don't you have somewhere to be?"

"At your side." His voice made it sound like there could be no other answer.

"No, I'm serious." Several assistants walked behind her as she made her way through the halls. Several military guards walked in front of her.

"So am I." Tigen's tone didn't change. "If you think I am leaving your side with an alien invasion coming, you are mistaken."

"I have other guards." Worthia turned left, went through a steel doorway that shut after their group was through, and turned right.

"None of them are me." A puffing of the chest accompanied the statement.

"And what makes you more qualified?" The question was somewhat playful.

"I love you more than anyone else here does."

"So you would give your life for me?"

"I would give all those aliens' lives for you. I've got too much to live for."

A small laugh came from Worthia just before entering the war room, but a serious expression soon came over her face. "Where are they?"

"They'll be here in about five minutes," Captain Zaheia responded. With raised eyebrows, Worthia walked over to the woman and stuck out her hand.

"Captain Zaheia, nice to see you again. What brings you to Denver?"

"You don't think we're going to fight aliens from another planet and I'm not going to be involved, do you?" One eyebrow rose with the question.

A broad smile graced Worthia's face as she withdrew her hand. "No, I expect not. You met one of the messengers, correct?"

"Yes, M. President." Zaheia stood with her hands clasped behind her.

"Impressions?"

"Automatons. Totally under the direction of the main aliens."

"Which make them unimaginative, as individuals, that is."

"That would be my assessment."

"Hopefully that will make them easier to deal with. Thank you, you may return to your station."

"Thank you, M. President, and nice to be here with you." Zaheia turned and walked back to the displays.

"That's a tough woman," Worthia said to no one in particular.

"You could take her," Tigen said softly next to her.

"I'm glad I don't have to find out."

"Ship on approach," a voice called out from the monitors. Everyone turned to the main display, which almost filled one wall. It showed a scene of the countryside east of Denver. Calm and restive, the only stain on the scene was a oblong, silver smudge that grew larger as they watched. As the ship took definition and grew larger, the camera zoomed back to prevent the ship from filling the whole view. Soon the outskirts of Denver could be seen.

"Any idea yet where it will land?" Worthia asked.

"It appears to be heading to the northern green," came the reply from the monitors.

"Of course," Tigen huffed. "I swear those Puritans kept that plaza empty just so the ship could land there."

"You don't think the area being scorched to bare earth made

people nervous about rebuilding?" Chadan asked.

"After all this time?" Tigen replied in disdain. "No, I think they wanted to make sure that ship parked on our doorstep."

"Either that or they just got used to the idea of a park being there." Secretary Coons gave him a smile. "Or they just didn't want to live that close to us."

"Fine by me," Tigen said with another huff as he turned back to the display.

The speed of the ship could be seen in the effect it had on the trees that it passed over, bending them like a strong windstorm. "They're going to overshoot," someone called from the monitors, but then the ship rapidly decelerated, causing the trees to bend back the other direction and sway for a few seconds. Halting precisely over the green, the ship hovered while the air settled.

"Altitude?" Worthia asked.

"One thousand meters."

"Thank you to whoever has been providing the information." Worthia made the comment without looking away from the monitor, her hands unconsciously squeezing each other.

"Of course, M. President," the voice replied, a small amount of shock included.

"It never hurts to be polite," she said softly to Tigen.

"The military? Not sure they really know what polite is, to civilians that is. To those under your command, doubtful." Worthia could tell from the tone of his voice that he had puffed out his chest.

"Please try to stay serious," she said with a half-giggle.

"Me? Always." The comment brought another half-giggle. Feeling the short stares around her, Worthia cleared her throat and resettled her weight on her feet.

As people watched, the sound of slow breathing resumed in the group. The wind around the ship had calmed, the trees stopped swaying, and birds could be seen returning to their nests. The ship still hovered.

"Are they going to hover all day?" someone in the crowd asked.

"Last time they were here," Chadan's voice offered, "they hovered for a whole day before descending."

"They sure like taking their time," a female voice said.

"Probably a characteristic of a collective mind," Chadan said with ease. The rustle of people turning toward him followed. "Because they are telepathic and from their previous behavior, we surmise that they are a collective mind of equally intelligent beings. This may lead to long decision times."

"Either that or they are scanning the city and our defenses," Tigen answered.

"Or that," Chadan said with a shrug.

"Always the optimist, huh Tigen?" Url Pernent added.

"Military mind," Worthia offered. She could feel the short stare Tigen gave her.

Those in the room continued to watch while the ship continued to hover. Every so often a comment would be made.

"Maybe they are checking for mines in the green."

"I thought of that but I was over-ruled," Tigen answered. Several laughs of various types were elicited by the comment.

"Maybe their equipment needs time to adjust. I mean, they did just perform a maneuver that our ships can't do."

"True."

"Maybe they are playing mind games with us, making us sweat," Tigen offered.

"Is anyone sweating?" A large sniff followed Worthia's question. "Okay, cancel that question."

After an hour, the ship had still not moved and people grew restless, some finding chairs and others pacing. Worthia walked over to Captain Zaheia.

"I assume the projector is ready at the north gate."

"Yes, M. President. Technicians are standing by." Zaheia started to salute, but stopped herself.

"You can call me Worthia in private conversation," Worthia said with a smile.

"Not in these circumstances, M. President."

Returning a smile, Worthia walked back to the wall monitor and looked around. Some people looked tense, others looked bored. Military personnel stood at parade rest with no expression on their faces. Taking one last glance at the monitor, she turned to address the crowd.

"I'm going to stay here," she said in a voice loud enough for all to hear without shouting. "I am going to sit in that very comfortable chair over there and wait. I see no reason for everyone to stay, but I am not kicking you out. Please be assured we will tell you as soon as something happens. And, if you stay or go, make sure you get something to eat and drink, if only a little. We don't need people fainting from lack of nutrition or dehydration."

Laughter mingled through the crowd as Worthia made her way to her chair. At her approach, it floated up to a comfortable height to sit into. Behind her she could hear Tigen's footsteps. The chair gave a view of the room and the wall display, floating higher after she sat so that her head was above the crowd. She watched as several people left, mostly lower echelon. Some, she noted, were still transfixed at the display, causing her to turn her head to Tigen.

"Do you think we need to get some counselors down here to talk to people?"

"Might not be a bad idea, if we can find some that aren't traumatized themselves. Or aren't already swamped."

"Talk to Stanley. Hopefully he had some on reserve." Worthia turned to face her husband and smiled. His brow squished.

"What?"

"This is one of the few times I am eye to eye with you."

Tigen opened his mouth to say something, but stopped. The sly smile on his face told Worthia it was good that he didn't. "I'll go talk to Stan." Turning, Tigen stepped away as if he already knew where to find the Surgeon General.

"I do love to watch that man walk," Worthia said quietly to herself.

After three hours, most of the crowd had left, a couple in step with a counselor. Those who remained were military personnel, but Chadan, Lorda, and Url remained also. Worthia lowered her chair and stepped out, stretching her legs before walking over to Chadan. The periodic work of the muscle stimulators helped but could not replace weight on the legs. Chadan turned as she got near.

"I bet if I ordered the military to drag you out of here, you would go kicking and screaming," Worthia said with a laugh.

"Will you allow me to go outside the city to the green?" Chadan raised one eyebrow.

"Of course not," she replied with a huff.

"Then yes, I would." Chadan smiled and raised one finger. "Scientific discovery must not be interrupted!"

"Not much to discover yet." The comment came with a shake of her head.

"Except that none of our sensors, including the ones we based on their technology, seem to be able to penetrate the hull." Chadan appeared happy with the statement.

"And that means what?"

"Maybe it means that since we can find no interruption in the hull, they can't scan us either." Chadan gave his eyebrows two shakes.

"So they are just sitting there?"

With a wave of his hand, Chadan tilted his head. "I could speculate a lot of things: the stress of travel, assuming a defensive posture first, etc. But without information, it is meaningless."

Looking up and to the right, Worthia focused on nothing. "Are they trying to telepathically scan us?"

"Always," Chadan replied. "Our sensors can detect that. It has been constant since they arrived."

"From the ship?"

Chadan's shoulders sagged. "Undetermined. Either they can hide the source or it is from all directions."

Turning suddenly, Worthia made a brisk walk to Captain Harjo. The captain saluted as Worthia came close. "Have we found any satellites that the aliens have placed in space?"

"No, M. President," Harjo replied in a crisp voice. "But with the technology that allowed them to get to Earth without us knowing, I would not be surprised if they did."

"Have we tried looking for what's not there?"

The questions caused Harjo's face to scrunch and tilt. "I'm not sure what you mean."

"If a satellite passed in front of a star, it would block the star's light, correct?"

"Yes," Harjo said in a tentative voice. "Assuming it wasn't

something else."

"We could look, though, correct?"

"Yes, we can, but it will take hours, if not days, to scan the sky and that assumes it happens when we are looking."

"Then get started." The command in Worthia's voice was clear.

"Yes, M. President. We cannot promise results."

"It's better than doing nothing." Worthia turned as Harjo saluted again and then turned back to her people. Walking to Secretary Rans, Worthia took a breath and exhaled.

"Keeping people busy?" Lorda asked in a cheerful voice.

"I'm surprised they hadn't started looking before." A shake of Worthia's head accompanied the comment.

"That's because you have no idea what you just asked for. Do you know how much computing power that's going to take?"

"There's only a limited amount of space they have to check," Worthia said defensively.

"A very large limited amount of space, plus you have to wait until something goes missing and then determine if something we have up there or know about could have caused it. And then you have to wait for a second occurrence to tell what direction and how fast it is moving. Big job." Lorda sighed in sympathy.

"We have plenty of computers. They might as well be busy too. If the aliens attack, it might be the last thing they do."

"True." Lorda's head bobbed and she smiled at Worthia. "Anything I can do for you?"

"Not that I can think of, but give me time." Worthia returned the smile. "Why did you stay?"

"My department's whole area of responsibility is out there." She pointed at the screen. "Not much for me to do at the moment. Besides, you might need moral support."

The comment caused Worthia to let out a single laugh. "Be careful. Tigen might think you are barging into his territory."

"Has he gotten more protective lately?"

"You have no idea." A heavy sigh followed the answer.

"Shoot," Lorda said as her head swung back and forth. "If you want protective, you should hear my mother. She wants the whole family to hide in an underground bunker until it's all over. Was calling me constantly to try and convince me. I had to block her."

"I bet she loved that."

"I have no information to confirm or deny." Lorda raised her chin.

Laughing, Worthia shook her head. "When you do talk to her, give her my sympathy."

Activity continued everywhere except on the display, where the scene remained the same. Worthia went back to her chair. At the appropriate time, food was brought in and distributed to people. Many people ignored the food placed next to them but Tigen had no loss of appetite. Worthia ate a modest amount, careful not to fill her stomach completely. Time was the most active agent, the seconds marching by in their regular cadence, ignoring people and aliens.

As night began to replace the day one shadow at a time, Worthia stopped at the command station. Everyone turned to her. "If these aliens follow their previous pattern, nothing is going to happen until tomorrow morning. I suggest that everyone get as much rest as possible. Tomorrow, most likely, will prove to be a busy day. Thanks for all your efforts today."

"Of course, M. President," came from Captain Harjo and was followed by others.

The sound of Tigen's footsteps followed Worthia out of the room. She didn't say anything until an elevator closed around them. Once closed, she leaned on his chest and laid her head just under his shoulder. "Can I be tired?"

"Of course, my love." His voice was soft as he placed his arm around her. "You appeared calm and in control the whole time."

"I wanted to explode and yell at the aliens to get on with it." The elevator slowed and Worthia disengaged from the embrace. "If they don't come out tomorrow, it's going to be a really boring day."

"Maybe we should stay in bed?" Tigen gave her a communicative smile.

"That would guarantee they appear," Worthia said with an eye roll.

Chapter Twenty-Four
Near Neighbors

Well before sunrise, Worthia stood in the war room, Tigen just behind her. The room was almost as full as the day before. About half of the people looked like they hadn't slept, particularly the non-military ones. Forcing herself not to tap her foot, Worthia stood in front of the wall display.

"Sunrise in five minutes," was called out from command. At the edge of the display, sunlight was pushing across the far horizon's edge and lightening the sky. Nervous energy caused feet to shuffle and people to mumble to themselves.

Sunrise came fast across the eastern plain. Shadows fled with light speed from the scene. The alien ship held on to some tree shadows for a while, but even these were soon banished in the bright sunlight.

"Olly, olly, oxen free," Worthia muttered.

"What?" Tigen's head twisted.

"An old kid's saying," she replied. "It means everyone can come out now."

"Maybe we should knock." Tigen's voice was cheerful.

"You'd need a tall ladder," Chadan added to the conversation from Worthia's right. He turned and gave a friendly smile.

"A shotgun might work," Tigen shrugged.

"See, that's why you're not President." Worthia straightened her back, pulled down her blouse, and clasped her hands together in front of her.

One half of the ship now glimmered in silver glory, giving the ship a yin-yang look. As people waited and the sun rose, the ship became more yang until the yin had been banished.

"Strange how there are no shadows on the side away from the sun," Chadan commented.

"Yes." Worthia turned her head as if to get a different view. "There should be some difference in brightness on the far side. How are they doing that?"

"The hull must propagate the sunlight around the ship, like a conductor. It would be fascinating to know how and why its function is. Besides the communication theories, that is."

"Are there any alien signals that we can pick up?" Worthia said loud enough to be heard by command without turning her head.

"No, M. President," came back.

"Maybe they're 'charging up'?" Chadan added.

"Maybe they just like a shiny ship," Tigen offered.

"Taking pains to be impressive has been a historic strategy from the beginning of civilization." Chadan nodded his head.

"Or they're just conceited." Worthia's tone implied finality of the subject.

"Ship descending," came from command in a voice with a little excitement.

"How fast?" Worthia stared at the display. "I can't tell it's moving."

"Fifty centimeters a second."

"At that rate they are going to take forever to reach the ground," Tigen grumbled.

"Obviously they're not in a hurry," Chadan replied.

"Rate has increased to one hundred centimeters a second."

"They must have heard you," Chadan said in a playful voice. Tigen huffed.

An altitude number was added to the display. It slowly grew faster and then slowed once the ship was halfway to the ground. Pads extended from the ship at two hundred meters. As the pads touched the earth, they sank into the ground half a meter before the ship stopped. Worthia turned and walked across the room.

"Projectors up and running, Captain?"

"Yes, M. President," Captain Zaheia replied, back straight and arms to her side.

"Then I will be in the communicating room. Hopefully our guests won't spend too long leaving their ship."

The clear glass doors of the communications room slid open at Worthia's approach, and then closed and darkened as she entered. The lights in the room came on at the same time. Soft lighting came her direction. The room was only about five meters across with a wall display on the far side that showed the ship from the north gate's view. Chairs could be called from the floor as well as a table or a podium, but Worthia decided to just stand. She waved at a light in the floor to activate holographic projection, but did not stand in the direct light yet.

"Always let the enemy commit first," she said to herself.

To her surprise, the wait was not long. It was only a few minutes before a ramp rotated down from the ship and a body could be seen exiting through the haze of the ship opening. A humanoid form in a long white robe walked down the ramp in an unhurried manner and then toward the north gate. He appeared to hold no weapons and no wings were visible from the front. Holding his arms clasped in front of him, the being kept a metronome pace, stopping ten meters from the gate. Worthia stepped into the projection area.

"Welcome to Earth," Worthia said in a diplomatic voice.

The 'angel' looked at the gate, one side and then the other, and stared for a few moments at Worthia's hologram. It peered past the gate as if looking for someone.

"Can't it see me?" Worthia asked.

"Its behavior indicates it sees something. Maybe it knows that it is not a person and is ignoring it?" Chadan's voice offered. "If it is not relying on strictly visual indications, it might know the difference."

The angel walked forward and touched the transparent shielding that covered the gate, pushing on it to test its strength and flexibility. Then, taking a step back and still not looking at Worthia's hologram, its mouth started to move.

"I can't hear any words," Worthia commented.

"Neither do we," Captain Zaheia answered via Worthia's interface.

"Maybe it has no voice," Lorda's voice said over the interface.

"Interesting!" Chadan's voice had the winding-up sound it made when he was discovering something. "A species so dependent on telepathy that they have lost speech. Much like the blind fish in caves."

"It's going to prove hard to communicate with them if they can't speak," Tigen inserted, "particularly since we are not removing our inhibitors."

"First things first." Worthia stepped from the lighted area back to the door, exiting the room. "We need to get someone down there, face-to-face, and…"

"It's not going to be you." Tigen's whole body was set for impact, from his face to his well-planted feet. "I'll go."

"Actually," Chadan interrupted with one finger pointing up, "I believe this is what we have a vice president for."

"Thanks for throwing me to the wolves." Storm Allin's feet made little sound as he neared the gathering group. "But they are right, M. President. We can't risk you going out there and, quite frankly, I won't pick the Chief of Staff for this either. No offense."

"None taken." Tigen looked back at the smaller man in his ever present crisp suit styled in the latest fashion. This one was dark blue, much like his current mood.

"I'm leaving now." Allin turned and raised his hand as he walked at a brisk pace. "If I don't return, you can drink the brandy I hid in my office."

"I can't figure out if that man is brave or foolhardy." Anne Coons shook her head.

"Dramatic," Worthia replied.

"I find the whole speech situation with our visitors fascinating." Chadan turned from watching Allin leave and addressed the small group. "Not only does it confirm so much of what we thought from our last encounter, but it raises questions that would prove a wondrous study. Were the aliens ever able to speak? Did they develop telepathy first and thus have never had the need to speak, or did their technology advance to the point that speaking was not necessary? The whole evolving of such a situation would be worthy of much investigation."

"If they weren't trying to steal our best people," Tigen put in with a huff.

"Plus," Chadan said as if ignoring Tigen's comment, eyes bright, "did they somehow put this ability into humans' evolutionary development or did they know that we would develop such ability? That assumes, of course, that all races don't eventually develop it. Now that would be fascinating! Telepathy as normal evolutionary progress." Chadan was almost hopping up and down.

"The basic fact appears to be, though, that we can't communicate with them without the inhibitors and we are not removing those." Worthia's statement contained force to kill the speculation and cut the conversation back to an even keel. "Plus the aggression they have displayed before would indicate they aren't keen on sitting down and discussing species evolutionary development. I doubt we could even get them to tell us where they took the twenty-five thousand people one hundred and sixty years ago."

"We could look at their records after we take their ship." Tigen provided an evil grin with the comment.

"You're assuming, of course, that we would even know how to access the data and read it." Chadan wagged his finger. "We have never dealt with an alien language before, except for those odd samples from when they were here before, and we still have no idea what they mean. Besides, you are thinking in speaking and hearing terms. The aliens' data bank might be such that we would not even recognize them, particularly if they use telepathic communication somehow to store the data. Now that would be fascinating!"

"Give us enough time, we'll figure it out." Tigen pulled down his eyebrows and gave a slight shake of his head.

"All of which doesn't help us now," Worthia continued in her command voice. She moved to Captain Zaheia's location. "Are we recording communications from the ship?"

"Yes, M. President, but we have no idea what they are saying, only the volume of traffic."

"How is the volume?"

"Heavy. I have no idea what I am talking about, but it looks like a heated conversation between multiple people to me."

It was Worthia's turn to scrunch her eyebrows and cock her head. "Like multiple 'people' trying to give commands to that drone out there?"

"It could be," Zaheia said in an unsure voice, "or maybe they are having the conversation in its head, like they are all there with it, so to speak."

"Damn." Worthia shook her head as if to clear it. "That would give you a headache. So you are saying they are, like, using the same channel? No, that's not exactly what I mean…"

"Like multiple pilots using the same heads-up display," Zaheia offered.

"All in control at the same time?"

"We have no idea." Zaheia kept her voice calm. "We are only guessing."

"Maybe that is why they take so long to make up their mind and do something. Is there any way we can tell how many there are?"

"I'm sorry, M. President, but until we can translate there is no way to tell."

"That is fine. Any information is useful. I assume all turrets are ready."

"Yes, M. President."

"Do we have any soldiers down at the gate to assist Vice-President Allin in case something goes wrong?"

"Yes, M. President."

"Then I guess that's all we can do for now. Thank you, Captain."

"Of course." Zaheia turned back to the monitoring stations.

Walking a slow, tight circle, Worthia drifted to the wall display, looking at the ground and tapping her fingers together. One corner tracked Allin's progress to the gate, sitting in a vehicle with two infantrymen. A broad smile filled his face.

"He looks like he is going to a party," Worthia said to no one in particular.

"He's a strange duck," Chadan offered blithely from behind Worthia.

"Yes, but he's a good man, particularly when things go sideways. I don't think anything phases him." She gave the image a small smile.

"That can be a useful trait. Did you pick him as your running mate?"

"Sort of. Not really. He came highly recommended and I couldn't find anything wrong with him. Plus, you declined, remember?" Her head turned and she gave the smaller man a stare.

Chadan chuckled. "I have no interest in just being the next heartbeat in line."

"But you could be out there now, talking to an alien."

"I will do that when it is proved safe." Chadan placed his hands behind his back and lifted his chin toward the display.

The small crowd watched as the vehicle pulled up behind the wall next to the gate out of sight of the angel. Allin stepped off the vehicle, gave a nod to the infantrymen, and walked, back straight, to the gate, tugging on his suit-jacket as he went. As if walking up to a neighbor's door, Allin stopped in front of the angel several feet from the protective barrier. Turning, the angel looked at him for a few seconds without reaction. Straightening its shoulders, the angel's mouth started moving.

"Is he saying anything?" Allin asked. "I mean, I should be able to hear him, right?"

"Instrumentation indicates that the angel is not making any sounds," Zaheia's voice said over the comms.

Waving his hand, Allin said with a tilted head, "Excuse me, but I can't hear anything. I don't think you're saying anything."

The angel stopped speaking. Its head twitched once before its mouth began to move again. Allin let it 'speak' for a few seconds.

"You," Allin pointed at the angel, "are speaking," he moved his finger from his mouth outward, "but I," he pointed at himself, "can't," he shook his head, "hear anything," he pointed at his ears.

Stopping in mid-word, the angel's mouth froze, along with his whole body. Then, closing his mouth and returning to his straight stance, the angel remained fixed in that position. Allin watched for thirty seconds before reacting.

"Did we break him?" Allin asked through the comm.

"We sense no change in his... being." Zaheia said the last word without surety.

"Guess we just wait and see." Worthia sighed.

They waited for another thirty seconds, and then another. After almost two minutes, the angel turned around and walked back to the ship with the same methodical pace that he had used approaching the gate.

"It's my face, isn't it?" Allin said in a high, pitchy voice and a slight smile.

"Stay serious out there," Worthia said.

"What do you want me to do?" Allin asked in a more serious voice.

"Go back to the vehicle and wait. If no one shows up in half an hour, come back."

"Yes, M. President."

Turning from the display, Worthia walked back to her chair at a modest pace and sat down. Closing her eyes, she tilted her head backwards. Chadan followed at a distance.

"Communication is going to be impossible if they can't vocalize." Chadan's voice was soft.

"I know. If they can't vocalize and we don't remove our inhibitors, seems we're at an impasse. I doubt sign language will suffice for negotiations." Taking a breath, Worthia lowered her head. "The next move is up to them."

"In Chicago, they used one of the Puritans to talk to us." Worthia had not heard Zaheia approach.

"Why not do that now?" Chadan asked.

"It was the father of the boy. Maybe they thought we would give him up because it was a parent. Since that didn't work, maybe they decided to do something else."

"What time is it?" Worthia asked.

"Only oh-seven-fifty," Zaheia answered.

"Damn. If they don't try again until tomorrow morning, it's going to take forever to have a conversation." Worthia looked over the small group. "Any ideas how long we wait until they do something else?"

The only one who spoke was Chadan. "All indications is that we will not hear from them until tomorrow."

The comment drew forlorn looks from everyone except Tigen. "I'll stay and watch. I'm used to it."

"Of course you will." A knowing smile crossed her lips as she stood up. She patted him on the arm. "Let me know as soon as something happens. I mean that. Right away."

"Of course, M. President." Tigen's serious voice was accompanied by the same kind of look.

"Well, people," Worthia said, scanning the crowd, "I am sure there are a multitude of things waiting for me that I have neglected the last couple of days. Plus I should make an announcement to the public right away. I'm sure my speech writers already have it prepared. Why don't we get back to our other duties while we wait for the aliens to decide what to do next?"

She didn't wait for their answers before heading to the exit. The cabinet members who were there followed in her wake, small bits of more normal conversation passing between them.

Worthia sat in a high-back chair facing the holo-projector. Dressed in a business suit, her hair had been forced over the last two hours to an uncharacteristically modern style. The technician's nod was her cue.

"Fellow citizens. I know you are all concerned about the alien ship sitting just north of our city. I want to make it clear that we have seen no aggressive actions from the aliens. As you may recall from history, the aliens can be very insistent on what they believe to be theirs. I want to let you know that no one will be forced to go with the aliens and we will not be kicking anyone out of the city just for our protection.

"Last time the aliens were here, humanity had no defenses or offensive capabilities to deal with the aliens. This time it is different. If the aliens become aggressive, I believe they will be quite surprised at the ability we have to defend ourselves. All of our defenses are on high alert and remain that way.

"I am not going to, at this time, tell people not to go on with their lives. But, if an alarm is sounded, please return to your homes or a safe area as fast as possible. Please keep track of those needing supervision so that you can help them if an emergency arises. And please help any friends and neighbors who may need it. We must all stay united as the community we are.

"Let me reassure you that there is no cause for alarm at this time. Last time, the aliens only took those who were willing to go. If you are such a person, you will be allowed to leave the city. But I believe we are more mature in our view of these aliens. The city will sit tight until they decide to leave.

"Thank you for your understanding and help during these times."

Chapter Twenty-Five
Waiting for the Knock

Words were not required as Worthia looked up from her desk in response to the door being opened by Tigen. As he entered the room, he was followed by Chadan, who then closed the door.

"No change yet," Tigen offered. "Taking their own sweet time, I guess," he said to Worthia's sigh.

"I had a thought about that." Chadan raised a finger as he spoke. "If the given biblical accounts are close to true and these aliens are the same as the Jesus described, then it would be reasonable to assume he had the power of speech before."

"Didn't those accounts have him being born?" Tigen asked.

"Why General Tonsten, your scholarship amazes me!" Chadan's eyes went wide. "I didn't know you were a religious scholar."

"I hear things," Tigen said in a dismissive manner.

"Anyway, since his early life is so sparsely documented, I am assuming that if it was our aliens, he showed up as an adult form. I don't think their body manipulating abilities go so far as a fully functioning, growing body."

"Couldn't they have been using telepathy that time too?" Worthia asked.

"I think if a ship was around, it would have been mentioned. I do not know how close the ship needs to be in order to affect telepathy." Chadan's head made small bobs as it traveled back and forth. "As I was saying, I believe it would be reasonable to assume the

Subordinate, who would appear to be the one to play the part, was able to speak. I find it interesting that he is apparently not able to speak now, at least not yet."

"Not yet?" Worthia's head did a slight turn to the right.

"It has been quite a while since those biblical dates so I assume the Subordinate reverted to his original form, or maybe he is inhabiting a shell, so to speak, and he left it. Either way, they may need to modify the Subordinate's form to be able to communicate verbally and teach it how to speak English. Of course I have no idea how long this might take."

"Maybe they need to make him a new body," Tigen said with a small laugh.

"Highly doubtful. If they were planning on returning right away, as it would seem reasonable to assume, I doubt he would take the trouble to dispose of the body he used."

"Where does this get us?" Worthia's head rotated down a little so she stared at the small man through the top of her eyes.

"It may explain the wait. And," Chadan became more animated, his feet starting to move along the carpet, "it gives us hope for a resolution to our dilemma. But just being able to speak is not enough."

"You mean he has to learn to speak a language we can understand, preferably English." Worthia's head nodded with the statement.

"Yes, but with their telepathic ability, I assume learning a language would be easy. Only the physical efforts to make the correct sounds would take time." Chadan gave a self-satisfied smile.

"You're assuming that the aliens can formulate the correct ideas to understand our thinking processes to select the correct words." It was Worthia's turn to point a finger. "Evidence from when they were here before is that different people heard different words."

"But they did get the same message." Chadan added. "Plus, if he is the historical figure written about, he has done it before. Either way, it will only be a matter of practice for sufficient communication."

"Wait," Tigen interjected, "didn't he die before?"

"According to the stories passed down." A shrug from Chadan dismissed the idea. "Besides, it's not like we are writing a legal document to be dissected by lawyers."

"Of course." Worthia gave a reluctant nod. "At least I hope it doesn't come to that. Damn, I wish they would just hurry it up and get on with it."

"That is most likely not in the plan and there is nothing we can do about it but wait." With his head bowed and his hands together, Chadan gave his goodbye and left the room.

Taking a deep breath, Worthia sagged in her chair and leaned her head back to look at the ceiling. "You were uncharacteristically silent."

Tigen shrugged. "I have no information to give so I had no reason to comment."

"Thanks. I knew I could count on you." The sarcastic tone was hard to miss.

"Always, my love." The comment came with a small smile when Worthia turned her head and peeked through her mostly closed eyes.

"Tell me there is something else to occupy my mind while we wait." Worthia's head went back to looking at the ceiling.

"Well, since you asked, the mayor has been begging for a minute of your time."

"Sure! Why not. Have him come in." Listening to Tigen leave, Worthia kept her eyes closed and head resting on the chair and waited. To her surprise and regret, she didn't wait as long as she wanted. It felt like seconds before footsteps returned to the office.

"Mayor Mellino, what can I do for you?" Worthia did not change her posture.

Mayor Sergio Mellino's suit was ruffled and his eyes looked tired as if he was not sleeping well. His hands were restless and his head kept turning from side to side. When Worthia sat back up and looked at him, the image of a nervous mouse came to mind.

"M. President." Mellino ran his hands down his shirt as if to settle his body. "People are worried, fearful. I'm afraid they might be close to panic." Mellino's weight shuffled back and forth between his feet.

"That's strange." Her head turned to the right as she looked at the man mostly with her left eye. "I'm not hearing this from anyone else. Are you, Mr. Tonsten?"

"No, M. President." Tigen used his military precision voice. "In fact, I hear just the opposite."

"They won't tell you!" Mellino's eyes got wide. "They put on a good face but I know that underneath they are scared as shit."

"Mayor Mellino, please calm down…"

"You have to do something!" Mellino's hands slapped flat on the desk. He started to lean forward but his neck was circled by an arm as thick as his neck and he was pulled back from the desk. His hands tried to grab that arm, but when that failed, he flailed at it. "Let me go, let me go."

After a quick look at Worthia, Tigen held the man until his body relaxed and went limp. Placing Mellino on the floor, Tigen arranged the man in a comfortable position before straightening back up.

"Make sure he gets some sleep, medicated if required." Standing, Worthia walked around the desk and stared at the unconscious mayor. "The man looks like he needs it."

"And a bath, shave, and change of clothes," Tigen added with a small scoff.

"Keep him under guard until we are sure he's back to normal." Worthia raised her wrist to her mouth. "I need a medical team for transport of an unconscious man, and a security person."

"And if he doesn't recover?" It sounded more like a suggestion for Tigen than a question.

"That's why we have a chain of command in politics, right?" Walking to the balcony, Worthia did not watch as the medics came and took the mayor away. Once the man was gone, Tigen joined her on the balcony. "Thanks, though you might have been a little enthusiastic."

"I am always enthusiastic about protecting you." Worthia could feel his smug smile without looking at him.

"You know what I mean."

"Usually." The smile was still there.

"Please have Lorda check on what the mayor told us. Wait, have Anne do it. She needs something to occupy her time since we are in communication lock-down. She must be pacing the heck out of her office these days."

"Just call her?" There was more than one question in the question.

"I'm… just not up to it at the moment. I'm pretty sure what Sergio said wasn't true, but it still rattled me for anyone to be like that. If I contact Anne, I might seem more worried than I should be."

"Plus it won't be good for anyone else to hear and start rumors."

"There's that too." Placing her hands on the rail, Worthia leaned forward and rested on the rail. "When I said I wanted something to distract me, that wasn't it. I meant something easy or at least fun, like a school event. Not someone going nuts in my office."

"Next time, be more specific." The comment earned Tigen a fist to the chest, which made him laugh. Worthia leaned her head on his shoulder for a moment before removing it.

"Go. Make sure the city is fine. It will make me feel better."

"Of course, M. President. I will return shortly."

As Tigen left, Worthia turned back to look over the city with the protective shell as background. The mountains in the distance could be seen, but as through translucent glass. It ruined the grandeur of the scenery. The city was the same, only less busy. Fewer vehicles traveled the streets and fewer people walked the parks and tubes.

"At least the city is still alive and functioning," Worthia said out loud. "Who knows what the aliens would do to us if we let them in. Scan everyone for telepathic ability I am sure and take those with it. To be treated how, who knows."

The tranquility lasted for five minutes before a ping was heard from her interface. Ignoring the first one earned her another after fifteen seconds. Taking a breath, she raised her wrist.

"Yes?"

"M. President, Secretary of State Url Pernent would like a word with you."

"Sure. Tell him I am on the balcony."

"Yes, M. President."

The view was still too good to leave even if the mountains only looked like far dreams. Staying at the railing, Worthia let Url join her on the balcony. He also put his hands on the rail and leaned into the view.

"Please tell me you have something pleasant to distract me with," Worthia said as a greeting.

"If that was a requirement, they should have warned me." Url turned his head to look at her over his shoulder. "My whole staff is dying of boredom with communications down. You want me to organize a bowling party or something? I know the staff would be up for it."

Laughing, Worthia shook her head. "Bowling with the president? That sounds like a campaign event. I think that would send a bad message at this time. But a nice foreign dinner would be great. Any of those tonight?"

"Actually, that might not be a bad idea. The diplomats trapped here are rather nervous being out of touch with their home offices and seeing you at ease would go a long way to calm them down. I am pretty sure several of them are trying to figure out how to sneak out of the city and get back home. Not that we are going to let them. How about an outdoor barbecue?"

"Seriously?"

"Sure. They're easy to arrange." Url gave her a smile. "I know Tigen loves ribs."

This time the laughter lasted a while before Worthia recovered. "Oh, you are so right there. If you are going to have a barbecue, you better have twenty pounds of ribs just for Tigen because there is no way he is not going to be there if I am."

"So I arrange a dinner for tonight? Casual?"

"Sure, why not? That's assuming our guests out there don't get active and we get to attend. But I guess you could always have it without us if you needed to."

"If the aliens do something, no one will be attending. They'll be glued to the viewers. I'll get started right away."

Url turned and walked from the balcony, a satisfied smile on his face. Worthia waited until he had taken four steps before speaking.

"By the way, what did you want when you came in?"

"To arrange a barbecue," Url called back with a wave as he walked across the room.

Chapter Twenty-Six
Darn Slow Aliens

Six o'clock in the morning once again found the war room full of people watching the wall display. After two hours of no movement from the alien ship, people started to peel off and leave. Since Worthia was at the front of the crowd, she had to wait for the others to leave before she could move, but at least the optics of the situation were good. Url Pernent took a few steps to stand by her side.

"Want me to organize another barbecue?"

"Heavens no," Worthia said with a small laugh. "I ate enough last night for all of today. If you keep organizing barbecues I will get fat."

"I didn't make you eat anything and besides, it was for social support mostly, not eating a banquet." Url's voice was light and airy.

"Something you obviously didn't tell Tigen. He practically had to be carried by the time we got home." The memory brought a smile to her lips.

"Me? Tell him? I like my face just like it is." Url acted horrified.

"Well, you can't have an event catered by Antoine's and not expect people to eat it, can you?"

"I had to choose them, they could meet the deadline." Settling his shoulders, Url raised his chin an inch.

"Right, tell me another I don't believe. So, tell me what you really walked into my office for yesterday." All lightness went out of Worthia's voice.

"Seeing as I am the Secretary of State, I feel it is my duty to at least ask this question, though I probably already know the answer." Url shifted his weight. "Would you like me to create a delegation to go out to the ship and attempt to talk to those in the ship? We could find people who don't know any of our plans and not much about our defenses and even include a sign-language expert if you want."

"No." The word came quick and with force. "I would never subject anyone to that duty."

"I am sure I can get volunteers."

"Still, I would never send someone into that. You know the first thing the aliens are going to do is remove the inhibitors, which then means they get to study them. Whether they could then defeat them, I don't know, but I won't take that chance. And sending someone without one would be like sending them into an interrogation."

"What about contacting the Puritans?"

"You contact them and you might as well walk out to that ship out there. No, this time they have to do things on our terms. At least until they can make us do it on theirs."

Url took a breath and let it out slowly. "I had to ask."

"I understand. How are your people doing? It must be hard."

"We are taking the time to catch up on items that normally don't get much attention: organization, proper archiving of data and agreements, checking agreements to make sure all the milestones have been met and delivered by parties, etc. It's tedious, but is keeping them busy for now. Not that they enjoy it but, hey, it needs to be done."

"And when you run out of that?" Worthia turned her head to look at the man who was still staring at the display.

"I've been talking to Anne over in Interior about joint projects inside the city. You know, get some interaction with the real people we are serving every day. Plus it will get people outside and out of the office."

"Good thinking. Make sure you have plenty of things to do because there might be others who join you." Worthia turned back to the display, which hadn't changed. "I hate the waiting."

"You always hated to wait." Url chuckled. "I remember during the first campaign when you had to wait for that doctor."

"Oh please, don't remind me." Eyes rolling, Worthia's head went back. Url continued to chuckle.

"I thought you were going to tear that receptionist's throat out."

"She kept saying 'Five more minutes, five more minutes,' for an hour and a half. Incompetence."

"She was probably just repeating what the doctor was saying."

Worthia shook her head. "I still think they were doing it on purpose. I'm sure he voted for the other guy."

"After the tongue lashing you gave him, I'm sure he did." Url took a deep breath to settle the chuckles.

"Is there any other unpleasant memories you wanted to bring up?" The stare that accompanied the question indicated it was not a question.

"No, M. President. I must return to my office." Url did a head bow.

"Sounds like a good idea all around." Worthia turned back to the display as Url left. Tigen took his place without saying anything. She let him stand there for several minutes in silence just to see if he would. When it appeared he would stand silently all day if required, she spoke. "Did you want to say something?"

"No. And I mean that." His parade rest stance didn't change.

"So you guarding me or everyone else?"

"Same thing." The statement was made in a neutral tone with no sense of playfulness. Worthia scoffed.

"Who made you so smart?"

"I've learned a few things after thirty years."

"Sometimes I think you are the only one." Her head rotated down to look at the floor. "Can I be tired already today?"

"Waiting is stressful, no matter what anyone says." Tigen's voice was softer. "Why don't you spent half an hour in the relaxation chamber?"

Letting out a single laugh, Worthia said, "That would guarantee that the aliens come out of the ship right after I get in there, right?"

"At least the wait would be over."

The comment caused Worthia's head to come up and her gaze to look at Tigen with a smile. "That's true, I never thought of it that way. Why not? You hold down the fort here and I'll try to relax for a while. Just don't let things go to hell while I am away."

"Me?" Tigen's face registered mock surprise. "I can't believe you would even suggest such a thing."

"I've learned a thing or two over the past thirty years too, you know."

Chapter Twenty-Seven
The Surety of Allies

Chairman Eiji had called the meeting in the war room for all of the previous attendees. A satellite view of the alien ship, prominently from the side, filled the display. Eiji stood with his hands behind his back, his hands tapping each other.

"We are still sure that there is one ship?" Eiji asked, his words directed toward the display.

"Yes, chairman." Smith's words. The other participants appeared more than willing to let Smith do all the talking.

"And the ship gives no indication that it intends to leave America?" Eiji's hands continued to tap.

"Not at the moment."

"How many did the ship take from our areas of interest?" Eiji asked.

"We counted fifty-three."

"Did any from the cities join them?"

"No." Smith gave a slight smile with the statement.

"And our people of interest are secure?"

"Yes." Smith's words were crisp. "They have been gathered and placed in a shielded location. All that we know of, that is."

"I assume their family members have been checked?"

"Every one. We thought of giving them a cover story for their relatives but with the aliens being able to read thoughts, it was not considered a worthwhile effort so we told them nothing."

"Excellent work." Eiji turned from the display, staring at the floor. "Our defenses?"

"Ready, but concealed."

"Do we know how many others the aliens took before reaching America?" The tension in Eiji's voice and body reduced as he talked.

"It was not possible to tell. They made six stops: India, Egypt, twice in Africa, Spain, and Greenland."

"Greenland?" Eiji turned back toward Smith, his surprise clear. Smith merely shrugged. "No stops in South or Central America?"

"None."

Eiji let out a small laugh. "I wonder if they are insulted or relieved."

"Maybe they plan to go there after the United Americas." Smith's head twitched a bare amount after saying the words as if regretting saying them.

Addressing the crowd, Eiji scanned the others in the room. "Anything else we need to be doing?" The manner in which he asked the question made it sound more like a progress report request than a real question.

"We could position satellites to cover the alien ship in America," a voice from the crowd suggested.

"Do the Americans know we have these satellites?" Eiji asked.

There was a pause. "No."

"If one can be positioned to cover both America and our eastern border, then reposition it. If not, I will not sacrifice our protection. Plus we would have to explain to the Americans where the satellite came from, which may be awkward." Eiji walked to the door, but stopped short. "Anything else?" When nothing was said, he added, "Dismissed," before turning and walking from the room.

Walking by himself, Eiji strode through the hallways of red walls and intricate molding to his private work chamber. The room was filled with antique furniture from past epochs and modern conveniences mixed in a dance of style and function, the modern hidden as much as possible. Taking a place near a chrysanthemum flower blooming in a pot of jade, Eiji appeared to study the flower. His studies were interrupted by a chime of bells from the door.

"Enter."

The door opened to allow Mr. Smith to enter. His measured walk stopped three meters short of Eiji. "You appeared to have other, unsaid, questions."

The comment caused Eiji to smile. "How did we find our people of interest?"

"Through complaints of malfunctioning inhibitors."

"And we didn't know about this before because…?"

"The company that made the devices did not report any incidences to avoid embarrassment when they could not find the fault." Smith's voice was the closest to a chuckle that it had been for a long time. "Of course, when we specifically asked, they gave us the data."

"How many individuals do we have?" Eiji's fingers touched the flower, rubbing a petal.

"Twelve. Their abilities are only detectable within a millimeter of their skull, at least with our instruments."

"Then either," Eiji said as he turned from the plant, "the aliens were distracted by the location they had already selected to check the whole globe or their sensors are limited also. Either way, we may have been lucky." Eiji walked for half a dozen steps. "I don't like relying on luck."

"Agreed." There was a slight movement from Smith that may have indicated that he regretted speaking.

"What about the rest of the population? There are those who do not wear the inhibitors on a daily basis."

"We could order that inhibitors had to be worn, but those in the hinter lands may ignore the law, those sympathetic to the alien churches in particular. Checking the whole population would be tedious."

"I don't care about rice farmers." Eiji made a swatting gesture. "The aliens can have them if they want them, particularly those with sympathies to the alien churches. I want a law issued that inhibitors will be worn and on at all times and all malfunctions shall be reported. Concentrate on those in cities and manufacturing areas, even those outside of the protected cities. If any are found to activate the inhibitors, they will be sequestered in the cities."

"And resistance?" Smith asked without emotion.

"Resistance shall be dealt with as any violation of the law is handled. The worst can be shipped to the desert. If the aliens want them, so be it."

"I will have the law drafted immediately," Smith said with a bow.

"Don't make the punishment too harsh," Eiji continued. "We mostly need to be able to take those of interest out of the unprotected areas so that the aliens can't sense them. Damage to those who resist can be minimal."

"It will be done." Smith exited the room with a brisk walk and a sly smile on his face.

"Now that we know what the aliens have been looking for," Eiji mused, "we can use them to our own advantages."

Chapter Twenty-Eight
About Time

"I'm almost beginning to believe we need to force the issue." Staring at the unchanging display, Worthia scowled and tried not to tap her foot. The urge to pace was strong, like the desire to keep watching the display while the sunlight growing from the horizon burned off the rest of the view.

"Permission to fire on the ship," Tigen said from behind her.

"Denied!" The irritation was not all at Tigen.

"Just a small shot to wake them up?" The tone of Tigen's voice made it clear he was not serious, though he did draw stares from others in the room and one brief smile. "How about I go out and throw a rock at them?"

"As much as I would like to, the answer is still 'no.' I am also starting to believe that they are doing this on purpose, but then that might be treating them too human." As the sun fully illuminated the ship, Worthia turned from the display and paced without direction. "And I'll be damned if I'm going to just sit here and wait for them to do something."

"M. President!" The call was from the monitoring stations but caused Worthia to look back at the wall display fast enough to cause sympathetic whiplash in observers. Breaths were held by all as they watched feet and a robe appear at the top of the ship's ramp. The slow pace revealed one of the messengers who lacked wings. As his feet reached the ground, a second set of feet appeared. The crowd watched as a second angel walked down the ramp, taking up a position to one side opposite the first. Their positions established, a third set of feet appeared. This robe was different, fuller, actually trailing a little behind.

"Finally," came from Worthia. A more humanoid figure, one that could pass for a person in the street if it was clothed properly, walked down the ramp and without pause turned toward the city gate. The two other figures followed one step behind and to either side.

Worthia turned and headed to the door at a quick pace. "Let's hope he knows how to speak. I want to be there before he is."

Concerned looks filled faces. Tigen opened his mouth, but shut it again when he recognized the determined look. Instead, he used his long legs to catch up until he was just behind his wife, giving orders on his interface as he walked.

"Where are you going?" Worthia asked.

"With you, of course."

"And if I ordered you to stay?"

Tigen huffed. "Fat chance."

"Fat chance I would order you to stay?" The question anticipated an challenge.

"Fat chance I'd do it."

"Just don't start a war, will you?" Worthia shook her head as she walked.

"I don't start things, I just finish them."

The statement brought a laugh from Worthia. "By the way, how's the mayor?"

"Receiving treatment and not the mayor anymore. Emotional collapse."

"I liked the guy, but he never did seem to be the most… reliable." Worthia's steps sounded a little harder as she made her quick way to the outside door. Opening the door revealed a vehicle, larger than the one that had driven the vice president, parked as close to the door as possible. Two security agents sat inside while one held the door open. A second vehicle with three more security agents was parked behind the first vehicle. Without slowing their pace, Worthia and Tigen stepped into the vehicle and took seats facing forward. The security agent followed, closed the door, and sat facing rearward. As soon as he was seated, the vehicle accelerated in smooth, ever increasing speed.

"Park where the vehicles can't be seen. I want everyone out of sight but me, and Tigen I suppose since he will insist on going with me." Though Worthia used a commanding voice, the agent in front of her reacted and spoke.

"But M. President…"

"I gave you instructions and I expect them to be followed. We are not doing a show of force." She paused a couple of seconds. "Besides, Tigen should be enough for that."

"Thank you, M. President." Tigen's voice sounded serious.

"Just don't make me regret you being there. So basically just stand there and don't say anything."

Tigen looked like he wanted to say something and then thought better of it.

"Everyone else can stay as close as they want as long as they stay out of sight. The barrier is up anyway."

"We don't know if it will stop one of their flame swords," the security agent said.

"If they draw weapons, then you can react, but not before. Understood?"

Heads nodded in front of them, though the nods were short and reluctant. Worthia didn't turn to see the reaction of those behind her, trusting them to obey orders. The stabilized seat's motion did not match the breakneck speed displayed through the windows. All traffic, foot and vehicle, had been cleared from the road and men in black suits sped past at periodic intervals, though Worthia could see the faces of people in windows and doors. She wanted to wave but refrained. Tigen must have seen the twitch it created.

"Don't want to look like you are waving goodbye?" he asked.

"Doesn't seem appropriate." Resettling herself, Worthia straightened her clothes. "Besides, if I thought I was not coming back, I would wave."

Smiling at her, Tigen answered. "Yes, you would at that."

The wall that surrounded the city came into view as the vehicle turned a corner and grew larger with haste. Worthia's and Tigen's seats spun a quick one hundred and eighty degrees and the vehicle made a rapid deceleration and slid to one side of the wall, the second vehicle sliding to the other side. As the seat rotated back, the door on either side came open. Wasting no time, Worthia and Tigen stepped out and walked to the gate.

Made of iron and glass, the north gate had an old-world style. In the middle of the gate, the iron had an open area, flat on the bottom and rounded on top, which had the look of a portal. That was the spot Worthia chose to stand. Beyond the wall and the shield, the Subordinate and his two escorts continued to make their way to the gate, though Worthia hadn't beaten them there by much. The Subordinate was slightly taller and walked with his hands behind his back instead of at his side like his escort. Clean-shaven with short hair, to all appearances the Subordinate looked human. The escorts' features were more general and indistinct. She could not see sword hilts on either of the escorts, but knew that meant nothing. The long robes all three wore rustled in the wind, but not enough to reveal the shapes of their bodies or anything else underneath.

Standing straight and tall, Worthia waited for the Subordinate to approach. He stopped walking little more than a meter from the barrier and stood silently. Letting him stand so for about ten seconds, Worthia spoke.

"Welcome, visitor. I am Worthia Amster, President of the Americas. How would you like to be addressed?"

"We are the EO-AY, but for your own convenience you may refer to this vessel as the Subordinate."

"Welcome, Subordinate. I am sorry I cannot invite you into our city. I hope the people outside of the city have treated you pleasantly." Worthia's face did not smile or show any sympathy.

"Why have you refused to commune with us?" The Subordinate tilted his head slightly.

"Are we not speaking now?"

"But we are not communing as is right. You do not hear us when we call."

Worthia couldn't help a smile. "We are not letting you into our heads again. Our minds are our own, you are not welcome in them."

"We own you. This world is ours and all on it are ours." For all his words, the Subordinate showed no emotional clues from his body except to sweep his right arm around half his body. It was starting to annoy Worthia.

"So you say. There is no way for this to be proved and we do not believe that intelligent beings should be owned by anyone else."

"Does not your own writing confirm this?"

"Writing that we cannot guarantee you did not put into the writers' minds in the first place. Besides, we have grown and matured in our thinking from thousands of years ago. We are our own people, not yours."

Crossing his arms, the Subordinate stood while seconds ticked away, making no movements but to lower his chin. After a short while, it came back up. "Your words distress and sadden us. So many of your world have gladly accepted us for who we are and yet you continue to be stubborn and rebellious. Such behavior did not prove profitable to others when we were here before."

"You will find us much more capable this time. You've been away for one hundred and sixty of our years and we knew you would come back. We have prepared. You will not find us so weak this time. We have learned much."

"Yes, learning is one of the traits we appreciated most in you." The Subordinate lowered his hands from his chest. "Give us the boy Bridge and we will leave your city alone. He belongs to us. In our generosity, we will not punish you for this insult."

Keeping herself from laughing, Worthia maintained her stoic manner. "The boy has already stated he does not wish to go with you, but if you like, we will ask him again."

"We will await his acceptance." The word said, the Subordinate turned and walked back toward the ship. Watching, Worthia waited until he was one hundred meters away before turning back to the vehicle.

"Arrogant bastard," came from her lips as she entered the vehicle.

"People who think they are superior always are," Tigen said as he followed her. "Oh, wait, they aren't people, so maybe it goes more for them." He waited until the vehicle was rolling back into the center of town before asking his question. "Are you really going to ask the kid again?"

"Yes, but it was mostly a delaying tactic. Plus I didn't say we would hurry with it."

Tigen suppressed all but one bursting laugh, but it was enough. It still took him a minute to recover. "Beat on them with their own game."

"They never seem to be in a hurry, why should we?" Looking out the window, Worthia rolled the window down and stuck out her arm. This time when she saw faces in the windows and doors, she waved. Many waved back. "Driver, slow down some. We aren't in a hurry this time."

"Yes, M. President," came over her interface.

"Just can't resist, can you?" Tigen asked.

"Why should I? These are our people, our community. The worst thing we can do is be cut off and aloof from them." Several little kids who had braved the front porch created a large smile on Worthia as she waved. The kids waved back with enthusiasm. "See, I just made two kids' day."

Silence reigned in the vehicle and Worthia lost her smile as she turned back to Tigen. "I'm sorry, I know. It's the one thing I really regret."

Taking her hand in his much larger one, Tigen gave it a small squeeze. "It's not your fault."

"It's not yours either." Worthia put her other hand on top of his.

"That's not what the doctors said." Tigen took a deep breath. "Besides, if I hadn't been so reckless and…"

"Stop!" Releasing his hand, Worthia put her arm around his chest and laid her head on his shoulder. "You are perfect, and as President of the Americas, I declare it so. You are everything I love. Children were just not meant to be. Besides, after all this is done and I am not President anymore, maybe we can adopt one or two. Or three or four. Maybe five."

"And where are we going to find five orphans to adopt?" Tigen's head movement caused her to look up. "Besides, when did we agree on five?"

"One, I am President of the Americas, I have connections. And two, you know you should leave the number to me. You'd eventually agree anyway, so why fight it?"

As Tigen's eyes came up, he caught a glimpse of the security agent, who gave him a shrug with a slight head tilt. "You're on her side?" he directed at the man.

"Of course," the agent replied in a neutral voice. "It's my job."

"Well then, this conversation is being put on hold until you are not in office anymore, wife. I don't need your security detail ganging up on me."

"We're nearing the building, M. President," came over the interface.

"Thank you." Sitting back up with her back against the seat, Worthia let go of Tigen and composed herself. "Most likely we won't have time for the conversation before I am out of office, which will hopefully be at the end of my term and not the next couple of days."

"Don't talk like that," Tigen reprimanded. "The aliens are not going to defeat us and I won't let anything happen to you."

"I just meant that if we can't stop them, I might not be in office for long." The vehicle stopped and the door was opened soon afterwards.

"And Allin be President? Hell no." Tigen looked at the security agent as he exited, believing he saw pleading in the man's eyes. "See, even he agrees with me."

Walking into the building in a direct line, Worthia strode past the hallway that led to the war room.

"Where are you going?" Tigen asked.

"The bunker," Worthia said without looking at him or slowing her pace.

"We could have parked closer."

"I'm not taking any chances of the aliens being able to see through the barrier."

The walk was about a block and a half long with multiple guards stationed on the way. As they neared the door to the bunker, the guard opened it so they could enter without pause. It led to another door which opened when the first door had been closed. Inside was a small apartment. Wilmont Bridge and a security guard were playing a board game on a table between them. It was an old-fashioned one with no electronic parts but small metal game pieces. Their entrance brought the game to a halt and a worried look from Wilmont. Worthia raised her hands, palms out.

"It's fine, there's no problem," she said in a comforting voice.

"Have the aliens come for me?" Standing, Wilmont clenched his fists, his shoulders shaking some.

"The aliens are outside the city." Worthia put her hands on the young man's shoulders. "They are asking for you to go with them. We will not make you go, but if you want to, we will not stop you either. It is your choice. If you want to stay, we will defend you from them."

"I don't want to go with them." Wilmont shook his head with vigor. "People back home worshiped the aliens. If I went with them, I would have to spend the rest of my life with those people and that would be awful."

"Your reasons are your own. That fact that you don't want to go is enough for me." Giving the boy a smile, she continued, "I'm sorry, but we are going to have to keep you here for your safety and so they can't locate you."

"Yeah, I'm sorry about earlier..." The boy looked down at the floor.

"It's not your fault. I should have had you moved earlier. Besides, they would have figured it out eventually, I'm sure." Her eyes wandered over to the game board. "Are you winning?"

"I'm not sure, it's hard to tell." Wilmont gestured at the game. "Things change so fast."

"Just like life. If there is anything I can do for you, please let me know."

"Can my friends come for a visit?" Wilmont looked up with hope.

"I'm sorry," Worthia said with a frown. "It's safer for them if they don't know where you are."

"Darn. I thought you'd say that. At least I have Mich here." Gesturing at the agent sitting at the table caused the agent to give the boy a smile. "He's pretty nice. Sometimes I think he lets me win though."

"Less and less all the time," Mich replied.

"I'm glad you have someone." Worthia nodded at the agent in approval. "I wish I could stay, but there are many things I have to deal with. Take care of yourself."

"Thanks for coming by." The boy waved as Worthia and Tigen

left. Worthia waved back before exiting the room. As always, Tigen followed close on her heels.

The pace away from the bunker was much slower than it had been getting there. Letting Worthia walk in silence, Tigen kept his position to the right and half a step behind. His looks at the guards told them conversation was not welcome. They walked more than a block before Worthia spoke.

"I guess I have to go back to the war room. Everyone will be expecting me to talk to them, make plans."

"They heard everything you said. If you want to take some time, you can. They'll understand."

"Thank you, dear, but I might as well get it over with. When they find out I am going to let the aliens stew a day or two, they will either relax or explode. Hopefully the first." Raising her shoulders slightly, Worthia closed her eyes and breathed in.

"If they explode, I can deal with them." A small amount of gruff entered Tigen's voice.

"I'm tempted to let you."

"I am the Chief of Staff, you know. You need to delegate more."

"So you keep telling me." Worthia's pace picked up a little. "By the way, I'm sleeping in tomorrow no matter what happens, except for a full on attack, that is."

"I could handle that for you," Tigen put in easily. Worthia laughed.

"I'm sure you could. I would just hate to sleep through it." Pausing for a moment, thinking, Worthia added, "Can you imagine what my great-grandmother would have thought about me negotiating with the aliens?"

"She would be proud, I am sure."

"I mean, she did the original negotiations with the Puritans and now I am negotiating with the aliens they worshiped. Kind of like a family business."

"No one else I would want doing it."

"Not even yourself?" The question was asked with a playful element.

"I wouldn't negotiate," Tigen said flatly.

Worthia scoffed. "Of that I am sure."

As Worthia entered the war room, she found all the faces turned her way. To everyone's credit, they held their tongues, though it appeared an effort to keep the words inside. Walking up to the assembled group, she addressed all of them at once. "The boy does not wish to go with the aliens, thus we are required to defend him. I'm not telling the aliens this until the day after tomorrow. They can sit and wait for us for a change. Given that, I think we can relax until then. Of course we will keep monitoring the situation, but I doubt the aliens will do anything. And it will give our people a chance to get a good night's sleep before anything happens."

"Do you really think anyone is going to be able to sleep?" Anne Coons asked, doubtful.

"The aliens are expecting us to comply, so I'm not worried about hostilities." Worthia took a deep breath. "That and the fact that they don't ever seem to be in a hurry is why I am not worried. If you can't relax, take a pill. At the moment, let's get some normal stuff done today or at least make people feel better. That's all."

Chapter Twenty-Nine
Hello

Standing behind the gate, Worthia watched the Subordinate and his two attendants walk from the ship. They wore the same white robes they had worn before as if nothing ever changed.

"Are they going slower on purpose?" she asked as she watched.

"Do you really want an answer to that?" Chadan's voice said over the comms.

"All I know is that I would like to smack that emotionless expression off his face." Maintaining outward calm despite her feelings, Worthia kept a neutral expression. "If they attack, I call dibs on shooting him in the face."

Again, the attendants stopped short of the gate while the Subordinate approached within arm's reach of the barrier. He appeared to examine the barrier before speaking.

"Where is the boy?"

"He has decided not to go with you."

"It is not his decision." The Subordinate could have been talking about a chair for all the emotion he put into the statement.

"We believe it is. There are plenty of people outside the city, ask them to go."

"The boy belongs to us. All on this planet belong to us. We have stated that before."

"So you say, and yet you have no proof." A smug smile was hard to prevent. The corners of Worthia's mouth curled a little.

"We require not more proof than your own history and writings. We are EO-AY. You are ours. This world is ours." The words were almost monotone, like a teacher's in class.

"Assertions will get us nowhere in this discussion. With all the people on this planet, I see no reason this boy should be of particular interest."

"He is special."

Worthia almost laughed. "Everyone is special."

"He is what we have been waiting for."

"Ah, as we suspected," Chadan said over the comm.

"So you have been breeding humans to be telepathic?" Worthia asked.

"Tip our hand much?" It was Tigen's voice.

"We only wish to commune with you." The tone of the statement made it sound harmless.

"Then let the boy stay, let the abilities develop, and commune in the future with us."

The Subordinate appeared to take a breath and moved his head some before answering. "It would be done quicker under our control."

"You mean selective breeding. Eugenics."

After a pause, the Subordinate answered. "We are not familiar with that term."

It was Worthia's turn to noticeably inhale. "It refers to select breeding of people to emphasize a particular trait."

The Subordinate paused again. "That sounds correct."

"It was practiced on Earth by some of the most despised people in history." Allowing the disgust run through her voice, Worthia turned slightly to the right with her shoulders. "We do not treat people as cattle, we treat them as beings worthy of independent action based on their own choices."

Tiny shaking motions were made by the Subordinate's head. "People are not cattle. Why would one think so?"

"Still not fully conversant with metaphors, it would appear," Chadan's voice said. Worthia thought about explaining, but the Subordinate spoke before she decided to speak.

"What do you wish for the boy?"

The question caused Worthia's head to jerk back a fraction of an inch and pause in her response. "You mean like a trade?"

"Yes." The Subordinate appeared to straighten. "What do you wish to trade for the boy? Humans trade for everything. We will trade for him."

Worthia's mouth curled. "We do not sell people."

"Throughout your history, humans have sold people."

"Not anymore."

"But it continues today. This we know. Money is given for people to enter your cities."

"Damn east Asians." Chadan again.

"Puritans in some areas are compensated for the loss of farm hands. It is not practiced here in this country."

"Name it as you wish, people are bought and sold. So we wish to buy this boy." The expressionless face of the Subordinate made Worthia want to punch it that much more.

"*We* do not buy and sell people. We consider ourselves evolved beyond such practices. If you wish to buy someone from the Western Conglomerate, that is their business, not ours, though we do not agree with it."

"Such disparity is why you need to be guided by us."

"Why? So you can mold us into whatever is more convenient for you?" Worthia allowed a hard edge to her voice.

The Subordinate paused and remained still in the manner she had come to associate with communicating with the other EO-AY. The wait was not a long one.

"Your hostility is disturbing," it finally said. Worthia felt like laughing in his face.

"We have no wish for violence."

"Good. Neither do we."

Another pause. "We will counsel on ways to convince you."

With that, the Subordinate turned and walked away. Shocked, Worthia stood in place for a while. No one even spoke over the comms. Finally, Chadan's voice came through.

"What does that mean?"

"I don't know." Worthia slowly turned, keeping her eye on the Subordinate while she did. "But I am sure we will find out."

During the walk back to the vehicle, Worthia kept looking back as if expecting something to happen, even standing at the door waiting for a moment.

"Don't leave just yet," she said as she entered the vehicle. Tigen followed.

"You think something is going to happen?" Tigen asked, the concern unconcealed in his voice. "If so, it would be better if you weren't here."

"I don't think they are going to do anything violent," she replied. "I just have this feeling they came prepared for a 'no' answer."

"Prepared how?"

"I'm not sure."

"Someone's leaving the ship."

"And there we are." Worthia stepped out of the vehicle and walked back to the gate. In the distance, she could see a man walking from the ship. Almost hesitant, he did not appear to be in a hurry. "Who is that?"

"We believe it is Wilmont's father."

Worthia huffed. "Playing the parent card."

Waiting, Worthia looked over to the security agent who was out of sight and nodded at the airlock at the side. The man nodded and moved closer to the controls on the wall. The walk from the ship was annoying in its length. Wilmont's father was in no obvious hurry. Shaking her head, Worthia walked back from the gate to the vehicle, stopping at Tigen long enough to say, "You take this one."

Smiling, Tigen moved to the gate and took a military parade rest stance. The man coming toward him was a good size but not as big as he was. He gave the man a stare as he approached.

"What do you want?" Tigen asked.

"Can I come in and speak with you?"

"Why?"

"I am Wilmont's father, Agnar Bridge. I am here to escort my son out of the city. Being his legal guardian, I have the right to do this." Agnar puffed up his chest and pulled his shoulders back.

"Wilmont has asked for and been granted sanctuary." Tigen's expression would have made any lawyer proud.

"Sanctuary? From what?" It was clear that the statement took

Agnar by surprise.

"Religious persecution?"

"What? He was not being persecuted for his religion by us!"

Making the comment with a dry voice, Tigen replied, "No, the other way around."

It took a few seconds for Agnar to process the statement, but when he realized Tigen's meaning, his face grew red and his teeth grated. Tigen thought for a moment the man would charge the barrier, but Agnar calmed himself and regained his posture.

"Then we have even more to talk about," Agnar said. "I think I need legal representation also. I will return to the ship and secure legal help and return to this gate."

"Do as you feel necessary." Not waiting for the man to leave, Tigen turned and walked to one of the security agents. "Stay here and escort Mr. Bridge and his lawyer when they return. Take them to one of the conference rooms in the capitol buildings, Room 11. Let us know when you are bringing them."

"Will do, sir."

Without a pause, Tigen walked to the vehicle where Worthia waited and climbed in. She didn't say anything until the doors were shut and the vehicle was moving.

"So?"

"The lawyers for both sides are going to get together and talk about Wilmont's sanctuary status."

Worthia shook her head. "At least it will buy us more time. What do they hope to achieve? They have to know there is no way we are going to buy any of their legal arguments. What do the aliens gain by this?"

"That is a good question," Chadan's voice said over the comms. *"Maybe they feel if they can get us to capitulate to their demands, the other cities will also without a fight."*

"The fact that they are not immediately using a military option has to be a good sign," Army Chief of Staff Matilda Ruaridh added. *"It must mean they are not confident about their ability to take on the cities, or at least more than one."*

"So we get to be their test subject?" Worthia asked.

"It would appear so."

"I assume all of the satellites are in place by now?"

"Yes, M. President."

"Then their indecision has cost them even more. If they were smart, they would have attacked right away." Tigen appeared pleased as he made the statement.

"Maybe luck was on our side this time. Who do we have that can handle this, Anne?" Worthia was back to business mode.

"Don't worry, I have several people in mind. In fact, I'll ask several to take the case. I'm sure they won't refuse."

"I'm sure they won't. I leave it in your hands. Don't give away the keys to the city. President out." As laughs followed over the comms, Worthia turned off her interface and leaned back into the seat. "I didn't see that coming."

"I'll take it over an attack." Tigen leaned back also.

"True. Can I be tired already?"

"I think it's the emotional content. You'll be fine in a little while. Did you eat breakfast?"

"Are you kidding? And risk throwing up? No way."

"Then we need to get you something to eat." Tigen nodded at the security agent, who spoke quietly into his interface.

"Will there be candle light?" Worthia asked with a mischievous tone.

"At seven in the morning?" Tigen scoffed. "Only if they've lost power."

"What's wrong with candle light for breakfast?"

"Ah, sunrise?"

"Spoil sport."

Chapter Thirty
Talk

"Let me go and ask them." Agnar bowed before the Subordinate, his head down to his knees.

Why would we allow that? The impression of the voice inside his head had shocked Agnar at first, but the strangeness had lessened with time. This close to the Subordinate, it was louder than he had experienced with the creature in the town.

"I am his father and my son is still a minor. Not an adult. I have legal rights to decide where my son goes and what happens to him." Not able to keep all the quivering out of his voice, Agnar's voice did not sound as confident as he wished to his ears.

Why do you think they will listen to you? The lack of emotions by the Subordinate while he spoke was disturbing enough by itself.

"If they don't, we have a legal precedent to forcing the release of my son."

We have no concern with your legal system.

"But the other Puritans will know that our laws have been followed and will not be able to assign any fault to your actions." Almost raising his head to smile at the Subordinate, Agnar checked the motion, fear winning out.

We own the Earth and all on it. We do not answer to your laws.

Fear spread in Agnar as the Subordinate's voice boomed in his head. "I didn't mean to imply that you were subject to our laws, my lord." His voice stuttered for a moment. "I was only suggesting it for the benefit of the faithful, to reassure their minds."

There was a pause during which Agnar heard no voices. Past experience with such times had shown him that the EO-AY were talking to each other and it could be a slow process. Maintaining his position, Agnar waited and hoped. Several minutes later, the Subordinate spoke.

We have decided to allow you to attempt to retrieve the boy. Time is no factor and a non-violent solution would guarantee the boy's safety.

"Thank you, Lord, I will endeavor to make your will come to pass."

We do not anticipate your success. The Subordinate turned and walked toward the part of the ship where Agnar was not allowed.

A sign of relief did not steady Agnar's shaking. Standing only showed how much his knees wobbled. "Buck up, Agnar," he told himself. "Now you have to come through with your promise."

The conference room wasn't more than a table with comfortable seats on either side. Six table displays, at a slight angle from the table instead of perpendicular, had been placed, three on each side. There were no windows and only one door. The walls were a calming light purple color with trim in the corners but no painting or other decorations.

Sans Rutledge took the seat in the center of the table on the other side of the table from the door. He was early, but he liked being early so he could call up the relevant documents before the meeting started. Two other lawyers soon followed, Marie Dubois and Mikal Leonid. Sans gave each a brief greeting without standing, acknowledged by both with the same brief reply.

"Your visitors are being escorted from the gate," a voice said over Sans' interface.

"Thank you," he replied, still entering his document requests. He was more than ready by the time the door to the conference room opened again. All three stood when the two guests entered.

"Good morning," Sans said. "I am Chief Counsel Sans Rutledge. This is Marie Dubois and Mikal Leonid, my assistants."

"Good morning." The man wore a dark blue pin-striped suit flawlessly pressed and a light blue shirt with a red tie. Next to him was another man, larger, in pressed blue jeans and a plaid shirt. "I'm Guy Sheriton, attorney in the State of Colorado and legal representative for Mr. Bridge here." Sheriton gave a nod to the other man.

"Do you gentlemen require anything? Something to drink, perhaps, or the facilities?" Out of the corner of his eye, Sans noted that the security guard had not left yet.

"Some ice water would be appreciated, but we do not have to wait for it to arrive to start." Sheriton indicated a chair to Mr. Bridge and took the center seat himself. "Let me sync my interface here and we will be ready to begin."

"Of course." The three lawyers took their seats while the guard disappeared, soon to return with a cart holding two pitchers and five glasses. Mr. Bridge left his seat to retrieve two glasses and filled them with ice water, placing one by Sheriton. "Whenever you are ready."

It took less than a minute for Mr. Sheriton to call up his files and look up across the table. "May we begin by agreeing that this is Mr. Agnar Bridge and that the boy, Wilmont Bridge, is his son?"

"Agreed," Sans said easily.

"And can we also agree that before any of this started, they were both residents of the state of Illinois?"

"Agreed."

"Can you provide us evidence of the boy claiming sanctuary?"

"Of course." Sans's finger touched a file on his display and flipped it toward Sheriton's. "This is a recording of when Wilmont requested sanctuary."

The recording was a feed from the recovery room where Wilmont had been held. Doctor Ordanza and Wilmont could be seen and heard, though the recording did not contain much more than the actual event.

"You recorded my son while he was in your care?" Agnar's tone was indignant.

"Only when someone was in the room, for safety and legal reasons." Sans's voice held no emotion. "When he was alone, he was not being recorded. As you can hear for yourself, the boy was not prompted to ask for sanctuary. If you doubt this, we can provide all the recordings for your review."

"I don't think at this time that will be necessary." Sheriton reviewed the record a second time before closing the file.

Agnar cleared his throat, earning a small nod from Sheriton before he spoke again.

"Can we have the medical records of the boy's condition and treatment, please?"

A second file was flipped to his display and he was allowed time to examine it. Agnar had still not used the display in front of him.

"For Mr. Bridge's benefit," Sans stated, "the file states that the boy had a growth between his brain and sinus cavity that would have killed him if not operated on within a short amount of time, days most likely. This condition had been developing for some time. May I ask, did you know that something was wrong with your son, Mr. Bridge?"

"We are not here to talk about that. You don't need to answer, Mr. Bridge." Sheriton's eyes turned less neutral.

"I only ask because Wilmont said his father had told him that he did not need to go to the clinic and God's will would be done in his life. If this is so, it constitutes physical neglect under our laws."

"Mr. Bridge and Wilmont were not under your jurisdiction at that time." Sheriton's voice was firming up.

"I only bring it up to give perspective to the situation." Sans was still calm. "The medical examination also revealed evidence of past... physical discipline done to the boy."

"I have broken no laws," Agnar stated with a firm voice.

"I didn't say you had. Again, it is just for perspective, though it all makes us wonder why you did not take advantage of medical assistance before this." Three sets of eyes looked at Agnar.

"We believe God directs our lives, not your science." Agnar's chin rose a small fraction with the statement.

"So do you believe the beings in the ship north of town are God?"

Before Agnar could speak, Sheriton broke in. "We are not here to discuss Mr. Bridge's religious belief. Let's stay on topic."

"But I think I am." Sans did a good job of preventing a smile as he turned back to the lawyer. "If Mr. Bridge believes that God controls everything that happens in our lives, then won't Wilmont going to the clinic and claiming sanctuary be in God's plan?"

The question earned a loud scoff from Agnar and a stern look from Sheriton. "Again, we are not here to discuss Mr. Bridge's religious beliefs. We *are* here to discuss the legitimacy of Wilmont's claim of sanctuary, *nothing* more. Does Wilmont have some basis for wanting this sanctuary?"

"None is required," Sans replied in an almost quiet voice. Sheriton's head twisted to the side.

"Excuse me? For sanctuary, there must be something that the person is fleeing from. It is the very definition of the word."

"According to the treaty signed by your church and the citizens of this country," Marie interjected, "any person who requests entry and citizenship in the protected cities can be granted such citizenship. No reason is required."

"But Wilmont is a minor, not an adult."

"The treaty does not state any conditions based on the person's age. Do you wish me to send you a copy of the applicable section?" Marie was not as good as keeping a neutral expression on her face and a smug expression accompanied the question.

"Yes, I do." Sheriton looked uncomfortable. "I will need a few minutes to confer with my client."

Sans stood. "You may have the room as long as you need." Looking at his two companions, he added, "Shall we?"

An hour later, the three lawyers were back in the room. Agnar Bridge did not look happy and Sheriton had the look of a man who knew he was about to pound a rock with his fist. Unable not to smile, Sans presented a pleasant mood.

"Have you come to a conclusion?" Sans asked.

"We feel that the fact that Wilmont is a minor and still under the guardianship of his legal parents makes him ineligible to ask for sanctuary. Thus if Mr. Bridge asks for him to be returned, we feel it is your obligation to return him to his father."

"And, of course, we disagree."

"Would you withhold, say, a three year old from their parents if they asked for sanctuary?"

"Just because we have the right to grant sanctuary doesn't mean we have to. That said, if we felt the three-year old was in danger, then yes, we would grant it."

"Does this grant of sanctuary have anything to do with his uniqueness?"

"No," Sans said flatly, "it does not. It is a matter of law."

"You will forgive us if we do not believe you." A small huff accompanied the statement.

"You will believe what you want to believe. I handle matters of law, not of science."

"You do what your president tells you to do, I'm sure." Sheriton looked at Bridge, who only stared and then looked away. Sheriton sighed and turned back to Sans. "May his mother and sister visit him?"

"I am sure that can be arranged."

"And if they convince him to leave with them?"

Annoyance at the tediousness crept into Sans' face. "If Wilmont states that he wishes to leave the city with them, of course he can leave, but it will have to be of his own volition and desire."

"I just wanted to make sure the same standard would be maintained." A small smile started on Sheriton's face.

"Then it would appear we are done here." Sans stood up, followed by Dubois and Leonid. "I will inform the authorities to expect the visitors."

Chapter Thirty-One
Unexpected Diplomacy

"Stop fidgeting." Worthia's voice was not stern, but Tigen's restlessness was causing some annoyance.

"I don't understand why you are here to greet them," Tigen replied.

"Because I can and I want to be." Her tone was cheerful. "Why are you here?"

"Because you are." The answer caused Worthia to laugh.

"Still protecting me?"

"Until I am dead."

A woman and a girl were being escorted by two messenger beings. The woman was in her late forties and had a sturdy build. She had the same hair as Wilmont and carried herself with purpose. The girl looked to be about thirteen, thin, with long brown hair, and looked more apprehensive. Neither worried Worthia as being trouble-makers. When they reached the gate, the woman and the girl were let through the airlock doors to the side of the gate and then led to her.

"Welcome," Worthia said with a smile. "I am Worthia Amster, President of the Americas. I wanted to welcome you personally to our city."

"Thank you for letting us in," the woman said. "I'm Miriam and this is Abbey... Abigail, but we call her Abbey."

"Welcome, Abbey," Worthia said to the girl. "Before we can progress any farther, I have to ask you to put these on. They go on top of the ear like mine."

Two pairs of inhibitors were presented in Worthia's hand. Being off, they did not have the shields deployed. With only a short examination, the woman took two of the inhibitors and placed them on the girl's ears. The inhibitors automatically secured themselves in place, causing a small startle to Miriam. Recovering quickly, she took the other two inhibitors and placed them on her own ears, her head slightly bowed before they secured their position as if she expected a jolt. When one didn't come, she straightened up.

"Computer, activate all inhibitors in the area," Worthia said into her interface. Both sets of inhibitors on the women deployed their shields, causing the women to startle in union. Both touched the inhibitors, but then settled, wiggling their faces some.

"They take a little time to get used to."

"Are these the things that prevent the... you know who from hearing you?" Miriam asked in a quiet voice.

"Yes, they are." Worthia had to grin.

"So..." Miriam pointed at their escort. "They cannot hear us?"

"No. We are sure that the Subordinate is the only one who can actually hear our voices."

"No matter what we say, they will not react to it?" Miriam's voice was getting emphatic.

"Yes, you may say anything you like and they cannot hear." Worthia's brow started to descend toward her eyes and her head turned to the right.

Straightening up, Miriam spoke in a clear voice. "Then we would like to request sanctuary." The girl nodded her head at the statement.

Looking at the woman, Worthia tried to formulate coherent thoughts for about ten seconds. The woman started to look worried, shaking Worthia out of her stupor.

"Please don't be alarmed, it's just that was not something I had even thought you would say." Worthia took a breath and raised her head. "Can I ask why you are requesting sanctuary?"

"These... creatures have taken half my children without so much as letting me say goodbye to them." Miriam's voice was filled with spite. "When I protested, they said they owned us and could do anything they want with us. We're nothing but sheep to them. They wouldn't even tell me what they were going to do with them. My children! They don't care about us. They are not compassionate and loving gods. They are a fraud and I want nothing to do with them. Abbey here showed signs of what they found in the other children so they were interested in her. But I don't want to go back to them and I sure ain't sending her back there. Who knows what they will do to us?"

Breathing hard by the time she had made the speech, Miriam puffed air with effort. When she was finished, Abbey placed her arms around her mother with a hold that dared anyone to make her let go. Both looked worried, their calm facade having fallen away, and their eyes pleaded.

"Of course we will grant you sanctuary." Worthia wanted to hug them, but refrained. "We do have a process for all those who claim sanctuary, so please do not think it is personal or that we want to reject you." Worthia flagged security with her hand. "These men will show you to where you need to go."

"Can we see Wilmont?" Miriam asked.

"As soon as you are processed and we are sure you mean what you say, then I see no reason you can't. Please know, though, you can never take off those inhibitors. Do you understand?"

"If they keep those… things out of our head, we won't touch them."

Two security agents stood next to Miriam and her daughter.

"Before you go, can I ask about your husband? Is he wanting to claim sanctuary too?"

"Agnar?" Miriam scoffed. "He's an idiot. He's still trying to get payment for the children. The biggest thing he is worried about is the loss of manpower for the farm. To hell with him. He would have let Wilmont die in the first place!" Miriam paused and pursed her lips. "I have one more question. We left a daughter at home, Elizabeth. I'm worried about her safety. Could someone fetch her from our home so she will be safe?"

"The aliens didn't want her?" Worthia's eyebrows pushed down as her head tilted.

"No. I thought Agnar would stay with her, but I was wrong. I'm worried about her. You know, the boys in town with a girl all by herself?" Miriam's face became strained.

"I will make sure someone from Chicago goes to your house and brings her into the city. With the alien ship here, I don't think they have much to worry about there. Gentlemen, please take care of these ladies." Waving as the women left, Worthia added, "I hope to see you again."

Holding his tongue until the vehicle with the women left, Tigen walked up to Worthia. "Now that I never expected."

"Me neither." Worthia shook her head. "I wonder how many others are out there too scared to try for the city."

"Since we can't read minds, there is no way to know. But you have a bigger problem."

"I do?" Worthia's face twisted as she turned to Tigen. "What's that?"

"How are we going to inform the aliens that the women are not coming back?" Tigen gave her a quick smile.

Rolling her eyes, Worthia responded, "I'll let Chadan figure that one out."

Holding the envelope as if he didn't know what to do with it, Agnar looked from it to the Subordinate. It was white with only his name written on the outside in Miriam's handwriting. He held it by its corner.

"What is it?" the Subordinate asked.

"A letter from my wife."

"Read it." It was a plain instruction with no force or malice.

Tearing off the end, Agnar withdrew the paper inside, opened it, and began to read. His eyes went sad as he did.

"So she intends to stay with the rebels," the Subordinate said in a neutral voice. "This is not entirely unexpected."

"I am sorry, my lord, I had no idea…"

"Of course you didn't. It is of no matter. You will return to your home. Your usefulness here has ended." The Subordinate turned and walked away.

Looking around, Agnar found he was being abandoned by all present. Panic was clear on his face. "How am I supposed to get home?"

The Subordinate talked over his shoulder as two angels approached. "That is your task. Goodbye."

Chapter Thirty-Two
The Big Guy

Later, Vice President Storm Allin would describe the Subordinate's gait as determined but not hurried. As he watched from behind the gate, he couldn't help but smile at the approaching alien and his two retainers.

"He's got to be pissed," Storm said for the mic.

"I'm the one who should be out there," Worthia's voice said.

"Are you kidding? If we don't die, the footage of this will guarantee me the Presidency in the next election."

"And if you do die?"

"Then I wouldn't have to worry about the election." Storm giggled at his own words.

"You're a strange man, Storm."

"Thank you. I'll take that as a compliment."

Spending the rest of the time in silence, Storm watched the Subordinate finish traveling to the gate. The smile never left his face. The Subordinate wasn't smiling.

"Release the boy to us." The words had more force than Storm remembered from before.

"He has no wish to join you." Storm kept his voice flat.

"Let us talk to him and he will see the light and want to join us."

"You mean so you can brainwash him."

The Subordinate's head twitched a little as if trying to look at Storm from different angles. After a prolonged silence he said, "Why would we want to clean his brain?"

"I mean you want to forcibly change his mind to agree with what you want but make it appear that he is doing it on his own." Storm prevented himself from laughing.

"When he sees that light, he will be willing. You are all ours. You will do as we say or your rebellion will be punished."

"Let me ask you something." Storm shifted to a more casual position. "Why aren't we talking to your boss about this?"

"We are EO-AY. You are talking to us."

"But you call yourself the Subordinate. That means you have a superior, the Primary, do you not? Why aren't we speaking to him?"

"Storm, what are you doing?" Worthia's voice said in his ear.

"Gathering information," he replied quietly.

"The names we have given ourselves are for your convenience." At least the Subordinate did not seem irritated at the question. "We are EO-AY. We are one always."

"But you have taken this form? What is your natural form? Is it more like that one that appears more like a ghost?"

"The forms we take are only tools. They are not us."

"So you have no bodies? Are you an energy form?"

The Subordinate drew his head back. "This conversation is of no consequence. Return the boy to us now or you will be punished."

The Subordinate turned and started the trip back to the ship. Storm watched.

"Storm, get out of there."

"I have a little time." Waiting a little longer, Storm casually ambled from in front of the gate, but then ran to the vehicle once out of sight. "Let's go, boys," he said once inside the vehicle. Their compliance was immediate.

"They won't do something until the Subordinate is back in the ship." It was Chadan's voice.

"Of course," Captain Zaheia Gint added. "That's obvious. Shall I power up all turrets, M. President?"

"Not yet," Worthia replied. "Do you play poker, Captain?"

"Not well," the woman replied.

Everyone watched as the Subordinate and his escort entered the ship. It only took a few seconds for another to exit the ship, one of the four-faced creatures. Once at the bottom of the ramp, it flew to the gate, landing ten meters away. As it took the first steps, the people in the war room held their breaths.

"Activate the gate turrets," Worthia said. It took but two seconds for the covers to open and two pivot-mounted lasers extended from the wall and took aim at the creature. The creature walked to within two meters of the wall. Stopping, the creature put its hand into its robe and withdrew the hilt of a sword. Raising it above its head, flame erupted from the hilt.

"Fire," Worthia commanded in a calm voice. Two golden lasers crisscrossed the creature's body. The sword arm was cut at the shoulder. Yellowish fluid flowed from the deep wounds in the torso. As the arm fell, the creature fell to the ground. Where the flame touched the ground it was burned black, but the flame did not spread on the hard surface. The flame stayed on until the hand relaxed and the hilt rolled from the hand.

"Cat's out of the bag now," Chadan commented in a low voice behind her.

"Command, activate all turrets except the main turret." Worthia's voice had turned firm and business-like. On a separate display, green lights came on across the entire circle of a rough outlay of the city.

"Target the top of the ship with the medium turrets on the north side of the city," Captain Zaheia's voice said to her command. "Open fire as soon anything comes out."

The wait almost didn't exist. The top of the ship opened and creatures streaked from the opening. Two turrets fired golden beams across the opening, followed by a third in a few seconds. Parts of creatures continued on a lesser arc as they fell on the ship to slide down the sides and to the ground, but many more creatures passed unharmed.

"Get me a count!" Zaheia all but shouted. "Alive and dead."

The other turrets took aim and fired as four-faced creatures made a tight arc toward the city, flying in erratic paths toward the turrets. Some fell, but sheer numbers guaranteed that some made it to the turrets. When they did, flaming swords swung through the weapons.

One turret exploded in a yellow fireball, destroying its attacker.

"They're moving too fast to take them all out," an operator shouted from his terminal.

"Take out as many as possible. Ground troops will have to eliminate the rest." It was Zaheia's reassuring voice, though it was hard to tell from her command voice. "Have the turrets on the sides of the city fire through the barrier."

"But that will destroy the barrier," a voice responded.

"Which those creatures will do as soon as all the turrets are gone anyway." Zaheia stood firm, feet planted shoulder-width apart as she surveyed the main display and those of her subordinates, head always moving.

More explosions followed. Green lights disappeared from the city display and more creatures fell from the sky. Some slid down on the barrier, past the wall, to the ground. Others flew from the ramp under the ship, spreading out in all directions before flying up toward the city. One of the beams cutting across the top disappeared at the same time as an explosion so large that it could be heard inside the war room shook the walls of the room.

"Turret M2 is gone," was called out.

"Aim M1 and M3 into the ship if possible," Zaheia responded.

"We have a major breach of the barrier," another called.

"All units prepare to engage," Zaheia said into her interface. "Unwanted company is coming for breakfast. How many creatures have exited the ship?"

"Estimate is one hundred and fifty." The voice that answered was shaking.

"How many have we destroyed?"

"Estimates are at fifty percent." The voice seemed to take no comfort at the announcement.

More small explosions caused more green lights to disappear, leaving few on the northern half of the display. "At least we are taking them out as we lose turrets."

Privates Harn Fenrous and Stephen Manes stood with their backs to a wall and their faces and weapons turned up. The controlled shaking of their hands did not help their aim, but the speed of the targets was a larger factor.

"Damn, they're fast!" Harn said as his projector beam gave a passing creature only a glancing burn.

"Tell me about it." Stephen aimed at a creature flying between a row of buildings and delivered a longer scar across its body, but the creature continued to fly past. "What the hell does it take to take these things down?"

"Just keep hitting them. They can't take hits forever."

Harn turned to a rush of air next to him. In a flash of fire, his weapon was bisected halfway along the barrel, resulting in a cloud of bluish smoke obscuring his view for a moment. He heard more than saw Stephen being knocked from his place next to Harn to tumble down the sidewalk. The smoke was swept away by the air to reveal the face of a bull looking down at Harn. Hot breath was pushed onto his face as the creature grabbed him by his shirt and pulled him up to the creature's face. Harn's attention was held by the penetrating but lifeless eyes of the creature as its breath continued to wash across his face. His whole body shaking and his bladder filling his urine reservoir, Harn felt his lips quiver as he tried to speak.

"Don't... don't eat me."

Instead, the creature used his other hand to reach behind Harn's ear and tear off his inhibitor. The action took some skin with the inhibitor, causing a cry of pain from Harn. Before the pain had a chance to subside, the other inhibitor was ripped from his other ear.

The following sensation was not painful, if unfamiliar. Later, he would describe it as if he was a library and someone was walking through him, examining records as they went. Time was irrelevant, but was not long. As the feeling faded, the creature dropped Harn to the ground, turned, and flew off. Dazed but happy to be unhurt, Harn smiled to himself and laughed, but quickly stopped. Standing, he turned toward where Stephen had been thrown.

"Command," he said into his interface. "The creatures are taking inhibitors off of people."

"Understood," Zaheia responded into her interface. "Where are we with the jamming?"

"Working on it," a frantic voice said. The woman's hands flew across her heads-up display. "We never worked with the actual signals before. It's proving more difficult than expected."

"Get it done. I have a feeling we'll have visitors soon if we don't."

Powerful footsteps ran for the door. Tigen stopped long enough for it to open and turned toward the guards. "Emergency shutdown once I'm through. No one in or out and that means especially the President." As the door opened, Tigen stepped through, taking one last glance back as it shut.

"Tigen?" Worthia turned toward the door. "Tigen!" She rushed to the door to be caught by the two guards. "Tigen! Let me out! Let me out!"

"Sorry, M. President, the door is locked. We can't do that."

"Tigen." Worthia's body slumped as a tear fell. "No, no."

Activating his headset, Tigen reached behind his back with both hands. "Where are the creatures heading?"

North end of the building, came the reply.

"Roger." When his hands came back around his body, Tigen's hands were covered in metal, actuators, and a few lights. Bands clamped around his wrists as the lights turned green. As he started to run down the hall north, Tigen flexed the augmentation gloves. Passing two guards, he did not stop to speak. "Stay here. Shoot anything that comes down this hall that's not human."

"Yes, General," came two voices in unison.

Huddled behind the cabinets that separated the living room from the kitchen, the Daunets heard the crash of the glass balcony doors and the sound of beating wings when the creature entered. After the briefest of pauses, steps walked to the bedrooms. Too soon the steps were coming back. Lyle Daunet clasped his arms around his wife and son as hard as he could as if to wish the creature to leave, but to no avail. It was clear the steps searched the house, finally coming their direction. As they came around the counter, Lyle let go and turned to the creature to be met by a lion face on top of a robed body.

"We have nothing…" Lyle started to say, but the palm of a hand hit him in the chest, knocking him against the wall and causing his vision to blur and his arms to go limp. Tucking the boy underneath her to the extent possible, Renna Daunet put her body in-between the creature and her son. Since her head was turned, she didn't see the creature reach down, but felt it grab her inhibitors and tear them from her head, causing her to squeeze the boy tighter in a flinch.

"Where is the boy?" she heard the creature say.

"He's not here." Her voice quivered but her arms remained tight.

"Where is he?"

"The military took him. They didn't tell us where. You have no reason to hurt us."

Silence from the creature lasted a short eternity. The footsteps leading away caused Renna to look its direction. The face of a man looking behind the creature met her glance before it turned back toward the balcony. With an almost invisible flutter of its wings, the creature shot from the house, stirring anything loose. Renna reached toward her husband.

"Lyle? Are you all right?"

"Yeah." Lyle turned his head toward his wife in a slow sweep. "I'll be fine. Just a little shaken."

"You were so brave," Renna said as she stroked his cheek with her hand.

"*That* was pretty stupid, Dad," the boy voiced. The statement was full of worry and not contempt. Lyle laughed.

"Maybe," he replied. "Maybe."

Worthia wiped her eyes, stiffened her back, and took a breath before turning around. By the time she did, her face was hard as a stone gargoyle and about as pleasant. Her steps echoed in the room as she strode past silent people to the command station.

"Report," she barked out.

Zaheia did a smart pivot. "All the creatures have left the ship. We estimate two hundred. At least sixty are still active but the number is hard to judge. Almost all of the small turrets in the northern half of the city have been destroyed, along with three medium turrets, leaving three more. They do not act like they know about the main turret or don't care because it is not active."

"Have the medium turret fire on the ship itself."

"Yes, M. President." She did a smart pivot back to displays. "Turrets M3, M4, and M5, fire on the ship at the same location."

"Roger, Captain," all three turret operators responded at the same time.

"And get that damn jamming working!"

At the next intersection, Tigen stopped and listened. Sounds of gunfire led him down the left hall to find two infantrymen dispatching a creature that had entered a reception hall. He arrived just in time to see the creature fall into several pieces not five meters from the men. Swerving his rifle Tigen's direction, the man's eyes went wide with shock and then fear as he promptly pointed the rifle upwards.

"Sorry, sir. These things are hard to kill."

"Carry on."

Tigen's attention was drawn by noises farther down the hall. A length of flame came through the ceiling and traced a circle, cutting ragged edges into the ceiling. Breaking into a run, Tigen made for the hole, avoiding the circular piece of ceiling as it fell. A creature soon followed, flaming sword ablaze. As it landed on top of the shattered ceiling piece, Tigen grabbed its sword hand with his left gloved hand, twisting it in what should be an unnatural angle, and drove his right augmented fist into the lion face in front of him.

Staggered, the creature brought up its other hand as it tried to focus its eyes. It was rewarded by a metal hand raining repeated blows. The muzzle broke and yellowish liquid flowed from the face. The next blow missed as the head turned, revealing an eagle beak and eyes. A wing swept from behind the creature, causing a cut along Tigen's right arm. He responded by driving his fist into the body of the creature and squeezing his left as hard as possible. Rewarded by a sound that could have been breaking bones, Tigen twisted the hand further.

With a screech to pierce eardrums, the creature beat its wings, leaving the ground and kicking Tigen with both feet. Twisting his body, Tigen whipped the creature against the wall and followed with more blows from his right. He could feel the creature attempting to turn its wrist and felt the heat of the sword as it inched toward his head.

"Left hand blade!" Tigen shouted. From its sheath along his left thumb, a metal blade shot from its case and plunged into the wrist of the creature. Holding the body with his right, Tigen wrenched his left and was rewarded by the creature's hand separating from its arm to be thrown down the hall, scoring the floor as it went.

Wings beat at Tigen as he held the creature, driving his left elbow into its throat. As he did, the wings beat softer and the creature sagged until it hung limp against the wall. Backing off, Tigen watched the creature fall to the floor as if a rag doll. Turning, he noticed the sword still flamed. He kicked the body but it did not respond.

"To all combatants," Tigen said out loud. "This is General Tigen Tonsten. The sword hilt is the power source for the creature. Separate the sword from the creature and they soon lose all power."

"Finally, some info we can use." Wray Wellington's aim at a flying creature was disrupted by the explosion of a turret a couple of blocks from his position next to the main turret cover. The explosion was advantageous in that it caused another creature to pause in mid-air. Taking aim, Wray swept the rifle beam across its forearm. The severed limb and sword fell to the ground. After a momentary look at his arm, the creature dove to follow, but his wings soon lost speed and he plummeted, tumbling, from the sky.

"Whoo-hoo!" Wray bellowed. "Take that, you alien bastards."

"How the hell you able to hit these things?" Cedynia Altone asked through the direct communication link from the other side of the turret.

"You just got to be good, which I thought you were." Wray laughed, lining up his next shot, a long one. "Oh, so off the range you're a terrible shot. Not sure why they brought you along with the reinforcements from Chicago then." Wray laughed. "Good thing you have me around."

"Hey! I'm not terrible." There was a momentary pause. *"Just not the best under pressure."* Cedynia's voice was small and meek.

"Don't worry, babes, I'm here to protect you." Wray pulled the trigger. The beam burned the side of the creature, not killing it, but doing significant damage. "Not bad for three blocks away."

"You're supposed to be protecting the turret, not me. Besides, I didn't ask you to. Damn it, missed again!"

"You don't have to ask me, darling," Wray said in an old-fashioned southern drawl.

"Men."

The creature that Wray had hit flew in an arc, ending up flying directly toward Wary. Unphased at its approach, Wray settled into his kneeling position, lined up the rifle, and took a breath. As he let it out, he pulled the trigger back. The beam hit the fast-approaching creature in the head, burning through its forehead, through its neck, and into its body as it neared the tower. The wings went from a blur to almost still and gravity started its unending pull, but the velocity of the creature was high enough that it only lost a few meters of altitude before hitting the side of the tower.

The impact, directly under Wray, caused the platform to shake from side to side enough that Wray lost his balance and fell to the floor over to his left, his knee on the ground doing nothing to stabilize him. The continued shaking of the platform caused him to roll and panic when he realized he was rolling toward the edge hanging over the city. A desperate grab at the rail with his left hand left his right holding onto the rifle and his face looking down the one hundred meters to the ground below. As his vision started to waver, his stomach synchronized the motion, threatening to discharge anything left inside. The vision wavered more, making Wray think he was losing his grip on the rail, but he dared not let go of the rifle. Palms sweating, his mind raced for a solution, but his imagination kept sending pictures of him falling to the street below.

Just as his brain told him he was losing his grip on the rail, a hand grabbed the back of his jacket and pulled him back onto the platform. Turning onto his back, Wray took a deep breath, clearing his vision and settling his stomach. Cedynia's face looked down on him.

"You're wearing your safety harness, you know?" Her face contorted like a mother staring at her silly child.

"Doesn't mean it didn't scare the shit out of me." Wray closed his eyes and relaxed. "At least I didn't drop my gun."

Cedynia laughed. "You can hit a fly from thirty meters but can't stand to look at the ground. What are we going to do with you?"

"How about not letting me fall to my death for a starter?"

Cedynia slapped his shoulder. "Get up, you big baby."

"Look at the ship around where the projection beams are hitting," Chadan said, waving his finger toward the wall display.

"What is it?" Worthia asked. "We don't seem to be having much of an impact."

"See the slight rise around the impact zone?" Chadan waved at the display and it zoomed in to the point of impact.

"Barely." Worthia leaned closer to the screen.

"If you look at the light hitting the top of the craft, it looks like the metal is moving. I believe that they are somehow moving new metal from other locations on the ship to replace that which is being destroyed by the projectors." Chadan waved his finger as if explaining an equation to a classroom. "Fascinating."

"What? I mean, how can they do that?" Worthia's mouth stayed open.

"I have no idea, but they are clearly preventing internal damage at the cost of protection in other locations. I would recommend hitting the ship in multiple locations." Chadan waved the display to return to the original view.

"We have activity at the ship," one of the soldiers at the monitors called out.

"What kind?" Zaheia called back.

"More hostiles exiting the ship. I think they're messengers."

"Zoom in." Zaheia stared at the display. "They can still wield those flaming swords. How many?"

"Maybe fifty?"

"The aliens must be getting desperate to send them out." Zaheia almost laughed in glee. The statement was punctuated by the sound of an explosion.

"We just lost M4!"

"Crap!" No glee was included.

"Should we fire on the alien ship?" The Minister of Defense shuffled from one foot to the other as he talked.

"And then we would have to explain to the Americans that not only do we have space weapons we have not told them about, but we have one that can fire on targets over their territory." Eiji did not physically react to the question but continued to watch the display. "Do you want to be the one to explain to them that we have been lying to them?"

"But this is a special circumstance," the minister continued. "I would think they would be grateful for the assistance against the aliens."

"They appear to be holding their own for now, so we will wait. Besides, they have their own satellites in place, do they not, Mr. Smith?"

"Correct, Chairman." Smith's voice was as emotionless as ever.

"And they have not fired them yet, so I assume they do not feel it necessary to engage space forces. Who are we to disagree with them?" Eiji turned to look at the minister with one raised eyebrow. The minister shuffled his feet some more while looking at the floor. "I know you are scared. If the aliens destroy one American city, they have more. It will be interesting to see where they go next if they do destroy the city. The more alien forces the Americans destroy, the fewer we will have to deal with if it comes to that."

"If we destroy them now, we will not have to face them in the future." The voice was from the Foreign Minster.

"But we do not know if destroying this ship will bring others," Smith said. "I would be surprised if these aliens only have one ship and I doubt we could defend ourselves against multiple ships at one time."

"A good point. Better to conserve our resources at this time." Eiji turned back to the display. "Besides, this is the most entertaining event that has happened in a long time."

"Aliens are entering the building at location one dash eleven."

Breaking into a sprint, Tigen carried the alien creature's hand gripping the hilt of the flame sword in his right. Inside the hand the flame sword, still ignited, blazed as bright as ever. Two soldiers ran behind him, struggling to keep up. A turn around a corner ended in a skidding stop. Ten meters down the hall, three creatures filled the hall with more behind them. The total number was not discernible, but it was clear to Tigen that they were outnumbered by more than was advisable. To the soldiers' credit, they fired on the lead creatures as soon as they could take a firing stance.

"I have a mass of aliens in hallway one dash eleven," Tigen spoke out loud after twitching his chin to activate his interface. "We are withdrawing to a better position. Back the way we came, men."

As the two men stopped firing and withdrew, Tigen pulled back his arm and threw the alien hand and sword at the advancing group. The hand made small circles as it flew, causing the flame to make rotations in the air.

The spinning swirl of flame approached the aliens like a unbalanced spinning wheel. The lead creature, having taken a hit to the head from a rifle that left him more than half blind, swung his sword in an arc in an attempt to deflect the incoming projectile. His flame contacted the thrown weapon at the hilt, slicing through the hand as if it didn't exist and bisecting the hilt.

"Didn't know how the use the thing anyway," Tigen said as he joined the soldiers around a hallway. "Keep..."

With the force of a hurricane, a concussive wave of air rampaged through the hallway and knocked down the three men in the adjoining hallway. Face down on the floor, Tigen felt the wave of heat flow over them. In motion the instant after hitting the floor, he pushed off from the floor with his hands to get one foot under his body, grabbed the two soldiers by their uniforms, and ran down the hallway. He had made only a half-dozen steps before a second blast sounded, followed in step by an even bigger blast or what might have been multiple blasts at the same time. The sound was so loud it removed all others from the men's ears and set up guard against future intrusion.

All three men rode the shock wave down the hall. Tigen felt his feet leave the floor, giving way to weightless flight as the floor rushed past his feet. It did not last as the wave dumped them without ceremony on the floor. Dust and heat flowed above and around them, felt from their heels all the way to their heads. The walls shook and the ceiling cracked. Flame burned on or in the walls. Ignoring the pain and spared the sounds, Tigen again grabbed the two men by their uniforms and ran down the hall. The man on his right made attempts to get to his feet, but the one on his left made no voluntary movement. His lack of hearing left no warning as Tigen's shoulder was hit from above by something that rolled off his back. The man on the right became heavy enough to almost stop Tigen in his tracks. His efforts to pull the man along left only a scrap of material in his glove. Fleeing down the hall, Tigen used both hands to throw the remaining soldier over his shoulder, giving him the opportunity to run faster.

The explosion at the north end of the building shook the war room enough to cause all those standing to lose or almost lose their footing except Zaheia. As the lights flashed and fans scraped their cowlings, Zaheia stood like a unmovable captain on a swaying ship. Caught and steadied by one of the guards she had not seen following her, Worthia scanned the monitors with quick turns of her head.

"What was that?" Worthia asked.

"Large explosion in the north end of the building," came back a reply.

"How big?" Zaheia asked, turning her head toward the speaker.

"We lost the north third of the building. It's just… gone. There's structural collapse in other parts of the building."

"Cause?" Zaheia moved closer to the display of the area.

"Unknown at this time."

"Aliens in that area?"

"Aliens had been reported gathering in that area," a different voice added. "Twenty maybe. Count is not fixed. Looks like they were staging for an invasion of the building."

"Where are they *now*?" The sharpness of Zaheia's voice caused the low chatter from behind her to stop.

"Gone." The reply was filled with shock and amazement. "Everything is just gone."

"Well, someone find out what the hell happened! I want reports from any forces in the immediate area. Have them call in now." Zaheia's voice pushed activity into bodies.

"We also lost M1," a third voice added. "We have no turrets firing on the ship."

"Activate the main turret and fire on the ship." Worthia's voice forced its way through the gathered military monitors without panic or emotion.

"Activate main turret," Zaheia echoed. "Blast those bastards from the face of the Earth."

The energized electrons in the large-core wires sounded like millions of metallic ants quick stepping up the tower. It caused Wray's and Cedynia's heads to pop up and turn, first to the center of the turret and then to each other. Clam-shell doors fled into the flooring and a beam projector the size of a sixteen-inch naval turret rose.

"Get inside!" Cedynia screamed. It wasn't necessary, as Wray was already moving to the hatch that had opened at the same time as the central doors. Jumping feet first into the hatch caused the safety harness to be released and he fell through a drag tube the seven meters to a pad located in the auxiliary control room. Looking across the room, he watched Cedynia fall onto the pad across from him. Lights flashed on the control panels and doors snapped shut and locked. The metallic ants were marching even louder inside the room. Cedynia sprinted to the control panel.

"They're firing the turret," she said out loud to the panel.

"No kidding." Wray recovered his feet and took a few steps to join her. "At what?"

"The ship, I would guess."

"Oh, right."

* * *

Watching the display of percent charge on the turret, Zaheia spoke as soon as it hit one hundred. "Fire."

The main display showed a silvery-gold beam streak from the turret and hit the alien ship. The hull started to blacken and a small trail of smoke appeared. The beam lasted for two seconds and then disappeared.

"Keep firing!" Worthia called.

"It cycles to…" a technician stuttered.

"Continuous fire," Worthia commanded.

"Continue fire," Zaheia echoed. The silvery-gold beam re-appeared.

"The creatures appear to be headed toward the turret," was called out.

"Where the hell is my jamming?" Zaheia asked with force.

"Active… now!"

"Shit! They turned it back on." Cedynia's head and hands waved through the air.

"Ah, yeah. You didn't think one shot would do it, do you?"

"No, it's too soon. The cooling system didn't get a chance to work."

Wray took up a position next to her, staring at the display. "Crap. It must be bad out there."

"The temperature is already in the yellow."

"We have reports of alien activity coming to a halt," a voice reported with no appreciable response.

"Turret temperature is rising."

"Keep firing." Worthia stood, firm of word and stance, next to Zaheia.

"The turret can't do this long before overheating," Zaheia said softly. "If it blows…"

"If we don't destroy those aliens, it wouldn't matter if it blows.

Keep firing.”

"Shit, shit, shit. They're not stopping.” Cedynia was bobbing up and down.

"Override.”

"I can't yet.”

"They'll stop. If they don't, the turret will take a third of the city with it.”

"M. President?”

"Keep firing.” Worthia was unmoved.

"But if the temperature…”

"*Keep firing!*”

Cedynia turned to Wray as fast as any mechanical door. "Take the emergency chute. Get out of here.”

"Come with me.”

"I can't. I have to try and turn this thing off.”

"Then I'm staying.” Wray's response was firm and unemotional.

"It only takes one person to turn it off, stupid. Get out!” Panic crept into Cedynia's voice.

"No.”

"Yes! Get out.”

"Why?”

Cedynia couldn't help but take a look at the display. The bar representing the current temperature made a steady pace to the red region and thick black line. Too fast for any comfort.

"So you'll live, stupid, in case this blows.” Her hand hovered over a large red square on the display.

"What's the point without you there?”

Turning back to Wray, Cedynia found the flatness of the statement did not match the hurt and pleading in his eyes. A wave of emotion ran through her face, chest, and stomach and caused a small sniffle. Swiveling back to the display just as fast, she saw that the temperature bar had reached the red zone and marched in a determined manner to the thick black line.

Slamming her hand on the red square, the lights on the display and in the room flashed. The metallic ants stopped to be replaced by the sound of high-pressure liquid pushed through quarter-of-a-meter pipes and air rushing through ducts like teenagers into an opened concert hall gate. The temperature bar stopped, but Cedynia did not wait to watch it descend back to the safe zone. Turning one last time, she threw her arms around Wray's neck and pressed her lips to his with every ounce of strength she had.

"What happened?" Worthia looked at the display in confusion.

"Someone shut down the turret on site," Zaheia answered.

"Activate a space laser and hit the ship again." With the projection beam gone, a large black spot could be seen on the alien ship but no interior could be seen. The smoke had increased, though, from the earlier thin trail to a much larger plume.

"Yes, ma'am!" Captain Moraine Harjo replied. "SP1, activate and fire at that ship."

"Jamming is no longer effective," was called from the monitors. "Signal has changed. Attempting compensation."

"SP1 firing."

The bright, yellowish light hit the alien ship from above, darkening the ship where it hit like a plow cutting fresh, tan colored earth and leaving a stripe of darkness. Broader than the main turret, the beam moved across the ship, despite the compensated aim of the satellite. After only four seconds, the beam disappeared.

"What happened?" Worthia demanded.

"The projector is set on a cycle…" Harjo started to explain.

"Override it."

"We can't."

"Who the hell sets up these weapons?" Worthia pounded her fist on the nearest object.

"The scientists," Harjo responded in a low volume as she ignored the shaking monitor.

"Fire again."

"It will, very soon."

"You know, there are most likely people on that ship," Chadan said from behind.

"They made their decision," Worthia answered with disdain.

"The ship is moving," was called from the right.

"The aliens are heading back to the ship," was called from the left.

"But the ship is closed up," the first voice stated. "How are they going to get on?"

The particle beam reappeared from the same source, hitting the moving ship. This time, the blurred forms of the creatures and messengers flew into the beam above the ship, disappearing almost as fast as they entered.

"What are they doing?" Worthia asked.

"Sacrificing themselves to buy the ship time," Harjo responded.

"But one of those creatures can't stop much of the beam."

"Whatever they stop, it will be more than without them." Harjo stared at the screen and typed messages on her interface. "Would be considered brave if I thought they actually had a choice."

As they watched, the mass of flying aliens that remained dove into the beam like a swarm of bees and turned into ash. Not more than a second after the swarm was gone, the particle beam turned off. The alien ship accelerated, entering clouds.

"Seems to have worked," Zaheia commented with disdain.

"Don't worry, M. President, the other particle beams will fire as soon as the ship clears the atmosphere." Harjo's eyes scanned several places. "Which should be any second now."

The alien ship cleared the clouds with impressive speed. It was welcomed by three beams all hitting it on the left-hand side per the view. Sparks of hot metal and smoke poured from the ship and it took a rightward track as it cleared the horizon. White plumes of condensed water accompanied the black smoke, swirling into tiny yin-yang patterns. The beams tracked across the ship for a few seconds and then disappeared. The ship continued on course. Gases and smoke continued to vent from where the beams had struck.

"The ship has taken severe damage," Zaheia commented without emotion, a fact that caused surprise to register on several faces.

Chadan waved his finger at the display. "It appears that the ship is headed toward the moon."

"Taking cover from the space-based weapons," Zaheia said in a flat voice.

The space-based weapons pivoted, but could not match the speed of the alien ship long enough to lock on target with reliability. Several more particle beam shots lit up space, but two only made glancing blows. Gas no longer trailed from the ship. Worthia's heart fell as the ship rounded the moon. Lost to sight.

"Now what?" Worthia asked as she turned to those assembled in the room.

"Now we wait," Chadan said with a shrug.

"So they can rearm and come back?" Sharpness was abundant in Worthia's voice.

"From our estimate," Zaheia interjected, "all of the creatures that left the ship were destroyed. From their numbers, I doubt they could mount another such attack."

"But we have no way of knowing." Worthia's voice was firm.

"No. It's a tactical estimate."

"So we both take a breather and do it again in another one hundred and sixty years?"

Glances were exchanged by those in the room, but no words accompanied them. Worthia waited, but the others ended up looking at her as if expecting the truth. "Zaheia, find my Chief of Staff and have him report immediately to my office."

"Yes, M. President."

"If he's alive, I'm thinking of killing him myself."

While some followed, none walked next to Worthia as she made her way through the halls. The guards looked concerned, but said nothing. Once inside, she closed the door before anyone else could enter. She was not able to keep herself from turning on a screen to a satellite view of the moon that watched for movement from the aliens. For its lack of activity, it was a tense view. The opening of the door drew her attention away from the screen. When she saw who was entering, she turned and quick-stepped that direction.

A dirty, torn-uniform Tigen walked into the room. Gloves off, his arms past where they had been were red. His walk had a slight limp from this right leg and he held his left arm gingerly. None of the wounds garnered sympathy from Worthia, who hit him in the right shoulder when she was near enough.

"What did you think you were doing?" Her face clenched with the question.

"Protecting you." The reply was soft and low.

"You... you." Worthia threw her arms around Tigen's chest and clenched it without thought to any possible injuries. He could feel her softly crying into his chest as he wrapped his arms around her. Without any words, he let her cry it out. Though he had left the door open, no one interrupted or looked their direction for more than a moment, though several smiled as they turned away. The two guards next to the door acted like nothing was happening while closing the door.

"What would I have done without you?" Worthia asked when her tears faded.

"You think a few aliens can take me out? You ought to know better than that. I mean, I... You probably don't want to know that." Tigen's mouth twisted in mild panic.

"You mean you don't want me to know. I can always read it in your report." A small laugh gave brief movement to her body.

"Darn reports," Tigen grumbled.

"When this is all over, I'm thinking of resigning."

"Define 'all over.' "

"When the aliens are gone, everyone is taken care of, and the repairs have started."

Tigen squeezed a little tighter. "You deserve it. Plus, I don't think anyone will blame you."

"For leaving Storm in charge when I leave?" The question had an amount of lightness to it.

Tigen rolled his eyes. "Okay, they might blame you for that."

As the laughter rolled the stress from her body onto Tigen's chest, he felt her relax for the first time that day.

Early the next morning the door to their apartment opened with urgency. Chadan took one step into the room and stopped. Without reacting to the scene of Worthia and Tigen in robes, he announced,

"There's something coming around the moon. We think it's one of the alien's creatures."

"That was fast." Disengaging from Tigen, Worthia turned to Chadan.

"Yes. I would have expected to wait several days, or at least twenty-four hours. Projections from their previous decision-making delays, at least according to records…"

"Enough." Worthia waved her hand at Chadan as she walked from the room. "Let's get to the war room." She took a step and stopped. "As soon as we get dressed."

The war-room had been repopulated with all the previous day's tenants, or they hadn't left. The main display had a graphic of the moon and Earth with one point of light between. The light moved faster than Worthia would have imagined.

"Destination?" she asked.

"Too soon to tell," someone replied.

Standing still was not an option Worthia was able to exercise. She tapped her foot, tried to do something with her arms, but was unable to find a comfortable stance, paced a few steps, and huffed at the display.

"Do you want us to target the alien, M. President?" someone seated at a display asked.

"No," she answered, not looking the direction of the question. "I think we can take one angel if we have to."

After a painful couple of minutes, a voice said, "Definitely coming to Denver."

"Then we should greet our guest," Worthia stated as she turned toward the exit. She found Tigen in her way.

"You can't be serious?" Worry occupied his eyes.

"I don't think they sent one angel here to assassinate me and it would be a waste not to find out why it was sent." Her upright stance deflected the possibility of argument.

"I'm going with you."

"Never imagined otherwise." The tone of Worthia's voice was matter-of-fact as Tigen pivoted out of her way and she proceeded. No one else spoke until they had left.

"That's a determined woman," Zaheia said.

"Determined to get herself killed?" the lieutenant next to her asked.

"No. Determined to end this thing."

As they walked the hallway, Tigen asked, "Where are we going?"

"I was thinking of an appropriate place. Somewhere public. Center park, next to that statue I like."

"Ugh."

"Yes, I know you don't... appreciate it."

"And it is going to be immortalized in pictures for eternity now." Tigen's voice was almost painful.

"And no asking them to edit it out," Worthia said in a sharp voice.

"Dang your quick mind," Tigen mumbled. "Wait, how are they going to know to go there?"

"How do you think?"

A guard opened a door to the outside. A vehicle was waiting.

"No! We can't..."

"We can't communicate otherwise. Besides." There was a pause of only two seconds. "They don't want to know what I'm thinking right now anyway."

Tigen let silence be his shield for the rest of the trip. When they arrived at the park, they received an update that the angel was over Denver. Stepping from the vehicle, Worthia took off her shields and placed them in her pocket. The cringe from Tigen could be felt without looking, but she made her way to the statue. It was abstract, too abstract for someone like Tigen, but she felt herself relax around it.

"I wonder if they will even notice it," she said out loud as she turned her back to the bronze.

The four-faced creature came into view. Making one circle of the city, it then made a direct path to the park. With a high-pitched sound, it landed five meters in front of Worthia. Taking a stance, the front of the creature opened to reveal the Subordinate, who waited for the opening process to complete before exiting. He walked to within a meter and a half of Worthia.

"The destruction was not good for either of us." His lips moved with the words.

"We would have rather avoided it, but you insisted." The tone of the words and stare she returned were full of meaning.

"We put you here. We watched over you. You are ours."

"So you claim." Worthia took a breath. "Even if you could prove this, we would still not accept that we belong to you. We are independent, thinking, intelligent individuals. We will never agree to you taking us against our will or in the future ever again."

The Subordinate appeared to take a breath. "We have waited tens of thousands of your years for you to develop. After all that time, you deny us?"

"Take those who are willing. One time offer."

"That is not our way."

"It is now, unless you wish more destruction." The words were almost a blow sent from Worthia to the alien. "We give you one chance. After that, you will leave all humans alone. Forever."

"And if we disagree?"

A smile crossed Worthia's lips. "You've seen how far we've come since the last time you were here. How advanced do you think we will be the next time you arrive? Your defeat today will not bode well for your position in the eyes of those who worship you. Humans don't like losers. Your churches will be all but abandoned in a generation. If you go and return in another one hundred and sixty years, you will be nothing but a historic note, our first regrettable instance of contact."

The Subordinate stood for a moment. At least he blinked every few seconds. "We will take those from the towns without domes."

"That are willing," Worthia added.

"It will be… not advantageous for us to visit here after that."

"We agree."

Turning, the Subordinate walked back to the waiting angel. Worthia's head ticked in a small, sharp motion to the side.

"Where are those who you took with you last time you were here?" Worthia came out fast and insistent. "I asked you a question."

Walking backwards into the angel, the Subordinate said only one word as it closed around him. "Goodbye."

As soon as the angel closed up, its wings moved and it accelerated upwards. Its ever-increasing speed took it out of sight in very little time.

"Bastards," Worthia said as she retrieved the shields from her pocket. As she put them on, she turned to see Tigen slump. Moving under his arm, she placed her shoulder to support at least some of his weight. "I'll call a doctor."

"No," Tigen replied in a release of breath, "just been a long day."

"Let's at least get you somewhere to sit down," she said, moving toward their vehicle.

"Whatever M. President says," he replied.

Her help not only extended to the vehicle, but continued inside and back toward the war room. Tigen didn't complain, but emphatically denied her request to stay in the vehicle or go to a medical facility, claiming there were enough more deserving people to be treated. She couldn't argue that the facilities were more than likely packed already and Tigen didn't complain how close she stayed, so she demurred. When they arrived to the expectant crowd in the war room, things changed.

"It's finally over," she said. People came over to shake her hand or give her a hug, forcing her to leave Tigen's arm. Watching from the corner of her eyes, she saw a guard help him to a chair. She let the gaiety continue for a few minutes before using her arms to ask for quiet.

"I want to thank all of you for your support and help through this. I know it was costly but we won." Another cheer went up and she had to ask for quiet again. "I want a video of the aliens leaving to be distributed across the world as soon as possible. I also need to make a statement to the people of Denver right away. Before we celebrate too much, though, I would ask that everyone be involved in finding those who are hurt and getting them treatment. I assume that has started already, but I think we need to get out there too, showing our faces helping and celebrating in public. There are a lot of people out there whose lives were endangered, I am sure. After I see to my own injured," a laugh went through the crowd at the statement, "I will be joining you. Again, thank you all. We did this together and we will move forward together."

Applause rang out in the room. Shaking her head did not cause it to die down. Most shook her hand again before they exited the room. Even most of the military personnel exited. After too long in her mind, Worthia got back to Tigen, who sat with his head down while leaning his arms on his knees.

"How bad is it?" she asked.

"I'm mostly just exhausted." Looking up, he gave her a smile. "I'll be fine. You need to get out there and let the people see you."

Kneeling, Worthia looked into his eyes. "I need to see you too."

"You will, hopefully a lot more." Taking her face in his hand, Tigen kissed her. "Now get out there and let the people adore you."

"I adore you." Worthia's voice was soft. "I don't know what I would have done if I had lost you."

"Find some other aliens to kill?" A chuckle vibrated Tigen's throat.

"More like put up a memorial and make you into a national holiday." Worthia smiled back.

"Hell, no." Tigen's head shook. "I don't want my legacy to be Tigen Day."

Raising her eyebrows, Worthia asked, "And what would you like your legacy to be?"

Tigen smiled back. "We can talk about that later."

Kissing him again, Worthia stood and looked at a guard. "Make sure he gets looked at and rested. And I mean it. Take as many men as you need to make sure he stays down."

"Yes, M. President." The man's voice shook as he responded.

Chapter Thirty-Three
Future Plans

"Servitors Wray Wellington and Cedynia Altone reporting for assignment." Wray spoke into his wrist interface and Cedynia mostly stood and smiled.

"Your assigned station?" a voice asked.

"It took no damage and has been secured." There was a brief pause before an answer.

"Are either of you injured?"

"Negative." A small giggle came from Cedynia behind him.

"Proceed to area D-13 for civilian assistance and accounting."

"Roger." Wray tapped the interface.

"You didn't tell them," Cedynia commented.

"There's plenty of time to resign after all the cleanup is done." Wray shrugged. Cedynia grabbed his arm as they started walking.

"So tell me," she said with a lilt in her voice, "why New Zealand for the honeymoon?'"

"I always wanted to go?" He raised his eyebrows as he looked at her.

"Why didn't you?"

"Didn't have anyone to share it with." He gave his head a shake to the side as he looked forward.

"Well, now you do." A tiny skip crept into her step. "So where else have you always wanted to go?"

"The Himalayas, Victoria Falls, the Andes mountains…"

"Paris, Rome, Hong Kong…" A dreamy quality filled Cedynia's voice.

"No, not really." Wray's head shook a little.

"Trust me, you want to go." A squeeze to his arm accompanied the comment.

Seeing the destruction had a greater impact than being told what had happened ever could. Worthia could not help but feel overwhelmed when looking at the north end of the building she had been hidden beneath. It looked like a giant creature had taken a large bite out of the building, leaving debris strewn around the edges due to its inefficient bite pattern.

"There's less debris than I would have expected," Worthia said.

"The initial explosions appear to have atomized anything around them. The debris is mostly from collapse after the loss of support from the explosion." Zaheia rocked on the balls of her feet as she surveyed the building, hands clasped behind her back.

"How many casualties?" A grimace came with the question.

"We only know of a few from the collapsing building. There is no way to know from the explosions until we determine who is accounted for."

Worthia shook her head. "Not a very satisfying way to decide if someone is dead."

"Sometimes that is all that's left. We can check the ash for human DNA but even then it won't tell us who it was."

"You seem awfully calm for the subject we're talking about." Worthia's face was sad, not resentful.

"It's a reality of war, something a soldier has to come to terms with or it will drive them crazy. It could have been anyone in there." Turning, Zaheia looked at Worthia. "If anyone died in the explosions, they are a hero and they didn't die in vain. That's something for a soldier, at least."

"I know." Worthia looked at the ground. "Civilians don't like the idea of anyone dying, but I know that's unrealistic." Taking a breath, she looked back up. "I'll make sure I thank everyone for their efforts today. Not much else I can do."

"It does mean something, to us at least." Giving her a smile, Zaheia looked back to the building. "Do you intend to stay and watch?"

"No, I have other things I need to do. Please tell me if you find any good news."

"Of course." Zaheia started waving at the workers.

Stopping halfway around her turn, Worthia asked, "By the way, can you tell me where Tigen was when these things went off? How close to this, I mean."

"Do you really want to know?" Zaheia stopped all motion when she asked. There was a pause.

"No, not really." Shaking her head, Worthia added, "That's something I don't need to worry about."

Relaxing, Zaheia started waving again. "He made it back alive and functional. That's all that matters."

"I know. Part of me just wants the information so I can yell at him better." A laugh from Zaheia accompanied Worthia's exit from the scene.

"Is he going to make it?" Private Harn Fenrous asked the medic.

"My best guess is yes, but it depends on internal injuries." The woman closed up the transport tube and started pushing it toward the waiting vehicle.

"What can I do?" Harn ran after the woman.

"You did a good job up till now so let the experts take it from here." The woman pushed the tube into a slot at the back of the vehicle. A light turned green when the tube was installed and engaged. "You need to report to your unit."

"Yeah, yeah, I should do that. Hope they still exist." Harn's voice was dazed and he looked around without focusing.

"Your interface will be able to keep you informed." The woman grabbed his shoulders. "Get busy, do something. We got your friend from here. Go help someone else."

Nodding, Harn's eyes appeared to focus a little better. "Right. There's got to be plenty to do. Thanks." Harn raised his wrist as he walked away from the medic. The second medic of the team came to the back of the vehicle, shutting the doors.

"Shell shock?"

"Plenty of that going around. We ready?"

"All buttoned up."

"Then let's get them to where they need to go." Both medics headed to the front of the vehicle and jumped in. "Hospital."

As the vehicle took off under computer controlled route to avoid hazards and blocked roads, the second medic shook his head.

"You know, it won't surprise me if the hospitals are full already. A lot of destruction out here."

"The hospital to which we are headed is only at eighty-seven percent capacity," came a computer generated voice from the console.

"That's why you're not driving." A laugh accompanied the comment, but it elicited a frown.

The Daunets stood on their balcony overlooking the city. Glass was piled in one corner, though much more was inside the house than outside. Smoke rose from several locations and they had stopped counting the number of broken windows. A few people waved from other buildings when they saw the family, who waved back with cheerful smiles.

"I can't believe we won," Renna said.

"Of course we won," her son said with such a firm voice that it made Lyle laugh.

"Oh, the confidence of youth." He rubbed his boy's head. He responded with a questioning look.

"Why won't we win?"

"Last time it was pretty one sided." Lyle still smiled with the comment.

"But that was ages ago." More laughter.

A voice came from Lyle's interface. It was the building supervisor. "Lyle. Is everyone in your family all right?"

"Yeah, Roger, we're fine."

"I heard your place was broken into."

"Some broken glass and we'll need new balcony doors, but no

injuries."

"That's good." The relief was clear to hear in Roger's voice.

"Anything we can do for you?"

"Not that I know of yet. Just finishing the building check. I guess if the government needs help, they'll tell us. Right now, they're trying to keep everyone off the roads and out of the way of the debris bots."

"We've been watching them, though there's not much to clean up around here but glass. There's a lot of that, though. Don't expect they stocked up on it?"

"That would have been some real clever planning." Roger's laughter was heard over the interface. "I'll bring some plastic around as soon as I have a count. What I have at least."

"No worries. Might be nice to sleep with the windows open for a few days." Lyle looked at his wife, who smiled at him. "We might even barbecue."

"Might what?"

"Barbecue. You know, cook outside on the balcony, or at least close to it."

"With what?"

"Oh, I don't know." Lyle looked down at his son's beaming face. "We'll think of something." There was a pause in the conversation.

"I don't think I want to know. Anyway, I'll talk to you later."

The interface went silent. Renna put her head into her husband's shoulder. "And what exactly are we going to use to cook this food?"

Lyle took a breath and raised his shoulders. "A pot, some shelves to set it on, and something that burns."

"Like what?"

"We'll find something. Maybe some wood down on the commons."

"I have an old art project you can burn," the boy offered.

"Oh no, you're not touching that." Renna gave him a stern look. "That's mine."

"Darn," came the soft reply.

The speech was broadcast on every display, even the large outdoor ones in the common areas. People gathered outdoors to watch, but few would remember any exact wording, much to the chagrin of the speech-writers. What they did remember was the scene of the alien ship fleeing from the city under fire. Their reaction was the same as those who had been in the war room: held breath, rising tension, and jubilation when the ship disappeared as if the event was a surprise. Few even realized that the president was talking the whole time. The following celebration was immediate, loud, and long. Every type of noise-maker was dragged out and employed. People hugged, cried, and patted each other on the back. Security and military personnel soon felt their lives in danger from the enthusiastic thanks, most making themselves much less visible, though a few would require medical attention. The fact that firearms, particularly the gunpowder type that Puritans still used, were no longer kept by the general population was a comfort; logistics personnel were glad they did not have to increase their glass orders to other cities.

By the time Worthia made it back to her apartment, her back and hands were sore. Plus she was hungry, more hungry than she could remember in a long time. The sight of Tigen propped up on the couch helped her relax.

"Nice speech," he said as she walked over to kiss him.

"Thanks. You think anyone heard it?" She gave him a short kiss.

"I did." It was almost a defensive statement.

Laughing, Worthia replied, "I guess that's all that counts then. We have any food around? I'm starving."

"Ah… no." Tigen looked away as he said the words. "I'm sure the kitchen can make you something pretty quick."

"Guess it'll have to." Worthia turned to the kitchen area.

"Make enough for two," Tigen called out.

"Two of you or two of me?"

"Yes."

"Kitchen, can I get some chicken and noodles with Alfredo sauce quick?"

"Is ten minutes quick enough?" a computer voice asked.

"Sure. Four servings. You want any, dear?"

Tigen only huffed.

"Would you like to add broccoli to that?" the computer asked.

"Sure, why not." Worthia walked to the drink dispenser. "Kitchen, do we have any desserts?"

"There is cheesecake I can unfreeze. Chocolate."

"Probably the only reason it's still around. Sure, unfreeze it."

"How much?"

"The whole thing."

"Of course. You wish to have it after the meal?"

"I wish to have it now so start unfreezing it."

"I will do that."

Walking around the couch, Worthia picked up Tigen's feet, sat in their place, and set them on her lap, laying her head back. With her feet, she pulled the coffee table close enough to put her feet on it.

"You did good today," Tigen said in a soft voice.

"I almost blew up the main turret trying to kill that ship."

"That's what other people are for." Tigen shrugged, though Worthia did not see it.

"I think Zaheia would have let me blow it up."

"She's a soldier, good at taking commands. But it won't surprise me if she had some kind of backup plan."

"You weren't there." A small turn of her head followed the comment, but then it turned back without saying anything more.

"Someone turned it off. Probably the crew inside the turret. I'm sure she knew they would do that."

Sighing, Worthia added, "I just wanted to kill that thing before it killed us."

"Hey, we won. I assume Space Command is looking to see if there are any more out there?"

"Of course, but seeing how close that one got before we noticed, I'm still nervous." Worthia's hand reached over and started rubbing Tigen's lower leg as if on its own.

"If there was, I'm sure we would have seen it by now. Just my professional opinion, you know." Picking up a drink on the end table by the couch, Tigen took a long draw.

"There you go again, thinking like a human." Worthia's drink was held forgotten in her hand.

"Guilty as charged."

"Your food has been prepared," the kitchen announced.

"You want me to get it?" Tigen asked.

"No way. You're not using me as an excuse to get up and do things." Before standing and walking into the kitchen, Worthia picked up Tigen's feet and plopped them onto the floor without ceremony.

"Can I at least sit up?"

"Sure." Worthia's voice made it sound like a strain.

"Do you want to eat at the table?"

"Nope, none of that. No tricks." Wagging a finger at him over her shoulder as she walked, Worthia grabbed two large bowls into which the meal was divided. A spoon followed into her bowl and a fork into Tigen's. "Where's that cheesecake at?"

"It's dethawing."

"What's taking so long?"

"Dessert is normally served after the main course."

"And is best eaten first! Besides, you're not the president."

"Correct. I will get it dethawed right away."

"Are you bullying the kitchen?" Tigen asked as she handed him his bowl.

"When you're president, you have to be careful or everyone will start thinking they know better than you do." She made the statement in a serious tone as she sat down. "Like your Chief of Staff."

"That wasn't your Chief of Staff, that was your husband." Tigen pointed with his fork before plunging it into the bowl.

"Pf-ft." Worthia rolled her eyes. "He's even worse."

Chapter Thirty-Four
Clean Up

Arching the body to the right was the natural response when trying to look at the tower. When that proved unsatisfactory, some like Worthia would just tilt her head while they stared.

"It's bent?"

"Yes, by a few degrees." Chadan rocked on the balls of his feet much like a little kid. "Just enough to make the mind wonder."

"How? I mean, I've never heard of a blast bending a building." Worthia tilted her head a little more.

"*My* opinion is that it was made that way and we are now only discovering it. Of course the records do not indicate this."

"It's kind of hard to believe everyone has missed it until now." Straightening her neck, Worthia looked at the shorter man.

"Maybe people just thought they were imagining things. Besides, there wasn't much reason to check before now." He shrugged as he talked.

"Is it safe?"

"Totally."

"So we have the leaning tower of Denver?"

"Not exactly, but in essence, yes. Maybe it will become a tourist attraction." Chadan smiled at his own idea.

"I'm sure we'll get plenty of those anyway." The sound of approaching footsteps caused Worthia to turn and find Anne Coons. "How's the cleanup?"

"All the debris on the streets and sidewalks has been removed. Not bad for two days if I say so myself."

"Your arms must really be tired." Chadan shared a giggle with himself.

"You know my first job was driving excavation equipment out in the mountains, don't you?" Anne just stared at him while the giggle disappeared. "The bots had a tendency to fall down the cliffs. Of course, they're better now, which is why I went into government work."

"I learn something interesting about people every day." Bowing, Chadan left the two women.

"Well done," Worthia said in a low voice after Chadan had left. "It's hard to get one over on him."

"Thinks he knows everything." The scowl on Anne's face made her opinion clear.

"If anyone does, he does." A quick smile came and went from Worthia's face. "So, have we finalized the count?"

"As much as we can. There's still collapsed buildings to deal with, but the seeker bugs tell us no one is alive in the wreckage at least." Giving one more glance Chadan's direction, Anne's voice was a little dark.

"How many?" Worthia breathed in and pulled her shoulders back.

"Military or civilian?"

"Yes."

It was Anne's turn to breathe in deep. "One hundred and eighty-two soldiers dead, at least twice that many injured, but as I said, that number may go up. On the civilian side, we're a lot better. Only a handful of dead, but a lot more injured, mostly from flying glass. Too many for the skin recovery units to handle at once so some people are going to be left with scars. Not that some seem to mind, particularly the guys. Men."

"Didn't people take cover?" Worthia's face twisted clockwise on itself.

"Apparently they couldn't resist the temptation to watch out their windows. I think a lot of people are going to have the nickname 'Scarface' for a while."

Shudders ran through Worthia. "They're lucky they weren't

blinded."

"Some lost an eye but only a few lost both. They were the first admitted into replacement therapy after the life-threatening injuries. Maybe they'll learn something."

"For the next alien invasion?" Worthia's brows elevated.

"You never know anymore." Anne shrugged. "That's not why I tracked you down. We have a delegation of Puritans outside the east gate."

"Angry mob?"

"More like the hat-in-hand type. My guess is that they've seen the video and want to make sure it's genuine. After that, who knows what they'll do. Their god was just defeated. That's got to be hard for the true believers." The tone of Anne's voice indicated she had little sympathy for the situation.

Breathing in and out once, Worthia rotated her head around to exercise her neck. "Guess I better get over there and see what they want. Have the other cities reported anything?"

"Hard to hear much when that blast took out most of our official communication capability, but no, the limited information we have received has not indicated any civil disorder."

"So we get to plow new ground again. Thanks for letting me know. We're going to be busy enough with our own for a while, not sure how much we can do for those outside at the moment, but we can at least talk. Keep them busy out here." Giving the woman a quick smile, Worthia turned to walk to the waiting vehicle.

"That's my job," Anne called to her. "Of course, if you would like to change my title to Secretary of Interior Design, I could add some style to this city while we repair things."

A wave over her shoulder was the only reply Worthia gave. Inside the vehicle, Tigen waited, shifting with stiffness as she sat down next to him. "See," she said, looking at him, "you can wait inside the vehicle."

"There were no threatening aliens," Tigen said with smugness. Worthia tilted her head to the right and gave him an eye.

"East gate," she announced. In response, the vehicle accelerated almost unnoticed. "We have a delegation of Puritans knocking at our door."

"So I heard."

The statement earned a look and small shake of the head from Worthia. "How do you find out these things before I do?"

"It's my job." A short pause was followed by, "And people like me."

"People are scared of you," Worthia corrected.

"Either works for me."

Rolling down the window, Worthia watched the city go by. "At least it looks better day by day."

"We got off easy. A human attacker would have made a point of destroying more of the city." Tigen's breath caught as he took in air.

"Then I'm glad we were attacked by aliens."

"Any news from Space Command?"

"No other ships found so far. They did find some small satellites they assume were used to relay signals across the globe. Buggers were really hard to find and Command was pretty proud of themselves for finding them."

"Did they blast them from the sky?"

"Actually, they are going to recover them for study." The outer wall came into view.

Tigen tsked. "With all the alien debris around the city, I would think they have enough to study."

"You know scientists, always happy to have more things to study."

"Chadan must be chomping at the bit."

"I think he can barely contain himself waiting for data. I heard he might resign so he can research the alien tech full time."

"Not a big surprise there. Any idea what these Puritans want?"

Worthia sighed. "If we're lucky, forgiveness and direction. If we're not, someone to take the news out on."

"Don't worry, I still have some fight in me." Tigen grew a smile.

"Let's make that our last resort." The vehicle slowed down and stopped. Giving Tigen a look as she did so, Worthia stepped from the vehicle. It had parked next to the door next to the east gate. A guard stood next to it. Taking a breath, Worthia walked to the door and looked at the man.

"I assume they are not armed?"

"Of course, M. President."

"Mood?"

"Subdued."

"Open both doors."

"Ma'am?"

"You don't think you guys could stop them?" A stare went with the question.

"Of course, M. President."

The man touched his interface and the door opened without a sound. The 'airlock' was two meters wide with both doors swinging outward. Bracing her shoulders, Worthia walked through both doors and turned to her right. A crowd of twenty to thirty men stood within throwing distance, some who actually had their hats in their hands. Beyond them was a larger crowd of a thousand or more. They didn't appear to carry any weapons but they still looked like they could be dangerous if incited. Many looked toward the ground instead of at the city. Between the two groups, military personnel stood and drones hovered with clear indication of their willing to use force. The man in front of the closer group, with salt and pepper hair and a full beard doing its best to turn white, raised his shoulders when he looked at Worthia. Several others next to him followed suit, though none looked ready for a fight. Giving them a smile, Worthia walked to them.

"Good morning."

"Morning, ma'am," several of the men responded.

"What can I do for you?"

The men looked at each other before answering. The one with the white hair spoke. "Is it true? Are the pictures we saw true?"

"Yes, it is true. It would not serve us to lie to you, plus we don't do that."

The man shuffled his feet, looked at the ground for a second, and then looked at Worthia. "My name is Jedikiah. I have been a member of the church my whole life, becoming an elder in our local chapter. When I heard that you were defying... God, I was sure that they would bring judgment down on you. But it seems that you are the ones who have brought judgment down on them. You can understand, this is hard for my people to understand and accept. Most keep looking up to the skies to see another ship appear."

"Not all of us believe it." The comment came from a older, long-bearded gentleman toward the back of the group. His eyes squinted in a hard stare. "No one can defeat God. Your pictures are a lie. God will return and take vengeance on you for resisting his will."

"I can understand this is hard for your people," Worthia said in a gentle voice. "But the vid was not faked."

Jedikiah looked into her eyes. "I consider myself a good judge of people and can see no deceit in you. As much as I don't want to believe it, what you say is the truth."

"Then you are a fool," the other man countered. "This is not over."

"You can't trust non-believers." The words came from someone else inside the group.

"If they speak the truth, they can." Jedikiah said the words over his shoulder. "Or are we so hateful that we don't believe the truth based on who says it?"

The words brought silence to the group. Some looked uncomfortable but said nothing.

"We profess to live in truth," Jedikiah continued, "so let us live and speak it. You all saw the ship damaged and leaving us. You saw the lights in the heavens. Are any of you in doubt that if... those inside were not defeated, then they would have returned? The fact that they have not, that they have sent no message, tells us what the unbelievers have told us is true. All of this we have already discussed."

"We cannot accept this and still profess our faith," came from an older man in the group. Some mumbled, some shook their heads. "If you believe this, you will be excommunicated from our faith."

Jedikiah turned back to Worthia. "You see our predicament. Our belief was based on our visitors being God, but how can God lose to mere men? We, most, don't want to accept this, but what choice do we have? And if God has been defeated, where does that leave us?"

Waiting a few seconds, Worthia asked, "Are you afraid we will attack you, take back the country by force?"

"Some are." Jedikiah nodded as he spoke.

"We would never do that." Worthia shook her head in response. "We still feel that all people who live here are Americans and should all be citizens together. We do not attack our own people."

"Some would say you are a fool for believing so."

"Fool, no. Idealist?" Worthia's eyes flashed upward. "Maybe. If anything these two visits by aliens have taught us, it's that we can only trust each other. That means we need to work together, to be on the same side. If you want to live on a farm and plow your field with a horse, fine, I don't care. I will respect your chosen life and you respect mine. There has to be enough room on this world for us to do that or else we condemn ourselves to situations I don't want to think about. No one life has to be right for everyone. Don't you think a real God could cope with a farmer and a scientist in a modern lab?"

A small chuckle lived a brief life in Jedikiah. "If anyone could, God could. But won't God want us to believe the same things?"

"So all your people, Puritans across the whole world, believe all the exact same things?" Worthia asked.

As his head twisted, Jedikiah's mouth took on the appearance of a door trying not to open to the words forming behind it. The mouth won for a while, but as his stance calmed, it was opened. "Exactly the same, no, I cannot say that. There has been some heated discussion about some points of theology, I will admit. The differences are not as great as between you and I, for sure, but I cannot say they do not exist."

"And why would an infinite God, one who created so much variety on just our world, want everyone to be exact copies of each other? Does that even make sense?"

Several breaths went by before Jedikiah answered. "Your words are worth thinking about. But they do not answer the question that haunts us at this moment. What do we do now?"

A smile broke out on Worthia's face. "Stop living for some false God and live for each other. Value a person for how much they live for other people, what they do for others, not how much they force others to follow some doctrine. Let people have their differences, because that is how new things are discovered and how life gets better over time. Glory in who people are and not how much they conform to what you want."

Jedikiah looked like he had been slapped. "That... will not be easy."

"It's a process." Worthia patted his shoulder. "Start small, work your way up. You can start by listening to people instead of just telling them all the time. They might challenge your way of thinking, but enduring challenges is how we become strong."

"Don't listen to her!" came from inside the group.

"Not everyone will accept this." Concern filled Jedikiah's face.

"Of course they won't. Many people hate change even though it happens every day around us. You don't have to tear down the house. Start by cracking open the windows and letting in the breeze for a while. It might be refreshing."

"And what about you and the cities?"

"We will be here. We will help when we can. Please believe me that we never hated you. Made fun of you at times, yes, but we're only human too. We all can go forward from here. We have to if we are going to be ready for the future. It's up to your people to decide what they can handle, but let them decide for themselves."

"And if they defile the faith?"

"Be the beacon. Show them what true faith is, not oppress them or browbeat them. Act with love and concern, not fear and anger."

Jedikiah snorted. "You mean act more like my wife."

"And who do the kids run to when they are scared?" Worthia's eyes widened by only a little. Jedikiah sighed.

"You have a point. You give us things to consider."

"We're going to be pretty busy in the near future." Worthia's thumb hitched over her shoulder. "But we will help as much as we can. Just be nice to our citizens and remember they don't mean you any harm. We are not the enemy and have never tried to force you to change, only asked that you let those who want to change do so."

As he breathed in, Jedikiah straightened himself. "That is fair. Is there anything we can do for you?" The group behind him stirred restlessly.

The question caught Worthia off guard, causing her to pause for a moment. "Thank you, that is very kind of you. I really don't know, but will ask and someone will get back to you if there is."

"Thank you for seeing us. Go with..." Shock came across the man's face and then embarrassment.

"You can say it. I understand what you mean. Besides, if there is a real God out there, I doubt he'll object." She gave him a kind smile.

"We will talk again in the future."

Turning, Jedikiah scanned the faces of those who had come with him. Some were hard with resolve, others looked lost. A few gave meaningful nods toward Worthia. Turning back to her, Jedikiah asked, "Do you know the fate of any that were—who had joined the ship?"

Worthia shook her head. "I am sorry. I have no idea who was on the ship at what time."

"Of course you don't, but we had to ask. Thank you."

The crowd of men slowly turned from the city, making its way in small groups that milled back and forth, forming and reforming. Worthia walked over to one of the guards who had been standing between them and the city, a lieutenant.

"Make sure they get a decent meal and transportation back to their homes if they need it."

"Yes, M. President." The woman's words came out in a halting manner.

"That's not a problem, is it?"

"No, I, uh, just..." The woman snapped to attention. "It will be done, M. President."

"Thank you." Giving her a quick smile, Worthia walked back through the doors and to the vehicle. Tigen still sat inside, watching her as she sat down. "What?"

"Did you give them a key to the city?" he asked.

"No," she sputtered, "don't be silly."

"Did you invite them to dinner?" The vehicle started to move.

"Now that's an idea!" Worthia's eyes lit up with fake interest. "We could have them all over for a barbecue. I'll tell them it was your request."

"Pft. You would."

Chapter Thirty-Five
Windows

The machine traveled a few meters around the building, stopped for a few moments, placed a piece of glass into the window frame, held it there while another arm extruded quick-setting glue around the edge, released the glass, and moved on. As it deposited glass, a flying drone lifted more pieces of glass to its storage area.

"I'm saying, it just looks weird." Wray was looking up at the machine as it performed its task. "The thing was a window washer a few days ago and now it's installing the things."

"What's so weird about it? It was only a slight modification to it." Cedynia tapped her interface, checking numbers sent from the machines in front of them. "At least they didn't ask you to climb up there and install the windows."

"Shit!" The word came out in a rush. "They tell me to do that and I'd just defect to the Puritans."

Hitting his shoulders, Cedynia scoffed. "No, you wouldn't. You'd just go hide somewhere until they assigned it to someone else."

"No, nope," Wray said, shaking his head. "They'd need to be taught a lesson about handing out dangerous jobs."

"Right, right." Head bobbing, Cedynia looked up from her interface. "What exactly *are* you doing anyway, besides standing around complaining, that is?"

"I'm in charge of glass supply, remember?" Wray turned, his hands spread out to the side.

"I thought the computer was taking care of that?" Cedynia looked up through the top of her eyes.

"Except that when you put the pieces together, the computer imager has a hard time knowing one piece from another or how many there are total." He turned back and shrugged. "It gets confused easily."

"And of course you don't?"

"No. I have a human mind able to take incongruent information and turn it into logical information and correct decisions for my environment." Chin coming up as he spoke, Wray ended in a pose with a finger pointed into the air.

Cedynia's face crunched up on itself. "Where'd you get that from?"

Wray acted shocked. "You don't think I could come up with that on my own?"

"In one word, no." Cedynia went back to her interface.

Hands coming to his chest, Wray's mouth went wide. "Why, I'm hurt. Hurt that you think so little of me."

"Ha!" burst from Cedynia's lips. "In all the years I've known you, you've never talked like that. And now I'm supposed to believe that you suddenly have changed?"

Pouting and shaking his head first, Wray tilted his head and closed his eyes to slits. "Maybe you changed me."

The comment caused Cedynia to stop and bring up her head. A smile started to form but then stopped, her face changing. "Oh no, you're not putting this on me. I don't know what you think you're up to, but it's all you."

"There you go, hurting my feeling again." Wray scuffed a shoe against the ground. Cedynia's hand came up between them.

"Don't even, don't even. You just get back to… whatever it is you're doing and keep me out of it."

Tapping his interface, Wray ignored the hand. "How many more windows we need to replace?"

"Hey!" Wide eyed, Cedynia's face turned to Wray. "Glass supply is your area. I just install them."

Rolling his eyes, Wray just said, "Thanks a lot. Computer, how many windows required replacement on this building?"

"Four hundred and twelve," a mechanical voice replied.

"So how many more do we have to go, mister glass supply?" The snide comment was made without looking at Wray.

"Haven't you counted how many you've installed?" The question brought a stare from Cedynia.

Without comment, she turned back to watch the window installation. "Just remember, the faster we get this done, the faster we go on our honeymoon."

Raising his eyebrows to their maximum, Wray replied, "You think I forgot that?"

Watching the plane ascend into the sky, Wilmont shook his head, though a smile graced his face. He took a deep breath to take in the familiar scents of the farm around him.

"Is something wrong?" his mother asked. "Regretting your decision?"

"No." He turned to face her. "Just having trouble believing I chose to come back. In a way, that is."

"Me too." Miriam turned to watch the girls as they were greeted by the dogs. "But I do appreciate it. With your dad and the other boys gone, the farm will be a handful to run."

"You could have stayed in the city. You all could've."

"I know they would have let us." Miriam sighed. "It just didn't feel right. I mean, the girls love the animals and already missed them." Her arms swayed as she turned to look around. "Plus, this is their home, our home. How could I leave?"

"Was Dad on the ship?"

"Last I know, but who knows. If he wasn't, I doubt he'll show his face around here. Being rejected by 'god' would look really bad after he told everyone how he was sure he would be chosen." Miriam tsked as her head went side to side. "That man could be aggravating."

Wilmont made his own survey of the farm. "I guess we should tend to the animals first. Who knows when they were fed last."

"I sure hope the neighbors took care of them. If they didn't, they will hear from me. Abigail! Beth! There will be time to play with the dogs later. We have work to do. Let's go!"

"You know there are going to be changes around here," Wilmont said as he followed his mother toward the barn.

"Are you about to get us kicked out of the church?"

"Do you care?"

She smiled in return. "Not anymore."

Chapter Thirty-Six
Talk

The room was large with a high, domed ceiling bathed in reflected light on the semi-mirrored glass panels. The walls below the ceiling were marbled with stone that had intricate, random streaks of blue running through it. The floor was textured composite that gave just enough when walked on to prevent leg and back injury from long exposure. It was covered with an image of the world with the compass directions aligned to the actual globe. In the center of the room was a large, round table, hollowed in the center to form an almost complete ring. Arranged around the table were twenty flags of the major protected cities from around the world. The attendees, taking a break from their long time seated, milled about the room, sharing conversations in groups of two or three.

Standing next to the Chairman of the Western Confederation, previously the Western Pacific Conglomerate, Worthia felt the tension she had been carrying disappear as if it had left on the alien ship. Seen through the roof, the blue sky appeared to promise serenity to those below, though it had no idea of politics. Worthia wondered if that was the way it was supposed to be.

"It is considerate of you to share the technology from the EO-AY," Eiji Hata said in a casual voice. "I wish we could have helped in your conflict, but you are on the other side of the world."

"I understand. There were a lot of pieces laying around, more than our people needed to study, though I can't guarantee they didn't keep the most interesting bits for themselves." Worthia turned and smiled at the chairman.

"Assuming they knew which are the most interesting." Eiji smiled back.

"I enjoyed watching you face down the EO-AY. Took nerve."

Eiji laughed. "Nothing less was expected from someone in my position."

"So I imagine. Still, you took a drastic chance. I, for one, am glad you came through."

"One must chance to gain." Eiji pointed with one finger.

Puffing, Worthia frowned at Eiji. "You writing a play based on the experience?"

"Not me." Eiji rocked forward onto the balls of his feet and then back to his heels. "But there are greater things to be accomplished. We must continue to develop for whatever is next." Eiji took a sip from the glass in his hand. "We really should be talking about a moon colony. It has many advantages in protecting Earth."

"Talk to the next president about that." Waving off the comment with her hand, Worthia shook her head. "I'm sure Storm would love the idea. Plus it will capture the imagination of the people. Our nation has been talking about a moon colony for a long time. Funny the World Council never tried."

"They were probably too busy trying to decide who would be in charge and receive the contract awards. Storm is a much less practical man, easier to motivate." A smile joined Eiji's face. "Plus he will like standing in front of cameras talking about the project. Handshakes with scientists and astronauts, you know. What will you do when your term is finished?"

"Sit on the couch, watch entertainment vids, and eat bonbons." The seriousness of her voice made it sound like a done deal.

"I can't imagine you doing that for long."

"Just watch me. It will make Tigen happy too. Besides, I have a few hundred years of movies to catch up on."

"A few hundred?"

"I found some old recordings. A few go back to the original cinematics. Not up to today's standards, but it will be interesting to see how things developed."

"Make it an official study?" Eiji asked.

"Heck no," shot back the answer. "Too much pressure. I mean to relax and nothing else."

"Then I wish you luck in your endeavor." Eiji made a small head bow but doubt still showed in his eyes.

Epilogue
Somewhere Else in the Galaxy

"I'm not sure one spot makes much difference from the other," Shawn Yun said as he looked around. "It seems to be a giant crater, probably from a meteor impact. At least it's well watered."

"Half swamp is what you mean, but we can get around that." Manus Drednik, a civil engineer originally from Italy, made lines in the scenery with his finger. "We can cut channels in the low areas, drain the water while providing water-courses for transport. Just like beavers."

"I am sure our benefactors will appreciate our imitations of nature." Cloe Jones added, making her one assessment. "As long as we don't harm the ecosystem too much."

"We harm it by being here to one degree or another," Manus replied.

"But we must have a place to live." Shawn's head bobbed up and down. "So, brick house or wood? The wood will have to be brought from the surrounding hills, which is a distance, but doable."

"Since we don't have metal for structures, it will have to be wood. Any luck in finding metal deposits in the basin?" Manus asked.

"Nothing," Shawn replied.

"Nothing? Not anything?" Manus's voice made his disbelief clear.

"You would think that if it was a meteorite crater, there would at least be the core of the meteor, but we have detected nothing." Shawn shook his head. "It's going to limit our options."

"Almost like they did it on purpose, huh?" Manus asked.

"Why?" Cloe spit out with distaste. "So you can't make your weapons or vehicles or skyscrapers?"

"So we can't make a lot of things, like pots and pans too," Manus shot back.

"We can make those from ceramics," Cloe said with a dismissive tone in her voice. Staring at each man for a moment, she turned and stomped to the gathering of tents.

"She has some strange ideas," Manus said as he watched her leave for a few seconds before turning back to Shawn.

"Don't you impugn on her gods," Shawn replied with a small chuckle and smile.

"Gods?" Manus's brow wrinkled. "She really believe that?"

"Many do. Isn't that why you came?" The question came loaded with sarcasm. It was answered with huff.

"I came to go to another world, just like you. Just didn't think we would be starting from scratch."

"At least the aliens left us with enough to start off with, even a couple dozen of those walking robots to help." Shawn's thumb gestured behind him toward a gathering of three meter tall biped metal creations that had a rough appearance of a person: two legs, two arms, a head-like structure above a wide, thick body, and four digit hands.

"Yeah, but if you ask me, they left us with just enough to set up a town and plant fields. Not much else. No livestock, almost no computers, no weather satellites, no long-range communication equipment. It's like they want us to be farmers and nothing else."

"Maybe they will bring more when they come back?" Shawn offered.

"Back from where? Earth? And how long will that take?"

"No idea," Shawn said with a shake of his head. "They gave us no information about how long we were asleep or how far we traveled."

"Can't you tell from the stars?"

"All I can tell is that it is in the same vicinity as Earth as far as the galaxy goes, but that could still be quite a ways. Without proper equipment, I can't take measurements and get any idea how far we traveled."

"Again with the lack of equipment." It was Manus's turn to shake his head as he looked at the ground. "It just feels like it is on purpose. They want to keep us ignorant. Just do what they want and don't ask questions."

"At the moment, I am not sure the answers would matter. We can't get off the planet so we are dependent on them returning for anything other than what we have and what's here."

"It might help answer why we are *here*." Manus pointed at the ground. "This is obviously not their home planet, so why here? Propagating humans across the galaxy? For what end?"

"It may take more than our lifetime to find out the answer to that." Shawn put his hand on the other man's shoulder. "Look, we have plenty of things to take care of at the moment without worrying about the bigger questions. Once we are settled, we can spend time thinking about them. Right now we have to make shelters, map out a town, clear fields, find resources, and organize twenty-four thousand, three hundred and twelve people. Not a easy task."

Manus scoffed. "Particularly with those fanatics around. We're outnumbered like three-to-one, you know? They're already talking about setting up shrines and a house of worship, most more than one. You watch, they'll want to force everyone to attend their services and pray to the aliens, you'll see." Manus's words increased in heat as he talked.

"Who cares about shrines? Let them have their churches. They don't even have a defined religion yet and will probably be arguing about what it should be for a hundred years at least. And the longer the aliens stay away, the less people will be inclined to worship them." Shawn spread his arms in a giant shrug.

"Just be careful, man of science. You might end up public enemy number one." Manus's finger waved at the man.

"What's more important is the form of government that is chosen, and with the diverse group we have, I can't see anyone trusting one person to be in overall power. I'm sure it will end up being a big committee that takes forever to do anything."

"Committees can be dominated by one person, you know." Head tilted to one side, Manus gave the other man a knowing nod. Shawn waved him off.

"You worry too much. Now let's put that training of yours to work making our town. Maybe they will even name a street after you." Slapping the man on the back, Shawn turned toward the tents and started a slow walk.

"Just what I need, to live on a street named after me. Sounds redundant. By the way, did they ever tally the votes on what we are naming the planet? And please don't tell me 'Earth 2' won. We can't be stupid enough to name another planet the equivalent of 'dirt.'"

"Nope. 'Altaterra' won." A smile spread across Shawn's face as they talked.

"You know that means 'second earth' don't you?"

"Yes, I do." A small chuckle raced up his belly.

"Great. Humans are that stupid."

About the Author

Fulfilling his lifelong dream of becoming a famous author just before he retires, Dale McClenning is transitioning from a job as a mechanical engineer in controls and project work into the exciting and glamorous field of being a world-famous author (still waiting for the last part to take effect). With his wife of 37 years at his side and encouraged by his 10 year old granddaughter, who is still waiting for the book inspired by her to be published, Dale plods on putting out hard science fiction works in that little appreciated field (everyone wants fantasy these days it seems). But never fear, Dale shall continue to write in the literary desert of Indianapolis until he is sure that genre specialty again is fully appreciated.